HUNTED

"The world is full of monsters with friendly faces."
~HEATHER BREWER

Dedicated to

DAVID

The best writer in the family, forever in my heart

Chapter 1

Friday Jan 24th 1992

Mason drove his brand-new white BMW along the Hume Highway at a steady speed, not obviously slow but making sure he kept below the 110-kilometre speed limit. As he neared the forest, his anxiety began to ease. Not far now.

Once he turned off the main road and down the long dirt road, he felt even more at ease. The gravel driveway, which was now overgrown, finally came into view. Seconds later, the cabin appeared behind a row of pine trees.

As a child, Mason had always enjoyed his time at the cabin. It was the only place where his innocence remained intact. Maybe it was because the rooms were too close to one another for his father to try anything. Or maybe it was the fact that his dad was enjoying his holiday and his mum was happy in her own way.

During those summers, he felt like a real child in a real family, and it was a good feeling. The cabin was his escape from the world. Even now, it was the only place where he felt safe.

Now, he was returning to his safe summer haven.

For the last two years, Mason had spent nearly every spare weekend at the cabin. He had turned the ramshackle cabin into a tri-level liveable weekend property. He now had it just the way he needed it. It offered a spacious lounge room, complete with stone fireplace. The hexagonal meals area and kitchen both overlooked the large 20-acre allotment. Finishing off the middle level was a quiet study nook.

The spiral staircase was located in a corner off the meals area. The stairs, leading up, led to three bedrooms and the communal bathroom, while the stairs leading down led to an enclosed garage-cum-cellar. It had originally been designed to keep as an open carport. It had seen better days and was in need of more than a lick of paint. Fitting it out was where Mason had concentrated most of his efforts. It had to be perfect.

The narrow winding driveway that had originally led directly to the front door had now been extended to provide access to the undercover cellar. It was enclosed by two large barn-style swinging doors.

By the time Mason was finished he was happy it would suit his purpose.

Today would be the first time it would be used.

His attention was broken when the prize in the boot of his car began stirring and making strange muffled noises.

He had arrived just in time!

* * *

Rebecca Carrington had been walking, as she had for the last eight months, from her doorstep in Amelia Avenue to the police academy situated at the top of Jells Road. The walk included a shortcut along the bike path through the wetlands.

The wetlands were surrounded by shrubs and reeds. Mason had lain in wait for her among the shrubs, kneeling on one knee. As soon as he caught sight of Rebecca turning the corner, her backpack slung over her right shoulder, he prepared himself. With the tall reeds blocking Rebecca's view of the bike path ahead, Mason lay himself down across the path, clutching his chest. As he had known she would, she knelt down beside him and asked, "Are you all right?"

"I'm fine but you're fucked!" he said, pressing an object into her side. Rebecca didn't see exactly what the object was; he was too fast. But as soon as she felt the pain, she knew what it was. The taser hurt like a thousand large needles and incapacitated her. Then he injected her with his prepared syringe of Benzodiapine, which only took a few seconds to render her unconscious.

Mason picked Rebecca up, together with her backpack, and carried her towards his vehicle, parked on the nearby side street.

Only one person saw him, a fit young jogger who looked as if he spent too much time in the gym. "Is she all right?" the jogger asked as he passed Mason, pausing as he awaited an answer. "She has diabetes," Mason quickly responded. "Needs her insulin," he added. The jogger, satisfied, continued on his way.

Mason approached the getaway vehicle in less than a minute. He had removed the key from his pocket ready to open the car. The boot popped and the indicator lights flashed twice. The inside of the boot was covered in plastic, top to bottom, front to back. Mason glanced around quickly before placing her into the boot. Then he calmly closed it, walked to the driver's side and got in.

Mason had taken every precaution possible to ensure his success. He had stolen two sets of plates and a second car, a white Holden. While it was only a short drive to his own vehicle, transferring the girl to his car was the most dangerous part of the plan. Hidden off a back track at the base of some parkland sat Mason's own BMW. While transferring Rebecca from one boot to the other had risks, Mason thought detection was a lot less likely on a secluded track than in a side street.

He knew he might have been seen in the side street. Yet with his disguise of red hair and beard and stolen car, should anyone have seen the abduction it could not be traced back to him.

* * *

Rebecca, who had regained consciousness shortly before, felt the vehicle slow down, followed by a few bumps before it came to a stop. She had no idea how long they had been travelling and with her hands tied firmly behind her back, there was no way she could see her watch. She knew only that she was in a car boot.

Rebecca began to rub her hands frantically against what she believed was a jack. She stopped when she heard the sound of the car door opening.

'I hope you're ready for a fight because I'm not going quietly,' she thought. Again, she began to rub her wrists, hoping it was doing some good, but the rope was holding tight.

By now, she was expecting the boot to pop at any second, but she was surprised when the footsteps on the gravel outside slowly moved away. She then heard what she thought were footsteps on wooden steps or flooring. When she heard a creaking sound, she thought it must be wooden steps.

Rebecca rested her hands for a moment before trying to pull them apart, but the rope held tight. She knew if she didn't get free, she would be dead.

Frantically moving her hands around, she couldn't find anything useful that might help her free them. Then her ears picked up the sound of footsteps on the gravel beside her. 'He must have missed the weak step,' she thought, as she hadn't heard it creak upon his return.

Shuffling her body around quickly, banging her head on the lid of the boot as she did so, Rebecca positioned herself ready for her own little surprise attack. She placed her feet straight at the lid of the boot, ready to kick up hard as soon as she saw it begin to open. Hopefully, she would be able to knock the lid up and clip the fucker right in the face and send him flying. All she needed was the right timing and a bit of luck.

Rebecca heard a small beep and moments later, a beam of light and a rush of fresh air entered the boot. Rebecca's reflexes were lightning fast. She kicked. The boot flew up. She heard a thump and then a cry of "Ahhh!" Mason's chin was collected by the lid of the boot. With the boot ajar, Rebecca scooted on her arse towards the daylight. Her legs were hanging out and her shoulders were holding up the lid. She couldn't see her assailant anywhere. She pushed all her weight forward, rolling her body out onto the hard, gravelly ground. Rebecca spun her head around but could still see no one. Staggering to her feet, she tried to run, still noticing the effects of the drugs. Her legs were heavy, as if she had just run a marathon.

"You looking for me?" said a voice from behind her. Spinning on her heels, Rebecca turned towards the voice. An object struck her on the right shoulder, sending a sharp burning pain down her arm. He had hit her with such force that it sent her back down to the gravel. She rolled over and looked up at a man standing over her with a shovel clasped in his hands. He didn't look like the same red-haired man who she thought had kidnapped her.

Blood was dripping from a cut just below his mouth where the boot had connected. Scooting away from the shovel-wielding man, she felt the gravel graze her butt and her palms as she dragged herself backwards.

"There's no point trying to get away," Mason said calmly, digging the shovel into the ground with his foot. "Look around. You're in the middle of nowhere. Where will you run?" he taunted her, approaching his prize who sat slumped on his driveway.

"Come and get me then, you sick fuck!" Rebecca sneered, not wanting to show him her fear. Mason removed the shovel from the ground and headed towards the five-foot-six blonde.

She knew what she was up against. But she also knew she had a lot of fight left in her and she wasn't giving up. As Mason approached, she waited to make her move. Once he was within reach, she would take her chance.

He took another step towards her, his shadow now over her. 'Now or never,' she thought, kicking out her right leg as hard as she could.

The combination of the force of the kick and the loose gravel on the drive forced Mason to lose his balance and sent him crumbling to the ground before her.

Rebecca got to one knee and pressed her foot hard into the ground, ready for take-off, but before she could launch herself up, something connected with her leg and sent pain shooting up from her ankle. She cried out in pain and saw that the shovel was gouged into her heel.

Mason knew she was pinned and he was glad. The last thing he wanted in this heat was to chase some useless blonde through the woods.

Gathering himself, Mason got to his feet and removed the taser from his pocket.

* * *

Rebecca's hair was no longer tied neatly in a ponytail, as it had been when she'd begun her walk that morning. It was now clumped and smeared with dirt and blood. Her blue jeans were torn and stained.

Mason had leaned her against the balustrade at the top of the cellar stairs. When she awoke, she realised she was bound to the staircase by her hands and feet. She could see no way out.

"I told you not to run but you wouldn't listen, would you? Now your death will be more painful."

With her vision still blurry, she did not recognise the person speaking to her but she knew it was her captor. She blinked several times until she could see the man standing in front of her. He was holding something. She couldn't make it out at first, but then she saw exactly what it was. A sword, a samurai sword to be exact.

He began to wave it around in circles in front of her. Woosh! Woosh! The blade cut the air in front of her.

"What are you going to do to me?" Rebecca slurred, the taser still affecting her tongue and cheek muscles.

Mason offered no response. He simply began his work. Firstly, he sliced the two shoulder straps off her top. "Oops, I must have nicked you."

He laughed as blood began to flow down her shoulder onto her chest. "I'm new at this," he chuckled.

"Get the fuck away from me!" Rebecca began to shout. There was no hiding her fear now, which only grew as she saw the man in front of her change. It seemed as though the man behind the eyes had vacated the premises. His eyes were dark and she saw pure evil in them, which sent a shiver down her spine. She could smell death. Her death.

Mason firmly clasped the sword tightly in both hands and before Rebecca could absorb what was happening, he ran the sword through her stomach. Her mouth filled with blood and she gave a final, gurgling cry.

Then he raised the sword high over his head and brought it down hard, severing her head.

It was over.

Victorious, Mason had seen it happen in slow motion. It had been like watching himself in a movie. It was meant to have been perfect. The pressure gauge had been released a little but he still felt empty. No matter how much he looked at his handiwork, the satisfied feeling he was after remained absent.

Maybe when it was on display he would get the feeling he was looking for. He brought up a large jar from his cellar and unscrewed the lid. He picked up Rebecca's severed head by her hair and placed it in the jar, then filled it with formaldehyde. The last thing he wanted was for his work to go to ruin.

Mason placed the jar on the display shelf he had made specially for the cellar, stood back and admired his finished work. Finally, there was some excitement in his pants. Wasting no time, he began to masturbate.

Chapter 2

Monday September 15th 2003

"Now recruiting!" the TV blasted its high-spirited jingle for the Victorian Police advertisement. They had been recruiting heavily over the past few years, as many female officers had been murdered. Since the early 90s, the numbers joining the force had been in steady decline.

Female officers were clearly concerned about becoming the next victim of the madman who had been dubbed the 'East Side Slayer'. He was still out there and his love of killing was increasing. The Slayer's tally to date was six, with one still missing, suspected abducted and murdered.

The police didn't seem to have a clue as to his identity or how he was targeting his victims. The only common thread was that they were all policewomen.

I sat back in my leather chair staring at the TV mounted on my office wall. It was one of the latest LCD flat screens and it had cost me a small fortune, but it was a gift I had promised myself for my years of hard work.

I was now a qualified psychologist, majoring in criminal psychology. My major year had been my most enjoyable. I was able to secure a place for a four-week stay at the Quantico Behavioural Science Unit. It really lit the fire in my belly for criminology. While my practice paid the bills with the substantial number of normal cases, the criminal cases and requests for help from the police were more lucrative.

During my childhood, I had always wanted to be a police officer. Many of my friends wanted to be playing cricket for Australia or Aussie Rules, but not me. I always wanted to be a cop. My best friend was the same. Maybe that's what helped us stay such good friends. The only difference between Jake Miller and me was that he was fit and I was severely handicapped by the time I was 12. I had five major heart operations and after I turned 20, two more followed. It was before my last operation that Jake broke the news that he had made the cut at the academy. I was disappointed for myself, at first, but it was replaced with overwhelming pride for Jake's efforts. He knew how proud I was of him, but he also knew how hard it was for me.

It wasn't until after my last operation that Jake suggested I should pursue a psychology/criminology degree. Maybe I could fight crime that way. He was right. It would be the only way. I had trouble doing anything physical. I struggled to run any great distance. As unrealistic as my dream was, I still wanted to believe I could do it. After all, I was six foot four and I often wondered how big I would have grown had I not been afflicted by my heart condition. Although tall, I was slim with little muscle definition, due to a lack of oxygen over the years. I was a tall weed.

I sat in my office chair trying to have a quick break before starting my preparation for tomorrow. The leather was splitting a little along the stitching of the armrests. I sat tossing letters around my desk without opening them. I looked through the client's files I was working on for the next day. I knew I would have to make a start on them soon.

The blonde-haired newsreader on Seven Nightly News, Christine Hope, began her news report. "We have breaking news in the case of missing Constable Jan West. We will now cross to Mark Harrity on location."

"Thanks Christine. I'm on the shore of Rye Back Beach where earlier today, local surfers found a woman's remains. While they are yet to be identified, police believe they could be those of missing Constable Jan West. Police are seeking the public's help with this case and they stress that any information, no matter how small, could be vital in solving this series of terrible crimes!"

"Thanks Mark," Christine said, before the video cut off. "Moving on to other news."

I switched off the TV, threw the remote on the desk and stood in front of the window to take in the lovely view. The city looked beautiful at sunset. I caught the reflection of my bloodshot hazel eyes. My thoughts immediately returned to the Slayer murders. I stood there trying to imagine what type of person would be capable of such a thing.

When I was at Quantico, we'd spent many sessions studying profiling as a useful tool in narrowing the search for murderers. We had studied past killers like Bundy, Gacy and Sutcliffe. I had read all the books by John Douglas on criminal profiling techniques and while I was there, I was lucky enough to sit in on some of his classes. He was a quietly spoken but observant man. The interviews of past serial killers provided exceptional insight into why they acted the way they did.

Bundy, for example, killed in excess of 33 women. Many say he did it because he was insane, while others including me thought he did it so that he could finally be successful at something. But more importantly he killed because he liked it and once he got a taste for it, he was addicted. Addicted to the feeling of power he had over the women as they died.

I went back to my desk and sank back into the chair. Out of the matching filing cabinet, I withdrew the file I wanted and began to flick through it. I had kept all the newspaper clippings about the East Side Slayer and had created my own preliminary profile of him.

So far, I had compiled:

Late 20s-mid 30s
Professionally employed
Likely to have freedom in his job
Highly intelligent
Possibly a family man
Traumatic upbringing. Most likely a broken home.

If I had more information, I thought I might be able develop a more accurate profile. If I knew more about the killer's signature, for instance. Every killer had one, but the police had kept it out of the media for some reason.

I had also created two maps, one with locations where all the women had disappeared, the other of all the killer's dump sites. There was no pattern in either map.

The only pattern I could see was that this killer was evolving and becoming more confident. The cooling-off period between killings had decreased each time, the last two murders being only three months apart.

Chapter 3

September 15th 2003 (4.50pm)

Mason Belic stood in the park as twilight approached. He was dressed in blue jeans and a light brown knitted jumper. With the wind off the ocean beginning to pick up, he was glad he had brought the jumper.

His son Jamie laughed as he pushed him on the swing. "Higher Daddy," he called. Mason loved his son; he honestly believed that Jamie was the only person he ever could love, or feel attached to. He loved everything about him: his blond hair, his blue eyes, his contagious laugh. When he heard Jamie's laugh he felt almost human, a feeling he never had with anyone else. He often believed he was dead on the inside.

He loved being with his son although today he was not at the park for Jamie. Today he was there for his own reasons. He wanted to watch the police investigating the work he had done. He wanted to marvel in the glory of what he had created. The thought that he had caused this was the most fulfilling thing he had ever had. Soon, his whole plan would be laid out for all to see. Soon, very soon, he would feel the desire to kill again.

"Dad, keep pushing, come on, higher. Dad, more, you're slowing down."

"I'm sorry Jamie. I was daydreaming."

"You're being silly, Daddy," Jamie said as his father pushed him high into the air.

"Weeee!" he screamed, as he swung back towards his father. "You're being a silly billy," he sang. "You're a silly billy," he repeated several times between pushes. "Daddy, what are all the police doing? Why are there so many?" he asked, without waiting for the answer to his first question.

"I'm not sure, buddy," Mason replied, knowing exactly what they were doing across the road. He was the reason they were there.

"Dad, do you think they will take me for a ride in the car with the lights going?" His eyes were filled with excitement and he was grinning at the thought of riding in the police car. The only one more excited was the man pushing him on the swing. However, he showed no emotion at all.

"I think they might be too busy, I'm sure they have lots to do." Mason continued pushing Jamie. He had a real rhythm going now. Out of the corner of his eye, Mason could see a police officer approaching.

"Excuse me sir, I'm afraid you're going to have to clear the area, we have an investigation to conduct and we have to seal off the area. Sorry to spoil your day," the officer added as he removed a notepad and pen from his pocket.

"That's ok, Officer, we were about to leave anyhow." Mason bent over and grabbed Jamie off the swing.

"But Daddy, I want to play longer!" Jamie responded angrily, almost ready to throw a tantrum. Had the policeman not been standing there he was sure that Jamie would have been screaming at the top of his lungs.

"Before you go, may I just ask you a few questions? I also need your contact details in case we have any follow-up questions." The officer had his pen poised.

"Sure." Mason paused. "Do you mind if he plays a little while we talk?"

"Yes, no problem," the officer responded.

"How long have you been here?"

"I guess about 20 minutes, not too long," was Mason's quick reply.

"Have you noticed anyone or anything strange while you have been here?"

"No, I can't say I have. It's been really quiet. The only activity I noticed was a couple of people walking their dog but they looked like a retired couple on their afternoon stroll."

Jamie jumped off the swing and headed towards the merry-go-round, jumping up and down as he ran.

"May I just get your name and address?" the officer asked, surveying the area.

"Sure. It's Philip Andrews, 19 Chambers Road, Rye," Mason replied. The name and address were real, they just didn't belong to him. He even had the car registration and make in his head in case he was asked.

It was easy to get the information when you knew how. Mason had plenty of experience as a real estate agent. He'd learned a lot of ways to gain information. All he had to do was knock on the door of the home and tell them he had someone looking to relocate. Would they be interested in selling? In most cases, the owners said no, but when you mentioned that your clients were prepared to be very generous on the purchase price they seldom hesitated to give their name and contact numbers.

The policeman never asked for the registration or to see his licence. With very little information gained, he was finished with his brief series of questions. Little did he know he was standing just metres from the most wanted man in Melbourne.

As the officer headed back towards his colleagues, Mason began to laugh inside, or so he thought.

"What you laughing about, Daddy?" his son asked.

"I was laughing at you being a silly billy," he said. "Do you feel like a cheeseburger for dinner?" he asked as they walked out of the park together.

"I want a cheeby, I want a cheeby," Jamie sang and skipped all the way to the car.

Mason had parked two streets away. If the officer had asked him how they'd got to the park, he would have just said they'd walked from home.

"Daddy, can I get an ice cream too?" Jamie asked, as he hopped into his booster seat.

Mason thought his son must have been mustering up his courage all the way to the car. "Sure thing, buddy," Mason responded affectionately. It was fake affection and Mason knew it. Although he was pleased to see his son happy, his real happiness came from the scene of destruction he had caused.

Chapter 4

Friday 3rd October 2003 (1am)

Raindrops began falling on the windscreen. At first, the rain was light but after only a few seconds, it was almost hailing. "Shit Geoff, turn on the ignition so we can wind down the windows." Geoff leaned forward and turned the key into the accessory position.

Jake, who was sitting in the passenger seat, hit the window button. As the window slid down the water began to drip in, landing on the sleeve of his three-quarter length woollen black jacket. "We need to keep our eyes open here," Jake said, without offering a glance at the driver.

He sat with his right hand on his Beretta that was resting on his knee and his left hand around the door handle, his eyes fixed on the entrance to the Mobile service station.

It was their third night on watch. All three nights had been dead quiet so far. "It's not going to happen again tonight," Geoff said, sounding half-asleep and bored to tears. During the last five hours, every word spoken between them had occurred without either of them taking their gaze off the entrance.

"It will happen," Jake replied softly, as if willing it through some psychic force. It had to happen soon, he thought. After all, nine servos had been hit in 11 days and this was the only one that had been missed in the same area.

Every hit had been the same. Five guys. Two took the entrance, two hit the safes and one went after the register. The last one had been a BP station where the attendant had been shot and killed.

A lady in a black BMW X3 pulled up at pump six. In the back, a little blonde girl was asleep, her head slumped forward. From Jake's perception, she was probably a single mum who had been on a night out.

The mother finished pumping the petrol into the vehicle, replaced the cap, locked the car, and headed in to pay.

Jake wondered if parents understood the risks of leaving children in cars unsupervised. It could go so wrong so quickly. The mother exited the servo, got back in her vehicle and headed off.

* * *

Jake began thinking about his own childhood. He had been a big boy; six foot two at the age of 12 and he was the only year 7 student who could dunk a basketball, something that most year 12 students still couldn't do. He didn't grow much taller but he bulked up once he started hitting the gym.

When he went into the academy, he weighed 110 kilograms and was all muscle. He could not only move fast but also do a 15 on the beep test. Even as a boy, he had genuinely cared about people and wanted to see justice done. He was the type of kid who was good at all sports and yet could study little and still pass with high marks.

When he was in year 10, his desire to be a cop was confirmed and the notion of preserving justice really hit home. Karl, one of his classmates, was sitting innocently in his mum's car. It was nothing flashy but it was a new Holden commodore, valued at $30,000. He had been engrossed in the cricket. It was the final session on day 1 and Australia was 2/258. Dean Jones was nearing his hundred.

While Karl's mother was in the shop collecting groceries for the evening meal, a man came out of nowhere and drove off in the car. Karl and his kid sister Amanda were taken with the vehicle.

Police later found both Amanda and Karl dead on the side of a dirt track, shot at close range. The carjacker was a man named James Mitchell, on a three-day coke bender. He was caught trying to escape to Sydney. He was convicted of manslaughter and sentenced to only 20 years' jail, his lawyer successfully arguing that the drugs had affected him to such an extent that he did not know what he was doing, therefore he'd had no intent to kill.

The lenient sentence angered Jake and he promised himself to keep doing his job of getting criminals off the streets, while hoping the judges would start handing out sentences that reflected the severity of the crime.

* * *

Snapping out of his reflections, Jake took his left hand off the door handle and picked up the radio. "How are things going in there? I hope you've left some doughnuts for the customers?"

"I haven't served a hot chick in an hour," Bobby's voice crackled back.

"Now come on Bobby, you're supposed to be looking out for these guys, not searching for a future wife."

"Just trying to stay undercover. I thought I was supposed to pass for a dumb servo attendant and I bet all they do is perv."

"I'm sure you're right. Just try and stay alert in there, ok?" Jake tried not to laugh at his stupid remarks.

He placed the handset back in the cradle and reached into the back seat for the Thermos and the cups. It was coffee time. He was in the middle of undoing the lid when a group of five men, all wearing black Nike hoodies, turned the corner and entered the servo.

Jake's coffee time would have to wait. He threw the Thermos in the back. "Heads up, guys!" Bobby's voice said across the radio before gunfire rang out.

Jake was halfway out the door when he saw Bobby's head jerk backwards and his body disappear behind the counter.

"Stay here and call for backup!" Jake shouted to Geoff as he drew his second Beretta from its right shoulder holster. With Berettas in both hands, Jake headed towards the entrance. He could see all five men begin to disperse quickly throughout the store. The one who had shot Bobby was now behind the counter with one of his buddies, while two ethnic looking guys were heading to the back of the store. The last suspect was fat and slow and he was halfway down the chip aisle heading towards the ATM.

Jake opened fire.

He didn't even wait until he was inside the store before he unleashed the other Beretta. He fired at the slow one first, three quick shots. Two of them found their target, one destroyed a bag of Doritos. The big guy fell to his knees, paused and then flopped head first onto the floor.

Jake then showered the front counter with six more bullets. He didn't think any of them hit but the spray bought him enough time to dive through the doors and slide behind the ice-cream machine. It wasn't ideal, but it gave him enough cover to continue his fire at the counter and the door that the other two had disappeared behind.

Jake reloaded his Beretta. He had a feeling he would need every bullet.

He peered over the ice-cream machine to see what was happening at the front of the store. The man who had shot Bobby returned fire with a 12 gauge. It was loud and it packed a punch. The outer side of the metal machine was sprayed with pellets. Jake felt a pellet clip his ear.

A large Caucasian man slid across the counter. Jake estimated he was several centimetres taller than he was and probably 15 kilos heavier. He landed, pumped his shotgun and ran towards Jake.

Jake acted quickly, firing two shots from each gun. He hit the gunman three times, twice in the neck and once in the chest. The last bullet flew into the counter somewhere. The gunman hit the floor, dropping his gun and clasping at his chest.

The two ethnic guys returned from the back of the store looking to see what the fuck was going on. Both men stepped through the doorway and instantly began firing. Jake ducked for cover. They looked like brothers, maybe even twins. The two kept firing for what seemed like an eternity.

The door buzzer went and Jake heard two quick shots followed by a third and finally a fourth. Jake's attention immediately turned to Geoff.

"Let's get this fuck and get out of here!" one of the voices from the rear of the store said. He sounded like a Maori.

Jake looked around the left corner of the machine. They were no longer standing in the doorway; they had obviously split up.

Jake heard movement on his left but could see nothing. He knelt down lower and saw the ankles of one of the men. They were fat and wide and led to big feet and big shoes. Jake aimed and let fire a quick burst. He wasn't sure how many shots he fired. He purposely shot in a direct line from the ankle upwards.

Cries of pain filled the petrol station; Jake had hit him but he wasn't sure where or how many times.

His brother came running out of the middle aisle firing his weapon, a high calibre Magnum. The buzzer went again as someone exited. Jake stood and fired through the door. The brother, running backwards, returned fire, and glass went flying everywhere. Jake continued to fire with both pistols until there was nothing left to fire. The brother had almost made the pump before Jake's bullets stilled him.

It wasn't until the gunfight was over that he realised he had been hit. It might have been a ricocheted bullet; nonetheless, the damage was done. Jake sat behind the machine once again, his calf spurting blood. He removed his jacket and ripped off the sleeves from his shirt, folded them and placed them over the bullet wound. He used his tie to hold the self-made bandages and hoped it would stem the flow of blood.

Jake reloaded and hobbled out from behind the machine, checking the corners and covering himself in both directions as he went from aisle to aisle. He came to the other brother. He was still alive but Jake didn't think he would last long. He had been hit several times, including in the chest and side. There was a large pool of blood under him and blood had started to seep from his ears.

Jake slowly headed towards the counter that Bobby had occupied only minutes earlier.

He went around the cash register side and saw Bobby slumped against the wall. He had been shot in the head at close range with the 12 gauge and the damage was significant. The blood splatter was all across the wall. Jake was lucky not to dry retch.

Jake left Bobby where he lay and headed for Geoff. The assailant on the driveway was dead but there was no sign of the one who had fled. Geoff was sitting where he had left him, but there was a trail of blood leading back to the car. Geoff's breathing was shallow and weak. "Hold on buddy, help's on the way."

Geoff had obviously met the fleeing robber on the drive. Geoff looked like he'd got the worst of the exchange.

Jake knelt beside Geoff until help arrived and then Jake was loaded into the second ambulance to have the bullet removed from his calf.

Geoff succumbed to his injuries on the way to the hospital. His vital organs had been directly hit and the blood loss was just too great.

By the time backup arrived, there were two dead officers and four dead robbers.

One was still missing. His name was Tyrone, and he lay just metres away at the bottom of the dumpster where he was hiding and trying to figure out what to do next. He had taken a shot to the knee and had struggled to make it this far.

He had killed a cop. Fuck, he was in deep shit now.

He could hear the police outside surrounding him, his blood trail easy to follow.

Tyrone had made the decision he would not be going back to jail. His plan was 'death by cop'. It was his only way out of this shithole and he accepted that his time to check out had arrived.

Tyrone reloaded, stood up and opened fire. He only managed two shots in his last blaze of glory before he finally checked out.

Chapter 5

Friday 3rd October 2003 (6am)

I had arrived early to prepare for my clients that day. It was only early but the offices opposite me were already buzzing with life.

I wasn't looking forward to the day, as I had a sex addict client coming in. I was helping her understand that sex and love were very different, and sex was not the only way to feel needed.

I hated dealing with sex addicts and divorcees, because they often misread a sympathetic ear as a sign of affection.

In this case, the attraction was there, well, the physical aspect anyway. She was stunning and I was…how would you put it? Male, and single. However, she was my patient and that line would never be crossed.

I took out the notes of our last session, which I had taped, as always. They knew I was the only one who ever listened to them.

Halfway through the tape, I received the call I had always feared. It was Jake Miller's mum. My best friend had been shot in the line of duty.

He was the only survivor of a sting that had gone wrong. His mum quickly reassured me that he was all right and his injuries were only minor. Of course, that's the last thing you think when you hear the word 'shot'.

Jake had spent years in the police force moving up from traffic to desk jockey, before he made detective and then lead detective in vice. After that, he'd headed up the armed robbery taskforce for the servo bandits.

Even though his injuries were minor, I put down the files and left a message for my secretary to reschedule all my appointments for that day.

Jake looked like he was enjoying the time off when I walked into his room. He was sitting in bed with his left leg up, wrapped in bandages, watching television and eating some sort of cereal. "It's 8am and you're already eating?" I said without hesitating.

"I'm still groggy from theatre but the food is helping."

I knew what he meant. I had spent more hours in hospital than anyone should ever have to.

I'd only been there a few minutes when Jake's parents walked into the room. His mum had a newspaper under her arm and his dad was holding a Styrofoam cup of coffee. "We got you a coffee and the newspaper, darl," his mum said.

"Thanks Mum," Jake mumbled with a mouth full of cereal.

The events of Jake's night had made the front page. The article, headed 'Two Police Dead in Servo Shootout', focused on the two dead police officer heroes rather than on the criminals. Below the heading were photos of Geoff and Bobby. There was also a separate two-page spread detailing the events.

Jake didn't read the article or speak of what had happened. He just lay there drinking his coffee. His parents left soon after, and he and I didn't speak much at first, until I asked him if he wanted to do the trivia in the paper. We used to do it quite often. He would usually win, but I was always up for the challenge.

After Jake again beat me at the trivia, I headed down to the hospital café for some food. I was starving and ordered an egg and bacon roll with a bottle of OJ. It was surprisingly good, or maybe I was just too hungry to notice it was average hospital food. On the way back,

I passed the gift shop and bought Jake a book, getting a copy for myself at the same time. It was Stephen King's latest novel, 'Wolves of the Calla', the fifth book in his 'Dark Tower' series. We'd both started reading the series in the early 1990s. The last in the series, 'Wizard and Glass', was a cracker and we'd been eagerly awaiting the next instalment.

When I arrived back in Jake's room, he was watching some morning TV show about how to use a newly designed ladder.

"Looks like riveting stuff, maybe you'll find this more to your liking." I handed him the book. He smiled. I sat in the chair next to his bed and we both began reading the continuing saga of Roland, Eddie, Susanna, Jake, and Oy.

When a loud voice interrupted us, Jake didn't even have to look up to know the voice belonged to his boss, Richard Knight. "Sorry to interrupt your recovery. I just wanted to run a few things past you so you know what's going on.

"We're holding a state funeral for Geoff and Bobby next week. Their families are hoping you'll be able to make it. They're very appreciative of everything you did. They know you did your best."

"I didn't do enough." Jake turned his head and attention to the window.

"You know, Jake, we have people you can talk to. You've been through an extraordinary ordeal."

"I'll be fine, I just need some time." Jake's attention remained fixed on the window.

"I do have some good news for you. I had a call from the head of homicide this morning requesting you be transferred there. I said I'd speak to you about it. They want you to be the new lead detective of the Slayer taskforce, Eagle. You get to select your own team."

Jake didn't reply immediately, and Richard continued. "Have a think about it."

Jake looked at the captain. "I'll do it. Send me the files and I'll get started from here."

"It can wait a few days, Jake," Richard replied.

"Just send the files," Jake repeated. Richard nodded. He looked uncomfortable but he didn't seem ready to leave.

Jake returned his attention to his book.

"Are you ok?" I asked. He lifted his head and his eyes met mine. "Geoff and Bobby are dead because of me, I didn't do enough, Brodie, it's as simple as that." Tears welled in his eyes.

I offered no advice because there was nothing I could say that would help. We had been friends for years and he knew I understood his pain.

Jake put his bookmark in the book and put the book down beside him. "You know, if I'm heading up the Slayer taskforce, I'll need a criminologist. Interested?"

"Are you able to do that?"

"Of course. They'll need someone to have a fresh look and if I bring in fresh people, that will be even better. You're qualified, aren't you?

"Yes, of course I am, you know that. But I'm not a police officer. I can't just become one."

"I can get the commissioner to use his authority to make you one," Richard interrupted.

"Can he do that?" I asked, still unsure of the possibility.

"Believe it or not, section 27 of the Police Act allows for the commissioner to waive the prescribed requirements and appoint anyone as a police officer under special circumstances. I think seven unsolved police murders qualifies as special circumstances. Don't you think?" Richard asked.

"Well it's settled then," Jake said. "You're a qualified criminologist and I need to appoint one to my taskforce. And the chief will organise with the commissioner to make it official."

I sat there in shock. I couldn't believe that with this turn of events, something I'd dreamed of all my life was now a reality.

Jake pressed the buzzer for a nurse, who arrived shortly

afterwards. I could tell he was taken aback by her looks. He tried to read her nametag without giving the impression he was staring at her breasts. I saw that it read 'Hayley'.

"What can I help you with, Detective?" Her voice was soft and sweet. Her curly blonde hair would have reached just below her shoulders had it not been in a ponytail. She was reasonably tall, about five foot eight.

Jake remained frozen before finally regaining his senses. "I was wondering if I could get a video recorder hooked up to my TV? I'm expecting some case information to come in. If not, I can arrange to have it done."

"No, that's ok. We have some around. I'll get it hooked up for you."

"No rush, I'm not expecting the information for a little while. Just when you get a chance."

Hayley checked his chart and then left the room.

"You were a bit speechless there, buddy. You ok?"

"She was amazing, don't you think?"

I nodded. "Female nurses and paramedics always seem to be hot." That had been my experience, anyway. "The best thing is, she's single."

Jake frowned and looked at me. "How do you know?"

"Firstly, no ring, and secondly, she was extremely well presented for a day at work. She's 'on the market'," I said, nodding. "But don't get too excited, you'll be competing with all the doctors and they earn more than you," I added.

Jake started to reply, then stopped, as if about to argue the point but then thinking better of it.

It took only about 20 minutes before the VCR was brought into the room and hooked up to the existing TV.

Jake knew if he didn't ask her out, he would never forgive himself. Maybe the events of the night before had affected him more than he knew. Subconsciously, life had suddenly become more precious than it had been just 24 hours before. "So, Hayley, what do you do when you're not working here?" Jake asked sheepishly.

"Is that a way to ask me out, without asking me out, Detective?"

My head was buried in my book and there was no way it was coming out until this little bit of banter was done with.

"Would you like to go out for dinner sometime?" Jake asked, still unsure of what her answer would be.

Hayley smiled, "I would love to, thank you. But we might have to wait until you're back on your feet." She continued smiling as she finished taking his obs and adding the details to his chart. "I'll come and see you again later. We can exchange numbers then." She turned and left his room. Her smile had not faded.

"I told you she was single," I said, keeping my head in my book. Stephen King had introduced me to a new word, 'roont', meaning ruined. He never let me down when it came to new ways of enhancing my imagination.

Jake raised his eyebrows and offered a quick, simple response. "That's why you're the profiler," he said with a slight smirk, going back to his book.

When a uniformed officer arrived carrying a filing box, Jake knew the information he was waiting for had arrived. He set his book aside. He was already ahead of me.

He asked the officer to place the box on the chair next to his bed.

I stood up from a chair on the other side of Jake's bed. "I'd better go and leave you to it."

Jake looked from the box to me. "After I've looked through this stuff, I'll get it sent over to your office," he said, removing the lid.

"No problem, I'll be in to see you again in the morning." I patted him on his good leg and left his room.

* * *

Jake removed the first manila folder from the box labelled 'Rebecca Carrington'. He opened the file clipped to the left-hand side protected by a clear A4 plastic folder that contained a set of crime scene photos.

On the right-hand side of the file was a stack of paperwork. The crime investigation report.

Rebecca had been on her way to work. It was only a short 15-minute walk from her house to the police academy. Her husband, Simon Carrington, said she always left at approximately 7.15am to ensure she was at the academy by 7.30am.

Simon had been ruled out as a suspect very early in the investigation. He had a solid alibi and when the second murder occurred, it was clear to investigators that they were dealing with someone far more dangerous than a possible jilted husband.

Rebecca was still considered a missing person despite the fact investigators believed she had already been murdered.

Jake leaned back against his pillows and placed the pen in his mouth, thinking.

Then he wrote a single note on a blank sheet of paper.

'First victim – mistakes made? Reason why she hasn't been dumped?'

Jake put the Carrington file to one side and withdrew the next file from the box, 'Karen Fitzgerald'. Karen had disappeared less than two years after Rebecca went missing. Although she was slightly younger, Karen's features were similar to Rebecca's. They were roughly the same height and had the same long blonde hair and hourglass figure.

Karen's disappearance was eerily similar to Rebecca's. Karen had been on her way home from the Prahran Police Station, and was last seen getting off the bus only 500 metres from her home. It seemed extremely likely that the same person was responsible for the disappearance of both women.

Two things concerned the investigators.

1. This offender seemed to have no geographical boundaries.
2. The offender was directly targeting female police officers.

Three weeks later, Karen's body was found floating in the Yarra River in the suburb of Warrenwood.

According to the coroner's report, her body showed marks most likely caused by an electrical current, from either a stun gun or a cattle prod. There were also traces of Benzodiazepine found in her system, a drug with sedative and muscle relaxant properties.

Cause of death was listed as multiple stab wounds – 81 in all. Many of them had occurred post mortem. Overkill, as it was commonly known within police circles, often pointed to a sadistic killer where the act of killing was the reason for the killing.

The existence of overkill led Jake to believe that this person had had time on his side. He must have been in a place where he wouldn't be disturbed. You don't stab someone 81 times on the street.

Jake continued through the autopsy report and noted a second important piece of information. Karen had been dead for up to 19 days before she was found. This confirmed to Jake that the girls were being taken somewhere to be killed.

None of Karen's belongings had ever been found.

Jake wrote several more notes.

1. Using stun gun and sedative on victim.
2. Victims being moved after death.
3. Time taken with murder.
4. Offender non-geographical.
5. Overkill present.
6. No witnesses, no suspects.

Jake then examined the evidence register in the file.

It was blank except for one note at the bottom of the page. 'No trace evidence found due to victim being submerged prior to being found. Victim may also have been washed prior to being dumped.'

Jake placed the files and his notes on the side table, lay his head back and closed his eyes. It had been a long day and night. He was exhausted and his body desperately needed sleep but his mind was racing.

Soon enough sleep came.

Chapter 6

Monday 6th October 2003 (8am)

J ake had told me that he would send the files to my office, but I was surprised when lobby security advised me I had a delivery when I arrived first thing Monday morning.

Norm was far from the fittest security guard who worked in the Northbrook office building. In fact, from what I had witnessed, he looked as if his lunch was usually a combination of hamburgers and coke with the odd guilty-occasion wrap and diet coke. His belt buckle was on the last hole and the shirt buttons looked as if they were about to pop and fly through the air at high velocity.

"I'll have one of the guys bring them up to your office on a trolley, Brodie." He tapped the top of the box.

I thanked Norm and headed up to my office to get a head start. My office consisted of a reception area with a medium sized room adjoining it, which I had converted into a waiting area. Then there were two offices, one temporarily being used for filing until my business was big enough to put on a colleague. My office was by far the bigger of the two, with room for my desk, a bookcase, a couch, and plenty of space. Each office in the building was also equipped with a small kitchenette, although the bathrooms on each floor were communal.

Minutes after I'd arrived, a security guard who I had never met before arrived with a trolley carrying several boxes.

I picked out a file at random. I didn't need to start with the first murder. I knew that the first victim was still missing and that finding her would be the key.

Then I flicked through the other files. The cases were all similar to one another. I placed the victims' photos on the desk side by side. I wondered if there were similarities in the dump sites, or whether the bodies had been posed after death.

Apart from the method of decapitation, common to all the murders where the victims had been found, the sites were all different in style and location. Also, the bodies had been dumped, not posed.

One thing concerned me: whoever had done this was very confident. Usually, serial killers were geographical, only killing and dumping where they were familiar with the area. This person had shown that he could abduct and dump all across the city.

Apart from letting me know that he was confident, it also led me to believe he knew his areas. Perhaps he had a job that involved a lot of driving?

I jotted down some professions that could give freedom of movement.

Truck driver
Salesperson
Retail merchandise supplier

Then my mind went to the victims themselves. Why police officers? Why these girls? The girls were from all over the state. All were blonde and had similar features.

He had a type. What did this tell us?

I sat back in my chair and pondered, then added to my notes.

Blonde women all similar in appearance.
Past police officer upset with the force, maybe a disgruntled ex-cop.

Suffered abuse as a child.

A hatred of police. Family involved in crime?

Maybe lost a family member at the hands of a police officer and looking for payback?

Any of these reasons could have been the initial trigger.

However, if my studies had taught me anything, he continued to kill because he enjoyed the power it gave him over the women. He liked to be in control. He enjoyed the thrill and the rush.

He was hooked.

His next victim fed the addiction but like any addiction it would become insatiable.

* * *

I spent the next two days in and out of the hospital visiting Jake. When I wasn't at his bedside reading our new book, I was looking at the case files hoping I would come up with something. Some miracle breakthrough: some vital clue everyone else had missed.

However, the few days I had spent on the case had so far revealed no such result.

Jake and I had agreed not to discuss the case until he was out of hospital and I had finished my review. A lunch would be good for both of us, we decided.

Chapter 7

Monday 12th October 2003 (12.30pm)

After a week's rest, Jake was still on crutches and I picked him up from his apartment in Docklands. His apartment was architecturally designed and elegant and its location was ideal, just a short stroll from the Telstra Dome, a place we both loved to visit when either of our teams played and time permitted.

Jake took it slowly coming down to the car, still getting used to his crutches. Our restaurant was only minutes from Jake's apartment and while it wasn't the cheapest place for a steak, you were guaranteed a great meal. I was sure Jake would be craving a good feed, as usual.

We hadn't even ordered our drinks before Jake started on the shop talk. "Before we start, congratulations are in order. You're officially a detective." He slid my badge across the table. It was majestic, I never thought I would hold one let alone be given one. "You don't get a gun until you've done the safety course and have spent time at the range. So, Detective, what do you think?"

I wasn't used to being called detective and it was something that would take time to get used to. Clearly, Jake had been chomping at the bit to discuss the case. I was just as keen to discuss my thoughts.

"I think you're correct in assuming your missing person Rebecca Carrington was in fact his first victim. I think the reason she hasn't yet been found is because something went wrong and maybe he worried he would have left evidence behind. He dumped the other women because he believes he got his method right. But be assured, the dumping of the women is not just to get rid of the bodies. He's dumping them to send us a message."

"There were no messages left with the bodies though. What message is he trying to send us?" Jake responded quizzically.

"He's not trying to communicate with us directly as some serial killers do, although that may yet happen. His message is simple. He's saying, "I'm in control. Look at what I've done.""

"Ok, so he's in control, why then is he cutting off their heads? I think he's saying 'I'm a fuckin' nut bag'."

"I think you'll find that the removal of the heads is also a control thing. Jeffrey Dahmer kept parts of his victims. He didn't want them to leave. He even ate some of them so they'd be with him forever."

"You serious? Man, some people are fucked. You saying this guy could be eating the heads? You wouldn't want to look in the toilet bowl the next day. You might have an eyeball staring back at you."

Humour was a way Jake dealt with stress.

"I don't know if he eats them but I would think he's collecting them in some way. I also think he maybe visits the dump sites. I wouldn't be surprised if he enjoyed watching us fuss over his latest conquest."

The waitress arrived asking if we were ready to order. From his order, I think Jake had been ready days ago. His was goat's cheese tortellini for entree and a rib eye for main with chips and salad. I ordered the same for entree but went for the rack of lamb as the main. We both had soft drinks because of our various medications warning against mixing with alcohol.

"There are a few things that I think are particularly important to this case," I said. "One. Why is he choosing policewomen? Most serial killers choose victims like prostitutes or backpackers, easy targets who are usually not reported missing for days or weeks.

But this guy picks girls who can defend themselves and yet will be reported missing immediately. There's a reason for his selection, although what that is, we may never know.

"Two. He is methodical. These are not opportunistic victims. Somehow, he's targeted them specifically. He washes the bodies clean and then dumps them at a predetermined location. He plans everything.

"Three. He loves what he's doing and he'll get better. The wounds on the victims show overkill, which means he enjoys the act of killing."

"I think it shows he had time with the victim, time to do what he wanted," Jake said.

I nodded in agreement.

"Four. The fact that our victims are not raped doesn't mean the killings aren't sexual. I'm sure he gets sexual pleasure out of every kill. Maybe that's why he keeps the heads to relive the fantasy."

"So how do we catch him then?" Jake asked.

"Unfortunately, unless we get lucky, we're going to have to hope he makes a mistake. But that means there'll be more victims."

Jake nodded and had another sip of his lemon squash.

I continued, "There are a few things I think we can do. Look at any ex-police officers and parolees incarcerated between February and October 2000 who are now doing a job that involves a lot of travel, especially driving."

"So what happened in 2000 that I'm missing?" Jake asked, as the waitress brought our entrees.

"Would you like another drink each?" she asked. She'd already removed my last drink without asking, and I hadn't even finished it. Nothing annoyed me more, but she looked young and probably didn't know any better.

"Great, thanks," Jake replied, digging into his pasta.

"Make sure your tip is a dollar less. You still had a quarter left." Jake had a way of knowing just what I was thinking.

"Back to 2000," I continued. "It was the only period over the past 10 years that there were no murders. Something happened that made him stop for a while. We need to look at that carefully."

"I thought you said he wasn't going to stop?" Jake said, as he scraped the last of his burnt butter sauce onto his fork.

"He didn't stop. He paused for a while. A cooling off period. Maybe he couldn't find anything that excited him. Maybe he was in custody."

"Ok, we'll look into the jail records see if any names on our radar appear." Jake wiped his mouth and pushed the plate to one side, then asked, "And why did you say he must have a job involving driving?"

"Because he only dumps bodies in areas he's familiar with. Based on the big distances between dump sites, he frequents a lot of areas."

We spent the next hour arguing about how people became serial killers. I believed they were a product of their environment, upbringing and circumstances. Jake believed that some people were just born evil, with all goodness missing from them.

That thought was just too simplistic for me. When our discussion became heated, we agreed to disagree. We were good like that. No matter how much we disagreed, we always put the friendship first.

With the serial killer discussion abandoned, conversation turned to Jake's stay in the hospital. More precisely, his upcoming date. "So, when is the date?" I asked as my main arrived, and it looked beyond delicious. The rack was set on a bed of mashed potato and minted peas and was served with a red wine jus. Not waiting for Jake to answer, I hoed in. When I looked up from my first mouthful, I realised Jake hadn't answered because his mouth was also full.

"Sorry bud, so looking forward to this. Next week, sometime, we haven't nailed anything down exactly yet. It will depend on how I feel."

I got the impression he wasn't too keen on discussing his potential date. Maybe he was worried he would jinx himself.

"So how are you enjoying 'Wolves of the Calla'?"

Jake was getting through his steak, answering with a mouth full of beef. "Awesome. Almost finished. It's going to be another cliff hanger," he added, cutting into his next piece of meat. "I have about a hundred pages to go and I'm hoping to knock it off tonight. It's getting exciting."

I scraped the last of my potato and lamb onto my fork. Nothing was going to waste. "I think I have two-fifty to go. I find it hard to stay focused with everything that's happened over the last few days."

"It's been crazy," Jake agreed.

We finished off our lunch with dessert and an in-depth analysis of who was favourite for the NBA title and which players would rise to stardom in the next few years. We both agreed that LeBron James would be a star, as number one picks should be. We both had doubts over the number two pick, Darko Milicic. I would have chosen Chris Bosh. Jake said he would have gone with Dwyane Wade.

"Only time will tell," I said.

"I'll be proven right," Jake said, always wanting to stir the pot a little.

On the drive home, Jake organised a meeting for the next day with the outgoing lead detectives of the Eagle taskforce. It was the official handover, but Jake used the word 'briefing' so as not to offend.

Chapter 8

Thursday 16th October 2003 (1pm)

Mason sat in his car just down from the police academy in Glen Waverley. It was the second Thursday he'd done this. Although he was facing south, he was looking north, in the rear-view mirror. The recruits were beginning to leave. Most left in cars, but some on foot. It seemed today there were more entering than leaving. He hadn't seen anything he liked. Nothing close to his type had triggered his dark desire. But she should be coming soon. Any minute now, he thought.

The academy had produced three of his six victims and his big concern was that it wasn't the best place for him to consider again, given the heat his endeavours had caused. But as he always told himself, high risk, high reward. As if on cue, out she walked. This one took his breath away and excited him like none before her. While the uniform and the blonde hair triggered his desire, it was the thrill of the kill that kept him looking for more.

Mason hoped she would follow the same routine as she had last time.

The hunting phase was the most enjoyable part, except for the end. Mason thought he liked the hunt the most because it gave him a god-like sense. As he sat there, he wondered what this girl's name was, what her hobbies were and what family she had.

Finally, Mason thought, 'it's funny how fate finds people.' Everything this girl had done in her life so far had led her to this point. Nothing but the intervention of God himself would stop him from adding her to his collection.

Mason waited until she was almost out of sight before he started his car and began to pull away slowly from the curb. He drove past her as she continued her walk. Mason turned his vehicle into the next side street and pulled over. He kept his vehicle running and leaned over to his passenger door and removed his Melway Street Directory, which sat neatly in its own leather-bound protective cover. He opened it to the Glen Waverley pages and began to pretend he was lost and checking his whereabouts.

Mason expected that he would soon see her turn into the street.

He was overwhelmed with joy. The thought of confirming where 'Blondie' lived was like winning the lottery. Even though he had seen her leave the police academy, it didn't mean she was enrolled there.

After all, receptionists, bookkeepers and other admin staff also worked there.

Mason removed his spiral-bound notebook and flicked through to the page with the folded corner. He paused, watching her, hoping she would enter a home soon. He was still pretending to be looking up an address as he watched her continue walking to the end of the street. Suddenly, she turned left and entered a property. It was in the distance, but Mason could make out a double-storey house with an orange, tiled roof. He would have to drive past to get the number. He waited a few more minutes to ensure she was inside.

Leaving his notepad open on the passenger seat, he started the ignition and headed towards the orange roof. The number '4' was written on the page and Mason simply ticked it.

* * *

Mason sat in his study while his son played and his wife cooked dinner. His family knew that once the doors of the study were closed, it meant he did not want to be disturbed.

Every piece of furniture in his study was opposite in style to the rest of the house, which was decorated in Edwardian style. His study was furnished in Georgian style. Mason's desk had been specially made to suit his needs. It had been crafted out of mahogany and it matched the green Chesterfield lounge suite in the corner of his office.

A large grandfather clock with a gold chime pendulum stood in the opposite corner. It chimed resoundingly every hour, on the hour. It had originally belonged to Mason's grandfather. On the wall behind his desk hung his estate agent's licence, the only item hanging on the wall of his study. Mason paused, remembering the day he'd graduated. Finally, the days of the fast bucks had begun.

His mother had wanted him to be a police officer, like his father and his two brothers. He couldn't think of anything worse; after all, it was the police force that had taken his father from him at the age of nine. Mason recalled that night as if it was yesterday.

But he remembered the two years leading up to his father's death more clearly. Maybe remembering them wasn't exactly correct. Maybe haunted by the two years leading up would be a better way of thinking about it, Mason thought, correcting his thoughts as he continued his stroll down memory lane.

He had just turned seven the first time he'd been woken in the middle of the night by his father sliding into bed next to him. It sent a shiver down his spine even as he thought of it now, all these years later.

He'd meant to ask his father what he was doing but he never got the chance. His father placed his hand over his mouth and began to remove his Superman PJs. The rest was a painful blur that would be repeated many times before his father's death. Even though the first time didn't last long, it was long enough to scar him for life. Mason didn't understand what had happened exactly but he did know it was wrong.

His dad left his room that night with the only sentence spoken between them. "If you ever say anything, bad things will happen to your mother and you wouldn't want that, would you?" Mason shook his head, desperately clinging to his doona. "This is our secret," his father reinforced, as he closed the bedroom door behind him.

After the second incident, his father brought him home two Huskie pups. Mason knew the real reason behind the dogs. His mother just thought he was being a good dad.

The pups were beautiful. One was all white and Mason named him Snow, while the other was grey with touches of white. He named this one Storm. He loved those dogs and considered them the two best friends he'd ever had. He never had any real friends at school. He often spent school lunch times sitting by himself. He even had trouble connecting with his brothers, who chose to spend time with each other rather than with him. He was definitely the odd one out.

By the end of the second year of his father's midnight visits, Mason had decided enough was enough and despite his dad's threats, he was ready to tell his mum.

It was a Friday night, and he was happy that there was no school the next day. It was past midnight. Mason remembered seeing his clock radio showing 12 but he couldn't remember the rest of the display. Usually, Mason would pretend he was asleep and just think of his favourite things when his father began his routine. But on that Friday night there was to be no pretending: everything would be out in the open. As his father climbed into his bed, Mason rolled over to confront him. "Not tonight, Dad. Not any night ever again: it stops here." Mason's voice was weak and jittery but the words came out clearly enough.

"I think you've forgotten our deal, Mase," he replied quietly.

"Not at all, Dad. If you ever touch me again, I will not only tell Mum but your captain, and I know he's hanging out for any excuse to boot your drunken arse off the force. Imagine how happy he'll be to send you to jail." His voice was no longer weak or quivering, he was firm and confident. "Leave now and I'll never say anything to anyone."

Mason's father looked ready to speak but then, as if reconsidering his position, he paused for a moment, and then left his son's room.

Mason had the best sleep he'd had in years and it felt good.

Saturday morning was brighter than any of the Saturdays he could remember in a long time. He had a spring in his step and his secret was no longer his shadow. His father was sitting at the head of the table eating his eggs and reading the paper. Steam rose off his freshly made coffee. His mother was in her usual Saturday house-work clothes and she was standing at the stove making porridge. "Morning hun. Would you like some porridge?" she asked in her happy Saturday voice.

Before Mason could reply, his father spoke, his head still buried in the morning paper. "Looks like someone tried to break into the shed last night. Storm must have disturbed him. He was cut up pretty bad, Mase. Unfortunately when I found him this morning, it was too late."

His mother turned from the stove. "Oh George! We need to call the police. That's horrible." She turned off the stove and headed over to hold Mason.

"I am the police, dear. It was most likely local kids trying to steal some tools. We'll never find them." His father was trying to put an end to the conversation.

Mason broke from his mother's grasp and headed towards the back door, tears welling in his eyes. The path to the door had become blurry.

George stood up and grabbed Mason by the arm before he reached the door, pulling him in for a consoling hug, or so it would seem to his mother.

"Don't threaten me again, nothing stops," he whispered, then released him.

Mason would never forget when he first saw Storm lying in the dirt, his fur smeared with mud and blood. His throat had been cut and his body had been punctured many times. It had been a painful death, Mason thought.

His father had left Storm's body for Mason to see and for Mason to bury. Only a monster, like George, would do this to his nine-year-old son.

Mason spent that sunny Saturday morning burying Storm. He knew the perfect spot, a quiet place on the farm that enjoyed the sunlight as well as the tranquil sounds of the stream. He had spent many days sitting on the grass by the stream playing fetch and enjoying the quiet. It was his spot and his alone and it was going to stay that way.

Mason expected his father to pay him a visit that Saturday night but when 2am had come and he was still alone, Mason decided he had to make sure his dad never visited again.

Mason removed the doona, put some track pants over his PJs and pulled an old windcheater over his singlet. As the floor creaked beneath him when he moved throughout the house, he was sure he would wake his parents or even his brothers, but no one woke. No one came to investigate the rumblings within the house.

It was cold and frosty out. Mason pulled up his hood and headed towards Snow.

He approached Snow quietly so he wouldn't be startled and begin a barking frenzy that would be sure to wake everyone in the house. "Here boy," he called softly, holding out a treat in his palm.

Snow approached excitedly. Mason put his hands around him and hugged him tightly, never wanting to let him go. Snow returned the love with a generous licking of the face and ears that seemed to be propelled by his wagging tail.

Mason took Snow by the collar and led him away from the house, to his spot by the stream. The same spot where he had finished laying Storm to rest only hours earlier.

Snow sat next to him panting. Mason sat on the damp frosty grass beside him and stroked his fur. He played with his ears and told him how much he loved him. His tears flowed for the second time that day. "I'm sorry, buddy," he whispered. Snow responded with another set of licks. Mason removed the knife from his sock, took Snow by the muzzle to muffle any sound, kissed him on his nose one last time. Mason took a deep breath then drove the knife deep into Snow's chest as hard as he could. Snow whimpered a few times before he fell limply into Mason's lap. It was the last time Mason ever cried.

Mason carried Snow back to his kennel and laid him in the mud where he had found Storm that morning. He removed the knife from his sock. To this day, he didn't remember decapitating Snow or slashing his dad's tyres, but he knew he must have done it.

Sunday morning it was Mason sitting at the table when his parents came out for breakfast. "Mum was right. We should have called the cops, those guys came back. They killed Snow this time and I think they slashed your tyres, Dad."

His father stood there, unemotional and silent. His mother had clasped her hand to her mouth as if to prevent herself from screaming.

His father's night visits stopped from then on.

Mason knew the events of that weekend had taken his soul. From that day forward, he'd felt removed from everything and everyone, as if he was in a constant dream. Nothing seemed real.

Less than a week later, death again entered his family.

It was a Friday night when his father was killed at work. His mum had told him there was an accident and his father had been killed.

The report said that George Mason and his new partner, Samantha Leirs, who had only recently graduated from the academy, were called out to Prahran on a suspected B&E. Upon arrival, they had surveyed the premises for any signs of unlawful entry. The back of the factory revealed an open roller door that was a quarter of the way up, enough for someone to slide under.

According to the report, George entered the building first, flashlight over pistol per standard police procedure. According to Samantha, they had only taken a few steps once she entered before they split. They were both making their way to the front of the factory, with Sam taking the left and George the right. There were pallets stacked floor to ceiling. There were no lights on in the factory but George could see light moving off to his left. He was hoping it was Sam's flashlight. George thought it best that he head over her way just in case she needed help. He turned off his flashlight and began to head towards the light to his left. A sudden burst of gunfire rang out, which was quickly answered by another short burst of gunfire.

The gunfire broke the eerie silence and almost pierced Samantha's eardrums. Before the echoing had stopped, Sam had taken cover, down on one knee, waiting for whoever had just fired at her to make themselves visible. George was also shocked by the sudden fire and noticed the lights he was following had disappeared. They had either killed Sam or they were now hunting her. George had immediately thought the worst and began to run towards where the light had been. His eyes had adjusted to the dark and despite his better judgement and police procedure, he left his flashlight off; the last thing he wanted was to be a walking lighthouse for some nut to pick off at ease.

With her knee resting on the cold cement floor and her back protected by the pallet behind her, a thought suddenly struck her. What if they weren't shooting at her? What if they had just killed George and he was lying in a pool of blood and they were coming for her? This question continued to run through her mind until the sound of running brought it to a sudden stop. The footsteps sounded quick and heavy. She thought it was only one set but then second-guessed herself. Then it appeared. It was distant but it was there and it was running towards her. She froze with fear, her mind blank. What was she supposed to do? She couldn't remember. The shadow moved closer, in fact it was running at her. Still she sat frozen to her spot. The shadow was holding something, a gun, it was definitely a gun. Soon the shadow would see her and she would be dead. She realised it was either shoot or die. She took a breath and pulled the trigger.

It could be George, she briefly thought as she squeezed but no sooner had it entered her head, than the explosion of her gun rang out. The shadow staggered. She fired again ignoring the nagging voice in her head. Her gun was empty. The shadow had finally dropped and was still. Her hands were shaking, heart pounding, chest tight, and she was struggling to regain her normal breathing. She placed her head in her hands and then it hit her.

It never occurred to George the shots he heard were aimed at him from his partner until the first bullet had hit him. Four more struck then struck in quick succession. He had heard a sixth shot but had not felt it hit him. By that time, he was beyond feeling anything.

Sam went into shock as soon as she saw George on the ground. She had killed him and nothing would undo it.

Several months later, an independent police enquiry cleared Sam. It was determined that George's decision to stray from following standard police procedure had significantly contributed to his own death.

While Sam was cleared, it was recommended that she be moved back to traffic for 12 months.

Hundreds of police were on parade at the funeral. His mum cried, even his brothers shed a tear, obviously their memories of night visits having begun to fade. Mason's were still too fresh to end in anything but hate. Mason had fantasised about putting his father in the ground himself, but now that opportunity was gone and they would all pay the price.

Everyone who spoke made out George to be a saint, a pillar of the community. Little did they know they were crying over someone who was roasting in Hell.

The only sad thought Mason had now was that there was no one to unleash his pain upon.

* * *

With the chime of Windows 2000 starting up, his memories faded.

"At last we have lift-off," Mason mumbled to himself.

He double clicked the Impact property logo and waited for it to boot. Impact was a perfect tool for his real estate career as well as for his side projects. It was like a reverse phone directory. He could type in the address and the program would show the owner's contact details, including all telephone numbers.

It would never have occurred to the programmers that the program might be used by a serial killer to find his victims. While it loaded, he looked at the two photos sitting on his desk. One was a photo of him on his honeymoon in 2000. He and his bride had spent almost a year touring the states. The other was a photo of the cabin after his renovations.

Mason typed the address into the search bar and a name and number appeared. Without hesitation, Mason picked up the receiver and began to dial.

"Hello?" a voice answered.

"Yes, I was after a Miss Janson?"

"Speaking," the voice replied.

"Miss Janson, you don't know me, my name is Bill Taylor. I'm from the Victorian Police. I'm just ringing our graduate classes to see if any of the students need any help or have any concerns."

"No, everything is fine, only a few weeks to go, so I'm really excited."

"Miss Janson…" Mason began again before she cut him off.

"Maggie, please call me Maggie," the soft voice on the other end of the phone said.

Finally, Mason thought, as he continued, "Sorry Maggie, I just have a few quick questions for you. As I'm with Human Resources here at the Victorian Police, I just wondered if you have any preference of station to begin your career?"

"No, I'm fine, I'll be happy anywhere."

"We have a lot of country positions available at the moment and we're always careful not to break up families. God knows this job is hard enough without being away from your partner." Mason paused, hoping she would butt in again. When she did, it was like magic, he thought.

Maggie replied, "No, I don't care where I go, I have no partner or kids, but I don't want to be too far from my parents if I can avoid it."

The smile on Mason's face had widened and he was becoming more excited with each word she spoke.

"It's tough for young people to be away from their parents, especially when they're still living at home."

"Oh God no. I moved out a year ago, but I see them all the time," Maggie replied.

"Well, thanks for the chat Maggie, I'll come and introduce myself at your graduation and I'll do my best to keep you local."

"Thank you, nice to speak to you, Bill."

Mason hung up the phone. He was excited. He was pretty sure she lived alone. There might be a housemate but unlikely, Mason thought. It would be worth the risk anyway.

He rocked back in his office chair, steepling his hands and holding them under his chin. Soon, Maggie, soon your path will cross mine and that's where it will end.

The golden handle of his office door turned and slowly opened. A cute face peeped in. "You busy, Daddy?" the little voice asked in a cautious tone so as not to upset his father.

"No Jamie, I've just finished," Mason answered.

"Good, come eat it before it goes cold, k?" There was no 'o' with Jamie, it was always just 'k'. Jamie opened the door a little further and stretched out his arm, motioning with his hand to come.

He had learned this gesture from his favourite TV WWF character 'The Rock'. Mason couldn't help but laugh. He was glad his wife was still cooking dinner. Had she known that he was allowing Jamie to watch wrestling, she would be upset. If she knew Jamie was copying the characters' moves, she would be furious.

Rising out of the chair, Mason picked up Jamie and headed to the table for dinner.

Chapter 9

Friday 17th October 2003 (8am)

Jake and I walked up the stairs of the St Kilda Road Police Station. It was where Jake was based and it would be the new home of the Eagle taskforce. We were there to meet the previous heads of the taskforce and revisit the current leads.

Senior Detective Warren James was the outgoing head of Eagle but he held no grudge about being replaced. He was a true professional, happy to help in any way he could.

Once we exited the lift, we headed towards what Jake called the control room. Jake led the way, through to a smaller boardroom. The room was full of laptops, whiteboards, notes, and pictures, clearly the information hub of the taskforce. The whiteboards contained names, dates and victims' details and then on a separate whiteboard were stuck two photos labelled 'suspect 1' and 'suspect 2'.

I peeled the tape from the whiteboard and took both photos with me into the adjoining boardroom.

I sat down at the boardroom table in the seat next to Jake. Warren sat opposite us with two men I had never met, one either side of him. His two colleagues looked a lot more put out about being replaced than their boss did.

After a general discussion, I posed the question regarding the two pictures. "What do you have on these two?" I asked.

"Well, suspect 1 is our best to date. However, he doesn't outdo the other guy by much. His name is Tony Donaldson. He's been in for three interviews and hasn't been unable to provide an alibi for any of the murders, although the medical examiner can't be exact on time of death, due to the substantial time some of the victims were exposed to the elements."

"What, not even for one of the days? He has no one who can vouch for him?"

"Correct," Warren replied, taking a sip of his coffee.

"The other reason he's our number one guy is that he has a previous record, did two years for rape 12 years ago and he's on the sexual offenders register. He was released just months before the first disappearance. We picked him up about six months ago. We had a call from his neighbour saying he was going out late at night, so we put a tail on him and found him trawling the streets. We grabbed him after he spent a night sitting in a bar for five hours. It was a police bar.

"While he hadn't committed any crime, his activity was unusual considering his past. Not many ex-cons visit known police bars. When we questioned him, he said it was simple, he was trying to find the killer. He wanted the reward money. He said the best way to catch a killer was to try and place himself in the killer's shoes. We asked him to partake in a polygraph but he refused and we don't have anything to get a warrant for one. We still have the tail on him, but our budget has limits."

"The other guy is Lance Silver. Again, he is a sexual predator who has done a stint in Port Philip for attempted kidnapping. Every time a victim has been taken, he's been out. Coincidentally, during the cooling-off periods in the disappearances, we discovered he'd been in the big house. He did two stints, one for six months for B&E and another of 12 months for stalking. Both times, there were no new disappearances that we believe are related to the case.

"Importantly, the person being stalked was an ex-girlfriend, who was also a police officer. She had no idea of his past.”

Jake and I looked at each other as if we both suddenly knew this was our guy. However, we both knew that being a depraved sex offender didn't automatically make him a killer.

“We've raided both their homes and found some items of interest, but nothing that links either of them directly to any of the victims. We found what looks like kill kits in both homes, plus in Lance's home we found a lot of porn, mostly bondage. He also had a fascination with serial killers. Found a heap of material on Bundy, in particular.”

I reached for the jug of cool water from the middle of the board table. As I poured the chilled water into the glass, something came to me. “You know, Bundy was well known for staging to catch his prey. He would pretend he had a broken arm and be struggling to get into his car at the college campus. Girls would come to help him any time he had his hands full and bang, he would strike. As they say, beware the man with a fake limp.” Their talking stopped. “It could be his inspiration.” I put the cool glass to my lips and the chilled water shocked my teeth.

Jake turned from me and requested Warren to continue his thoughts. “As I was saying, we have had them both under surveillance. It's up to you guys if you want to keep the surveillance going.” Warren was interrupted by a young brunette who seemed very shy and timid. I gathered she was probably new to the job and maybe a little shocked by the aggressiveness of her boss.

“Just place the files on the table, Sophie. They can look at them after the meeting,” Warren said.

“Yes sir,” she replied, doing as instructed and then leaving.

“These are the files of our two suspects. Feel free to have a read.” Warren stood up and offered his hand and his best wishes. We accepted the gesture and returned wishes for Warren's future.

Warren's two colleagues hadn't spoken during the whole meeting. Now, they stood and offered their hands in a thankyou gesture, still saying nothing.

Before I knew it, Jake and I were sitting at the table staring into space. As usual, not liking the silence, I opened my trap again. "Well that was weird. Obviously Bill and Ben didn't like us!"

Without even turning to face me, Jake replied, "They just got demoted, what did you expect?"

"I expected some courtesy and maybe a word or two, something, anything."

"What you said about Bundy was interesting. Do you think our guy is copying his method?" Jake asked.

"Maybe he also used fake injuries to lure his victims," I replied. "Bundy even used clumsiness against them."

"What do you mean clumsiness?" Jake asked.

"Often he'd pretend he was lost and ask for directions, or pretend that he couldn't read a map, things like that."

"Interesting," Jake replied. "So what do you think about our two suspects, Brodie?" Jake sipped the last of his cold coffee.

"I think they are both legitimate suspects. Maybe one of them is the killer, maybe it's someone else entirely. But out of the two, I think that Lance is more likely and I'll tell you why.

"One. Attempted kidnapping could have been his practice run. Two. Break and enter, robbery may not have been on his list. Maybe he was lying in wait. Without even looking at the case file, I would suggest the house was either owned or rented by a single girl. Three, and most importantly, he has heaps of material on Bundy and I would say he is using him as the example he wants to imitate."

"So you think it's him then. You think this is our guy?" Jake asked in an almost excited voice.

"I think he could be a killer, however, whether he is the Slayer or not, I'm not sure. You need to remember the person we're looking for is not the only serial predator walking our streets. One thing I do know is that our guy is showing likeminded nut bags it can be done. Look at all the press our guy gets. He'll spawn more killers, copycats, trying to get in on his fame."

Jake stared at me for a while and then asked, "So where do we start?"

I stood up and tucked my shirt into my trousers. "We start with the two leads we have, but the key to this case is Rebecca Carrington."

"Why her? Why is she so important?" Jake asked, confused.

"The first time is when they're most likely to make a mistake. She's the best chance we have of finding a clue. I don't want to have to wait until he makes his next mistake. Who knows what the body count could be by then!"

"I think we continue to watch both of them and organise a second search on their properties, if a judge will give us a search warrant," Jake said, taking the files from the desk as he finally stood up. "Come on, we can read these in the car. Let's have a look at these guys ourselves."

Chapter 10

Thursday 6th November 2003 (7am)

Mason doubled and triple checked Maggie's Thursday schedule for the last few weeks.

He had done this so many times he could not believe how precise his planning had become.

His alarm clock flashed 6.30am and as the radio came on, his wife stirred in her sleep beside him. He became excited as soon as he thought of his plans for the day.

By the time he had fed Jamie his Coco Pops and made his wife a coffee, it was 8.00am and he was ready to head off to work.

Mason was just leaving as his wife came down the stairs to watch Jamie. He kissed her as they passed. "I won't be home tonight, babe. I'm going straight from work to the airport. I have that conference and I won't be back till late Friday night.

"That's fine because I'm taking Jamie down to Mum's for the weekend and I might even stay until Monday. I just want to help Mum a bit. She's been struggling with Dad since the stroke. You don't mind, do you?"

"Not at all babe, I might do a bit of work on the cabin Sunday and maybe even Monday if I feel like taking a sickie."

"Take the day off, you've been working so hard," Sophie said.

"Have a good weekend. I'll call you. Say hi to your parents for me."

"Have a good weekend too, darling," Sophie replied, grabbing his arse as she gave him a passionate second kiss.

"See you later," Mason said, as he closed the door behind him.

Mason had been doing paperwork for about 45 minutes before the office had even opened. It was the only real estate work he would be doing today.

"I'll be out most of the day," he said to his receptionist as he was leaving the office. "I have some meetings with a couple of developers from Sydney."

"Ok, that's fine. I'll put all your calls through to your mobile," Vanessa replied.

"Could you just take messages, Nes? I don't want to be interrupted while I'm in these meetings."

"Sure," she said, as she wrote a note on a Post-it sticker to remind herself.

As Mason got in his car and plugged his mobile into the hands-free kit, he could still see Nes through the glass door, and he thought, 'that is one attractive receptionist'. She was the only attractive receptionist the company had hired in years. There had been many days when he thought she had caught him perving on her, but he didn't really care.

Mason pulled up outside the council offices and headed to the rates department. He placed his folder on the desk and buzzed for the attendant. A few seconds later, a rather plump woman arrived at the desk and stood there as if to say, 'why are you bothering me?'

"How may I help you, Sir?"

"I would like the address and names of the owners of this property," he said, sliding the paper across the desk.

She took the paper and looked up at Mason. "There's a six-dollar fee for that information, Sir."

"That's fine," Mason replied, smiling.

The plump lady turned side on and faced the computer and then typed in the address provided. Looking up from the screen, she said,

"There you go," and passed the piece of paper back to him along with a printout of the information he'd requested.

Mason placed the six dollars on the counter and took the paper and printout. He noticed a big mole on her right cheek and thought immediately of the scene in 'Uncle Buck'. It made him almost laugh aloud. "Thanks," he said as he walked away. As he walked to the car, he looked down at the piece of paper clasped in his hand. A smile spread across his face as he read the printout.

Property address: 4 Ascot Close Glen Waverley
Owner: Mr and Mrs P Jackson.
13 Laslowe Road Wantirna.

No mention of the tenant Miss M. Janson.
"Just as I thought," he muttered to himself. "You're just a tenant, Maggie."

Chapter 11

Thursday 6th November 2003 (10.15am)

Lance stood at the bottom of the stairs to his garage. He was a tall man, standing just over six foot. Despite his hair thinning on top, he was still handsome.

He stood motionless in the dark, cold garage. He could feel it building up again, like it had the time he was in that house. It would have been perfect had she not brought a man home and ruined his plan.

This time though, it felt more intense. He felt more pressure. Finally, he would kill. Nothing was going to stop him this time.

He walked over to the workbench and caught a glimpse of his reflection in the side mirror of the old Holden Monaro he had attempted to restore in his younger years. Despite the steam that was building up inside him, his outward appearance was completely normal.

Jail had aged him, but it had done nothing to deter his fantasy. If anything, the only lesson he had learned was, don't get caught.

"No mistakes," Lance repeated to himself several times under his breath, as he made his way over to the workbench. He flicked the light on. He then walked over to the Monaro that took up almost half the garage, hopped in the driver's side, released the handbrake, and rolled the car back, almost flush against the door. On the garage floor was a large mat. It served the purpose of protecting the concrete from the oil, but more importantly, it hid his hidey-hole.

Lance rolled back the rug, removed the flick knife from his back pocket and used the tip to find the crack in the concrete. Then he used the knife to lever the door open. Inside the nook was a bag that had once housed a four-man tent. Now it hid the tools of a dark mind. Inside the dusty blue bag lay rope, a carving knife and duct tape. Next to the bag was a leather-bound notebook. Lance removed the items and headed back to the workbench. He placed them upon the dusty and cracked bench and then opened the book. Each page contained clippings from newspapers. All of them were about the Slayer's victims. Lance was proud of his book; he had kept every clipping, had placed perfectly in order every article on every victim. It was his inspiration.

'All I have to do is find myself a policewoman and I'll have articles written about my work,' Lance thought. After a couple of minutes of entertaining this daydream, he realised it was potentially only hours away from becoming a reality.

Lance replaced the book in its original hiding spot. He rolled the mat and the car back into position. With his hands filthy from the trapdoor and the car, he headed to the old trough in the corner of his workshop, which had seen its fair share of grease.

As he rubbed the soap bar across both hands, he began to mumble to himself, "I must be better than him. No mistakes, and then they'll be talking about me, not him. I can be better than him. I can be better than him, better than him."

Chapter 12

Thursday 6th November (2.25pm)

Mason was sitting two streets away from Maggie's address. He had found a nice spot for his car in a very quiet little cul-de-sac, parking outside a house at the end. It appeared to be the best house in the street and he assumed it would take a professional couple to pay for it.

He reached into the centre console and pulled out some business cards of colleagues in the industry. Flicking through them, he stopped when he found the one he wanted. 'Perfect,' he thought. Brent Samuels from Stevens and Co. No photo on the card and a local agent. Minutes later, Mason walked up the drive of 4 Ascot Close and approached the door. He knocked and then stepped away from the door as if to appear less confronting. Mason was now Brent Samuels, and he held out the business card ready to prove it.

A few seconds later, the door opened and Maggie appeared. "May I help you?" she asked softly.

"Yes, I'm Brent Samuels from Stevens and Co, Real Estate." Mason handed over Brent's card. "I'm here for the 2.30 appraisal for Mr and Mrs Jackson." He opened his diary to appear as if he was confirming the details.

"Well, no one told me, so you'll have to come back another time. I do have rights, you know." Maggie began to close the door.

"I am sorry, miss. I was under the impression that the owners were going to make an appointment with you. I could do it now? It will only take me five minutes, then I'll be out of your hair." Mason was using every ounce of charm he had.

He paused while Maggie considered his request. "Really, I'll be gone in two minutes." Mason smiled as if to say, 'come on, better now than later.'

Maggie stepped aside and let in her killer.

Mason opened his little briefcase, removed a piece of paper and began to write notes. Then he placed the paper and pen on the table and began sifting through his satchel. As if he was looking for something.

"So, you're in the police force then?" he asked. He lifted his head slightly to focus on the police cadet photo on the wall behind her. Maggie turned to see what Mason was looking at and as she did so, Mason struck swiftly and forcefully as soon as her back was turned to him, placing the stun gun on the back of her right kidney and his left arm around her throat. The stun gun took effect almost immediately and after the first initial convulsing of her body from the electrical current, Maggie lay limp in his arms.

Alive but ineffectual.

He quickly injected the usual Benzodiazepine.

Mason lay Maggie on the floor of her living room and pulled on the latex gloves that he had at the ready.

Once the gloves were on, he removed a little rag and wiped everything he'd touched, including the Stevens & Co card, which he removed from Maggie's hand.

Mason again reached into his case and removed his biohazard suit. He had stolen it off the clothesline while doing an inspection at a vendor's home. The owners had assumed that some kid had taken it as a prank.

Mason walked over to the kitchen drawer and removed some garbage bags. Then he walked back to the limp, unconscious body lying in the middle of the lounge room. He placed her feet into one bag, which came up to her waist, and pulled the drawstring tight, closing it around her waist. He then moved to the other end of her limp body and lifted her head.

He placed the garbage bag over her head, ripping air holes into the bag so she could breathe. He wanted her immobilised, not dead… well not yet, anyway.

It took Mason about three minutes to do a quick search of her house before finding her car keys on the bedside table.

Obvious place.

He walked to the family room that adjoined the garage and opened the internal access door. He loved this. No one would see him.

It was so easy.

He was so smart, he kept thinking to himself.

He carried Maggie into the boot of her own car.

He doubled back inside, checking he had left nothing behind.

As usual, all clear.

He placed his case on the passenger seat beside him and opened the garage door with the remote that hung from the key ring. He waited until the garage door was just above the car before he rolled out onto the driveway, closing the door as he left.

It would seem to anyone looking that she had just gone to the shops.

Mason parked Maggie's 1997 white Holden Commodore right beside his car and popped the boot. Then he pressed the button on his remote, unlocking the boot of his car. He picked Maggie up and placed her in the boot of his car, then closed the boots of both cars and left hers where he had parked it, just two streets away.

Within seconds, he was headed for his cabin to finish off his eighth victim.

This time, it would be perfect.

Chapter 13

Thursday 6th November (1pm)

Jake and I stood in front of Justice Aaron pleading our case for a search warrant for Lance's property, for the second time. Considering we had very little to go on, getting the warrant wasn't going to be easy.

Justice Aaron looked up from our submission, removed his bifocals and looked directly at Jake. "I hope you have something else, Detectives?" he asked, almost pleading.

"No, your Honour," Jake responded quietly.

"I understand your need to search but unless I have some new evidence or a valid reason as to why you believe that in the next 72 hours Mr Silver will commit a crime, I don't know how you can meet the State's legal burden." Do you have such a reason or evidence, Detective Miller?"

"No, we can't say it's likely that an offence will be committed in the next 72 hours, your Honour. However, we would like to plead that this is an exceptional case that has resulted in many police officers' deaths."

After considering our plea, Justice Aaron continued, "Hypothetically, if I did give you the warrant and you found something, it is very likely that any decent lawyer worth his salt could have any evidence you found deemed inadmissible and thus any arrest or conviction that may occur as a result would be overturned. There-fore, despite my strong personal feelings, unfortunately I believe your submission fails to meet the requirements of the Crimes Act. Please bring me something new and you will have your warrant."

Jake and I stood and thanked him for his time and left his chambers. "What the hell are we going to do now?" Jake asked me as we left the courthouse.

"I think we need to try and get something more on him. Maybe we can keep an eye on him, see if he leads us anywhere. Hey, we might get lucky," I said.

"I don't think he's going to drop evidence in the street, Brodie."

"I'm not saying that, but he might lead us somewhere! What other choice do we have?"

Jake paused two steps ahead of me, then turned and nodded in agreement. "We might as well get started, but we should stop for snacks first." He removed his phone from his pocket.

By the time we reached the car, Jake had cancelled his date with his newfound love, Hayley. I could see he was stressed about having to let her down again. But work came first, especially now.

Chapter 14

Thursday 6th November 2003 (4pm)

We had parked the car on the opposite corner of the street from where Lance lived and had a clear view of the front door and the garage. We would see anyone entering or leaving.

Jake had arranged with two other senior members of Eagle, Steve and Darren, to watch the back. When we'd stopped for supplies, they had radioed in saying that they were about half an hour away. Within minutes of arriving at Lance's, Jake had got stuck into a bag of Cheesy Doritos. I sat there trying to take in the excitement of my first sting, anticipating something might happen at any moment.

Jake, on the other hand, looked as if he was not at all interested and continued to shovel in the Doritos.

That was the difference between us. He had done this before. I was a rookie and a nervous wreck; he was cool, calm and collected. "Where are they? Steve and Darren should be here by now," I said, without taking my eyes off the house.

"It hasn't even been half an hour yet, mate. Don't panic," Jake mumbled, his mouth half full of Doritos. It was a wonder he didn't choke on them.

Jake shuffled back in his seat, reached down and removed the bottle of OJ from the plastic bag provided by the kind service station attendant.

I couldn't believe how much Jake had consumed in such a short time, although I shouldn't have been surprised. It was 4.30 in the afternoon and Jake was just eating his lunch. He would have been starving again two hours after breakfast. He had always been that way even when we were kids in high school. He used to take lunch from home, always a couple of sandwiches, cake and drinks, plenty to keep him going for the day.

When I was about 14 and Jake was 12, we went to a Pizza Hut. It was all the go back then. Pizza Hut had just introduced the 'all you could eat' pizza for $5.95. They couldn't have known there were people who would eat as much as Jake. I sat opposite him and watched in amazement as he devoured 14 slices of pizza while I ate only four.

I looked over at Jake and began to snigger a little. Jake, who was finishing off the Doritos, looked at me with a 'what the fuck are you laughing at?' expression. "What's so funny?" He looked down at his shirt to see if he had spilt anything.

"Nothing," I replied, "just that seeing you eat those Doritos reminded me of when you ate those 14 slices of pizza at Pizza Hut."

Jake began to laugh, almost spitting the half-chewed corn chips all over the car. "How was that waitress? She couldn't believe I'd eaten almost two family-size pizzas by myself. She was ready to stop serving us."

I focused back on Lance's house.

Still no movement.

Then, out of nowhere, the garage door began to roll up, revealing the old Ford Ute. The Ute reversed and headed north towards the city. I started the ignition and began to follow Lance's vehicle. Jake radioed Steve and Darren and gave them the plate and description. While they were close, they had two busy roads to navigate before they would meet up with us. Lance headed out of Hawthorn and up Toorak Road towards the outer edge of the city. We sat a few cars behind so as not to draw attention to ourselves. The traffic for this time of night was heavy and it was getting harder to stay far enough away to not arouse his suspicions yet remain in sight of his Ford. The traffic lights at peak hour were on their short cycle. If we didn't stay a little closer we would lose him.

"Keep up with him, buddy, stay close." Jake repeated the sentence a few seconds later. As the last words of the sentence came out of his mouth, we approached a tram, which Lance's Ford had already passed in the middle of Toorak Road. The stop sign popped out and I had no choice but to stop or run over the passengers exiting the tram. As the tram began to pull away again and the lights ahead of us changed, I could not see the Ford Ute beyond the lights. Our tail was broken.

The lights and siren were not an option if we wanted to keep our cover. We accelerated up the hill. When we reached the top, we knew we were in trouble and that finding Lance would not be easy. Six different roads led into and out of the city. We would only be guessing. There was no sign of the Ute.

We had lost him.

Jake looked over to me. "Don't worry, mate, we'll find him. Let's head into the city and call in that we've lost him. One of the divisional units might sight him."

Chapter 15

Thursday 6th November 2003 (4.38pm)

Mason had parked near the front door. Leaving the car running, he got out and opened the doors to the enclosed garage.

Then he returned to the car and unlocked his boot. Maggie had begun to stir, beginning to recover from the effects of his jab. As Mason picked her up to unload her, Maggie began to kick and struggle.

Mason walked in through the open doors and into his garage. Her body thudded in a puff of dust as he dropped her to the hard dirt floor. Mason grabbed Maggie by her feet and dragged her further inside his cellar, her head hitting each step on the way down. Her cries and screams rang throughout the empty cabin. After a few seconds, Maggie began to squirm in the dirt again and Mason just stood back and watched his prey. He was enjoying every moment of his little game but soon it would all end. Well, for Maggie, anyway.

"Maggie," Mason said, as he removed the bag off her head.

"What do you want with me?" she asked, still trying to recover from the hours in the bag.

Mason knelt down beside her and spoke softly. "Do you know who I am?"

"Some fucked-up psycho. Where am I? Let me go, you fuckin'

sicko!" Maggie yelled, beginning to cry. "Just let me go, I'm a copper, you know. You're under arrest, you have the right to remain silent…" She began to sob louder as she continued to read Mason his rights.

"Listen, you little bitch, you're not in a positon to be reading anyone their rights, especially me. I'll tell you who I am. I'm the person you've dubbed the East Side Slayer and soon I'll be reading you your last rites."

Maggie's face froze with the knowledge that she was in the hands of a killer.

"Do you know why I'm doing this, Maggie? I'll tell you why. Because it's fun. I enjoy watching your eyes when you know you're going to die. I like having you pigs beg for your life and the best part is, your smart-arse cop friends don't have a clue who I am."

Mason walked over to a large covered tool cage hanging on the cellar wall with an array of swords and knives. "Let me show you something."

Mason grabbed her head and forced her to look. "Look!" he yelled, pulling Maggie's hair and pointing to the top shelf of the cabinet. "Show me some respect and look."

Maggie tried to worm away from Mason, shaking her head, the tears flowing.

"I said look, you bitch. Look at what you coppers have made me do."

Maggie again wriggled away and continued to shake her head.

"See what you people have caused."

Maggie could not avoid looking up at the top shelf. Then she began to dry-retch at the sight of seven heads floating in some concoction all staring back at her through glass jars. She guessed the liquid was to preserve the heads.

"You're next, Maggie. Soon you will join them. You will be number eight." Maggie vomited right down her front. "Don't worry about the clothes, Maggie, you won't be needing them much longer."

Maggie tried to move but Mason was far too strong.

He picked her up and slammed her against a steel pole. The back of her head took the biggest impact. Mason cuffed her right hand to a second pole and her left hand to the first pole. Then he pulled on a nearby cable, raising Maggie off the ground, leaving her hanging by her wrists.

Mason went back to the cabinet and removed a long sword and turned and smiled at Maggie. With that smile, Maggie knew her life would soon be over. She also knew the end would be excruciatingly painful.

Chapter 16

Thursday 6th November 2003 (6.23pm)

Lance parked his Ford in a secured parking lot a few blocks away from the Sweet Kandy adult club. The 'K' in the logo was a picture of a girl kicking a leg high in the air. Lance removed his tool kit from the pocket of his coat and placed it neatly under his seat. He could not get a lap dance with a carving knife in his pocket.

It was about a five-minute walk to the Sweet Kandy Club from the car park.

The unceasingly cold air bid Lance good evening and the wind rushed into his lungs, filling his chest with frost. Or so it felt. He began walking to the club. He had no idea how much his life would change in a short few hours.

Sweet Kandy was a well-known strip club. It had become very popular due to all the publicity it received when the owners applied for a licence. Many of the Melbourne City Council board members had tried vigorously to block it. However, it had received a majority vote and the operating hours had been passed. It was suggested by the media that some members of the council had been paid off. The publicity ensured that Sweet Kandy would be a success from the day it opened.

Some people went just once to see what all the fuss was about, while others like Lance were hooked by the beautiful girls on offer.

Lance had his favourite, Charlie. She was young and very pretty and possessed a very sexy body that looked amazing in a g-string.

Her dark black hair curved into her cleavage and she had a marvellous way of saying, "I want to fuck you", looking at you with her deep blue eyes. Of course, she said that to every guy in the place, to get them to pay her to dance. It was her job and it only paid well for the girls who knew how to sell it.

Lance knew that there was no way she would date him, but just having her perform for him was enough to get him off. Since he'd first had her dance for him, he had felt an extra special connection with her.

That connection was growing stronger within him, building up, pushing him to take his desires for her further.

He had felt the connection from the moment he'd laid eyes upon her, one wintry Friday night several months before.

A week later, he'd returned to the club just after dinner, only planning to stay an hour or so.

Charlie always worked Thursday, Friday and Saturday nights. Apparently, the tips were good. She was paying her way through uni and had no classes on Fridays.

He had just finished his first drink at the bar and was about to order his second when she approached him and whispered in his ear, "Would you like me to give you a lap dance?"

Lance was beginning to feel movement in his pants and he smiled and replied, "Anytime with you."

"It's good to see you again, cutie," Charlie answered. Lance wondered if she remembered him or if she just called everyone cutie.

She reached out and grabbed Lance's hand, walking him towards a booth where the private dances took place. She sat him down on the chair and began to dance. Charlie was wearing a bikini top, a short cheerleader skirt and a bright yellow g-string. Lance was a sucker for g-strings. He loved seeing women in them. When he spent his nights watching pornos, he was always excited to see a cute girl getting fucked in a g-string.

He was equally disappointed when the girls removed them.

He knew that his love for g-strings was becoming an obsession but he didn't care. He could have whatever fantasy he liked.

His thoughts were shocked back from his nights of porn when Charlie placed her ankle on his shoulder and thrust her pussy towards his face. Then she stepped back in time with the music and began to remove her bikini and push her breasts together.

She then lowered her head and as she moved closer to Lance, she began to tweak and lick her own nipples.

Then she grabbed Lance's head and moved it in between her breasts, rubbing the sides of his face with her breasts. His cock was now very hard.

The smell of her vanilla perfume kept him wanting more. He thought it must be some type of aphrodisiac. It was the club policy that the girls were allowed to touch the clients but under no circumstances were the clients allowed to touch the girls. The girls generally touched the customer's thigh and maybe gave them a kiss on the cheek at the end of the dance, but if they did more than that and the boss found out, they would no longer be employed by Sweet Kandy. Ricardo, the owner, did not want his girls exciting the guys so much that they became trouble and he didn't want his girls using his business as a hook-up place where they could prostitute themselves on the side. Charlie continued her dance, removing her skirt and beginning to wave her cute arse in front of him. The dance continued for four more songs due to the extra cash she had received at the start of the second song. When the third song began, Lance began to feel that little bit special. Charlie got down on her knees and rubbed his penis through his pants. Then, after looking around to see if anyone was watching, she unzipped him, pulled out Lance's dick and quickly placed it in her mouth, sucking it for just a few seconds then licking the top of it prior to placing it back in his pants. It was the quickest and best blowjob he had ever received.

Charlie again looked around, checking she was not being watched, lifted herself up off her knees, and kissed Lance's ear. At the same time, she rubbed her cheek against his and then slowly brushed Lance's lips with hers. As they met, Charlie's tongue softly entered Lance's mouth. "Don't tell anyone I did that. I'll lose my job. Let me know if you want any more dances today, ok?"

Charlie backed away, picked up her clothes and left the booth. Lance sat there for a few seconds, for two reasons. One, to give himself time to work out what the hell had happened and the other to give his boner time to go down. Nothing looked worse than walking out of a booth in a strip club with a rocket in your pocket.

Chapter 17

Thursday 6th November 2003 (7pm)

Lance sat nervously thinking about how to ask Charlie out.

In the end, he decided just to go ahead and ask her.

Charlie was leaning on the bar, still puffing after her aerobic shift on the main stage. Lance bought her a drink and flashed a hundred-dollar note. "After the drink, you got time for another dance?"

"Always for you, cutie," she replied in her excited voice, which Lance had begun to suspect was fake. He knew that tonight if he got her he would not be able to let her go.

The music pumped, Charlie began her dance and as she danced, Lance's desire increased. He wanted her and he wanted to be written about. He wanted to be hunted by the police.

Soon, he would replace the Slayer. Charlie was the perfect way to start his plans.

"Hey, Charlie, do you ever see any people from the club, outside the club, I mean?" he asked her, stuttering a little.

"Are you asking me out, sexy? Cos I'm not allowed to date guys I meet at the club, but if you don't say anything, I won't." She smiled and flicked her hair. "I don't get off until 12 so if you're not doing anything then, you could pick me up and we could go to my place for coffee if you like." She flashed that sexy smile and softly kissed his lips.

"That'd be cool, I'd love to, I'll meet you out the back then?" Lance had forgotten where he was for a second and as the words came out, he cringed at how juvenile they made him sound. How many 32-year-olds still used the word cool.

"Yeah, at 12, ok cutie," Charlie said, as she hurriedly redressed.

"Could I have another dance first?"

"I'd love to, cutie, but I'm due on stage. How about I make it up to you later?"

Charlie placed the hundred-dollar note in her garter, gave him a quick wink and left the booth.

Chapter 18

Thursday 6th November 2003 (7.33pm)

I sat there with my arm up against the glass of the driver's side window and my knee on the dash, waiting for a response from any patrol car that might have sighted Lance's car.

Our search had turned up jack shit. We had cruised the city for the last few hours without locating Lance's car. "Jake, I can't believe that no other police have spotted Lance's car either. Are they all fucking useless?" I asked.

"Easy, tiger," Jake replied, "we'll find him."

"Yeah, but I hope it's this year. Why are we just sitting here in the middle of King Street and not driving around looking for him?" I questioned.

My lack of police skills was showing.

"Mate, King Street has the most pubs and clubs. It's the heart of sleaze. More strip joints here than in the rest of Melbourne. If he's out on the town trawling, it's a good chance he'll be here. If his car is in one of those underground car parks, when he leaves, we'll see him."

"But there are heaps of other places he could be. There are other pubs and strip joints outside of this area as well. He could be anywhere."

"Yes, he could, Bruce," Jake acknowledged, "but here is our best chance."

Jake often called me Bruce. When he'd first started doing it, I'd wondered what the hell had happened to him.

Stroke maybe.

Then I thought I must have misheard. When he said it again, I asked, "Mate, why the hell you calling me Bruce?"

He smiled. "Mate, every Aussie has a best friend called Bruce, you're my best friend."

I thought it was both logical and stupid at the same time. That was why we were best friends.

I'd just let it ride ever since.

Chapter 19

Thursday 6th November 2003 (8.38pm)

The sun was almost set as Lance walked down the dark steps of the strip club and out into the bright lights of the city. He did not want to drive home and back before 12 so he thought it would be best to spend what was left of the evening in the city.

He was halfway down Collins Street when he stopped in the middle of the footpath and stared into the window of an adult shop. On display on the mannequin was what would make his night with Charlie perfect. He couldn't believe he hadn't thought of it until now. He looked up at the name of the shop. 'Adult Playground' was sign-written across a big pair of red lips, an eye-catching logo. Underneath the lips were the words, 'Making your playtime more exciting'.

Lance looked at the mannequin staring back at him through the window.

'Perfect,' he thought, entering the shop.

Lance walked in and stared at all the lingerie, toys and costumes.

"Can I help you?" the voice from behind the counter asked. After taking a few seconds to observe the cashier, Lance answered, "I was wondering how much the police costume in the window is?"

"It's actually on sale. It normally retails for $259 but it's only $199 at the moment. What size is the lucky lady?" the attendant asked in a friendly manner.

"I think she's a size eight or ten," Lance replied.

"Well, it comes in small, medium and large. Small will suit girls sized eight to twelve. The material is lycra and spandex so it stretches. A small should suit her then," she said, showing him one from the rack. "Would you like me to wrap one up for you?"

"That would be great. Do you take Visa?" Lance asked, hoping that they did as he had little cash left on him.

All his money was wrapped around a garter.

"Yes, we do, sir," the attendant replied. "Would you like the uniform in a gift box? They're only $5."

He nodded in acceptance. "Are the handcuffs that come with the uniform real or plastic?" Lance asked.

The attendant, who was now placing the item in the box, replied, "They're plastic, but we do have real ones on the back shelf. I think they're about $40.00."

Lance headed for the back shelf. Gazed at the wide selection that lay before him.

Most of the handcuffs on offer had a separate release tab that the prisoner could activate to let themselves out. He wasn't surprised, considering they were novelty handcuffs.

He had almost given up looking and then he saw them, second from the end. Real handcuffs with only a key to open them. Lance removed the box from the shelf and headed back to the counter.

"Take those as well?" the attendant asked, to double check before she scanned the attached tag and opened the gift box to place the handcuffs in.

"Yeah, that'd be great. All on the Visa, thanks," Lance replied, as he handed the attendant his card.

She put the gift box inside a black plastic bag.

Lance signed the receipt and thanked the attendant for her help.

A few minutes later, he was back out on the street. The sun was quickly fading on the city horizon. The air seemed colder now.

He continued to walk through the city. Seeing the casino in the distance, he decided that was the place to fill in the night until Charlie finished work.

The air had become incredibly cold and the wind pierced his lungs with each breath.

He passed the Crocodile Club with its unique green door glowing in the darkness, the usual line of drunken horny guys waiting on the footpath.

Lance looked over his shoulder and checked there was no traffic coming up behind him. He saw the lights of a small vehicle, waited for it to pass and then crossed. As it passed, a gust of wind generated by the passing vehicle blew a cold shivery chill up his back.

By 9.30, Lance had won over $500 on blackjack. Playing on would likely result in the loss of all his gains. He pocketed his chips and headed for the cashier. A meal and a bit of sport at the sports bar would be the perfect way to settle himself for the big night ahead.

Lance looked over at the bar attendant and as soon as he noticed her brown curly hair, the thought of spending tonight with Charlie came flooding into his brain and he suddenly felt hot and nervous at the same time. "Can I get you anything?" the young bar attendant asked, as she continued to remove empty beer and spirit glasses from the bar with her right hand and wiped the bar with the rag in her left.

"I'll have a Scotch and Coke on the rocks. Do you do counter meals?" Lance asked as she placed ice in his glass. He placed his Visa on the bar to cover his tab.

"Sure, I'll grab you a menu," the girl replied.

"It's ok, I'll have a parma if you have that?" Lance asked, glancing back at a TV screen showing football.

"Sure do. I'll get you one, Sir," she said, taking his Visa and placing his drink on the coaster in front of him.

She then clipped a ticket to the service line.

He assumed it was his parma order.

Lance's mind was only on Charlie even though his eyes were flickering between the EPL and the cricket in the Caribbean. The attendant brought his parma, but that and the Scotch did little to settle his nerves and nothing to satisfy his hunger.

"Can I get you another?" the bar attendant asked, holding up his empty glass.

Lanced nodded.

She placed the drink in front of him and went to serve a young couple who had just blown in from the street, bringing with them a gust of cold night air.

Lance could not concentrate on the game.

His only thought was, 'tonight is my night.'

Soon he would be the new East Side Slayer.

Soon everyone would be talking about him.

Writing about him.

Finally, he would get the respect he deserved.

Chapter 20

Thursday 6th November 2003 (11.45pm)

Lance had just finished his fourth Scotch and Coke. The EPL had finished and he wasn't even sure who had won.

He picked up his wallet and his package from Adult Playground to prepare for the bitterly cold stroll back to the Sweet Kandy Club. In the alleyway behind the nightclub, he stood shivering, thinking how cold it must be even though he was wearing his long jacket. Perhaps he should have worn a warmer jumper as well.

It was 15 minutes past 12 by the time Charlie came out of the rear steel door of the club. It had been 15 minutes that Lance had spent thinking that she must have changed her mind.

That it was all a cruel joke.

A hoax.

As Charlie came outside, she was followed by a large security guard who looked as if he had spent too many years in the gym and most likely on steroids.

"You know this man, Charlie?" the security guard asked, standing close enough to act if Lance were some perverted fuck who was hiding in the dark alley lying in wait ready to rape or kidnap one of the dancers.

"Yeah, I'm fine, Gus, this is just an old friend I haven't seen in a while." Charlie turned to Gus and blew him a kiss as if to say, thanks for caring. Charlie took Lance's hand and began to walk with him towards the main street. As she neared the end of the alleyway, Charlie raised her left hand and yelled, "See ya tomorrow, Gus!" She knew he would still be at the rear door watching her leave.

As they entered the main street, Charlie removed her hand from Lance's and lowered it to his arse, giving a slight squeeze of his butt cheek. "We can walk to my place from here. It's two minutes at the most." Charlie began to drag on his arm to lead the way.

"Ok, ok, I'm coming, I just need to get my bag. I have my phone and stuff in my car. It'll only take me a sec then we can go to your place for some fun." Lance started to pull her towards the parking garage.

Within a few minutes, they were standing at Lance's car.

Lance was looking for the car key on his key ring so he could open the door to get his tool kit from under his seat.

He sat in the car, adding the contents to the black plastic bag from Adult Playground.

"What's in the bag?" Charlie asked, as she tried to get a sneak peek. "You didn't have that when you came into the club."

"It's a surprise and you'll just have to wait until we get to your house," Lance replied, pulling the bag away from her and moving it into his other hand so that she would not have a chance to glimpse the contents.

They walked hand in hand all the way to Charlie's home and when they arrived, Lance was surprised at how nice it appeared from the outside.

It was a modern townhouse, of the type that had been all the go in Melbourne for the last five years. Many developers had built them, making open-plan living one- and two-bedroom homes and then selling them to young couples and young corporate singles who worked in the city.

Charlie unlocked the downstairs security door and closed it behind them. She and all the other tenants had been told at the last body corporate meeting to make sure they did this. Apparently, too many tenants had been leaving it unlocked and there had been three burglaries recently.

"Here we are," Charlie said, as she swung the door open to her apartment. The furniture was sandstone, which suited the modern look of the home. The main wall of the lounge housed a gas log fire. Charlie opened up two double doors that stood at the end of the lounge, revealing her large king-sized jarrah bed.

The posts were carved, joined at the top by an inch-thick piece of timber. Attached to the timber was a soft lace netting that draped to the floor. The bed was decorated with at least 10 large cushions, all covered in silk or satin covers.

Charlie simply nodded her head as if to say, 'come here'. Then she said, "Are you going to stand there all night or are you coming in?" as she removed her dress, leaving it on the floor at the entrance to her bedroom. She parted the lace and crawled onto the bed.

'Remain calm,' he thought. 'Your time of infamy is just beginning. The Slayer wouldn't panic and neither must you.' Soon, his vision would be complete and he would never be forgotten. He had to ensure that this was only the beginning.

Not his first and last. After all, anyone could kill.

'Only the great ones are remembered,' he continued thinking, as he slowly approached the bedroom.

Chapter 21

Thursday 6th November 2003 (11.57pm)

"Mate, I think he's gone. We've spent over seven hours and there's been no sign of him," I said, struggling to keep awake.

Jake turned his head towards me while still trying to keep one eye on King Street. "Maybe we should go and stake out his house. He has to come back sooner or later."

"Yeah, we're just wasting our time here, but I need a coffee and some fresh air if I'm going to stay awake for the rest of the night." I started the car and headed towards the freeway.

"No Brucey, you're better off going towards Toorak Road. That way we can go down Chapel Street, get a coffee, have a walk, look for Lance."

"With the thought of a hot coffee and the possibility of finding our boy, how could I say no?"

It only took about 15 minutes at this time of night.

We were soon cruising down Chapel Street. All you can do in Chapel Street is cruise. There were so many teenyboppers looking for clubs, pubs and dance spots that the traffic was bumper to bumper. As we slowed to a crawl in our police issued 2000 VS Commodore, a 1995 dark green Ford pulled up beside us. The car was crammed with six guys, most likely late teens. Obviously out looking for some fun or trouble.

Maybe trouble was fun to them.

The driver and most of the passengers looked Greek or Italian. The driver had the radio blasting and he was bopping his head in time to the bopping of the mmcha, mmcha, mmcha of the techno music.

The passenger looked over at our car. He was obviously not impressed that I was staring at him and their car. "What the fuck are you looking at?" he said through his wound-down window. "What's your fucking problem?" he repeated. He turned his head and began to speak to the four guys in the back, as if to rally the troops. He turned back towards me and leaned out of the window, shouting. This time one of the backseat passengers, who had also wound down his window, decided to join in the fun.

"You're fucked," the front-seat passenger said, pointing his finger at me, and the guy in the back added some smart-arse comment that I didn't quite catch.

Jake leaned over, took the CB radio out of its holder and called in for a divvy van.

"What the hell are you doing?" I asked, puzzled, as he began to open his door. "Just stop the fucking car. These boys are going to hurt someone or themselves if we don't stop them. They have too many passengers in the car and they're drinking in public. That's enough to arrest them, plus they've just pissed me off."

Jake removed his seat belt. "You can either stay here or come with me and kick some arse, but don't forget your piece."

I had only limited training with my Glock and I wasn't looking forward to having to use it. I also didn't want some big guy taking it from me and then shooting me with it.

Jake was out of the car before I had pulled to a complete stop. "Did you have something to say to us?" I heard him say as he went in front of the bonnet and headed towards the Ford.

"Yeah! What the fuck if I did? Whatcha gunna do about it?" I heard the passenger say. I looked in the side mirror and saw all the passengers opening their doors. Although I had never been in a fight before, I knew that these numbers were bad even for Jake. I took a deep breath and opened my door, making sure the safety on my Glock was off.

As I stood at the side of the car, I saw the passenger in the Ford turn towards me. He was a lot shorter and fatter than I'd expected. His hair was a long and greasy tangle beneath his dark blue bandana.

He looked like a typical street punk, long tracksuit pants and replica American football jacket with 'Raiders' across the front. As he approached me, I heard Jake say, "Well, I have something to say to all of you."

"Fuck you, man," the driver said, tossing his jacket on the bonnet to prepare for the fight that he foresaw. Jake reached into his inside breast pocket and removed his badge. "I said, I have something to say." He flipped open the black leather top of his badge cover.

"You have the right to remain silent, the right…"

"What the fuck! What are you arresting us for, man?" the passenger said as he realised the fight he was so desperately trying to start was not going to happen.

Jake finished reading them their rights. "Hands on the car, guys, all of you, now!"

"Fuck you, pig," the short passenger said as he leaned on the car. "We haven't done anything wrong. You have nothing on us."

"I have you drinking in a public place and that's against the law, threatening two police officers, and illegal use of a motor vehicle. I think that's enough to have you in front of a magistrate. Plus, I'm sure my colleagues will find drugs in the car when they search it."

A minute later the divvy van arrived to take them away and impound their car. I couldn't believe that we had got out of that without having to even pull a gun.

"How did you do that?" I asked as we made our way back to the car.

"Just punks, Brodie. They were never going to fight once they knew we were cops. If we'd just been kids, then there would have been trouble, of that I have no doubt."

Jake and I jumped back in the car and continued our search for Lance.

About 300 metres down Chapel Street, we finally decided to pull over and grab a coffee.

After that, we would check out the inside of some of the clubs to see if we could find Lance hiding in a dark corner.

I sat down on the bench seat in the booth and immediately looked out the window at the throng of passing women, all of whom looked as if they had just come from a fashion parade. I never knew Melbourne had so many attractive women. I certainly never met any in my own social life.

I had obviously led a sheltered life, I thought.

Jake had sat down but instead of looking at the view outside the café, he was preoccupied with reading the menu.

"You can't possibly still be hungry after everything that you consumed tonight?" I asked, surprised.

"You know me, mate, I'm always hungry," Jake replied, his eyes still firmly fixed on the menu. "I think I'll have some pancakes with my coffee, Brodie," he said, as if to seek my approval.

Jake was finishing his last pancake, making sure it had as much maple syrup on it as possible. He quickly whisked it around the plate before devouring the last bite. I went to pay, and then returned to the booth and asked him, "Shall we hit the clubs now, Jake?"

He nodded. I gathered my jacket from the booth and said, pointing across the road, "I think we should start at the clubs here."

"If that fails, then we head back to Lance's," Jake suggested.

I nodded in agreement and followed Jake across the road.

Chapter 22

Friday 7th November 2003 (12.27am)

Charlie sat in the middle of the bed with her legs slightly apart, flopped back and exposing her full, voluptuous breasts. "You coming over here, cutie?"

"Would you mind putting this on? I hope you don't mind, but I got you something." Lance held out the gift box to Charlie.

"Sure hun, whatever gets you going." Charlie raised herself up from the bed, her cute arse showing in her g-string, and took the box from Lance's extended hand. She opened the ensuite door. "I'll be right back. Get yourself ready," she said as she closed the bathroom door behind her.

Lance began to undress. When he was down to his boxers, he grabbed the bag that still held the cuffs and his other items. He placed them under the bed, making sure they were within arm's reach.

Charlie reappeared from the ensuite and Lance was stunned. She looked amazing in the lycra police uniform. She had even gone to the trouble of putting on the badge and was swirling the plastic baton around as she walked towards him.

"You're under arrest, Sir. I think I'll need to frisk you," Charlie said, giggling as she knelt on the bed beside him.

Lance had planned not to take part in any sexual activity with

Charlie. He knew that the DNA evidence would put him behind bars. Again. He knew he had to be careful, for this was just the start of his plan.

Charlie began to rub his thigh, moving her hand higher up his groin and at the same time, she slowly caressed his lips with her own. Lance began to feel more tempted with each kiss from Charlie. "Are you going to bend me over and fuck me?" Charlie softly whispered into his ear. It was those words and the rub of her butt against his groin that caused him to deviate from his plan.

Lance took Charlie by the hair and began to kiss her passionately. It wasn't long before they were both enjoying hot passionate sex. "Can I tie you up?" Lance asked.

"You like it, kinky, do you?"

Charlie moaned between thrusts as she ground down harder on Lance. Lance began to lift Charlie up and grab the sheets to tie her up in.

"Not yet honey, I'm almost there. Keep fucking me. Don't stop!" she yelled. She was grinding harder and faster, bringing herself to orgasm.

"Now tie me up, baby, and do what you want with me. Just make me orgasm again. You're so good!"

Charlie rolled on her back. Placed her hands against the carved headboard. Lance grabbed the cuffs from below the bed. "Ohh, kinky!" Charlie giggled. "Not too tight, cutie," she said, as she thrust her body back and forth waiting for Lance to start fucking her again.

"I don't want you to get away from me," Lance whispered, as he cuffed her hands around a groove in the woodwork.

Charlie was naked lying on her back, hands cuffed, waiting for more pleasure.

Lance bent down and grabbed his bag of goodies, removing the long knife. He rose to face Charlie, who was watching him with interest. "What you got there, cutie? Did you pick up some naughty toys from that store?" Charlie caught a glimpse of the knife as she finished speaking. She began to pull wildly on the cuffs that held her hands to the bedhead.

"What do you think you're doing! Let me go, you freak! Let me fucking go!" She began to scream as she again tried to pull herself free.

Without another word, Lance took the knife and slit Charlie's throat, spraying blood all across the bedhead and over her face. He then stabbed Charlie several times. From the reports in the papers, he knew the East Side Slayer stabbed his victims many times. Sitting on top of her, he stabbed her all over her upper torso. Once he was over his frenzy, he packed up his belongings, went out to the kitchen and wrote a quick note. 'Here is another victim for you. I will not stop. You will not catch me. East Side Slayer.'

Lance no longer wanted to copy the Slayer.

He wanted to become him.

Chapter 23

Friday 7th November 2003 (1am)

I sat at my desk in the corner of an old open office that was in need of a major renovation. It was obvious from my corner space that I wasn't thought of highly within the police system. The detectives had their own office with all the extras including timber Venetian blinds, laptops and in some cases, TVs and video players.

It didn't matter to me that I wasn't well respected, after all, my father always told me that respect should be earned, not expected. I was from the outside and had been brought in as an outside expert, and I hadn't done any of the hard yards. Most of the guys here had been through the academy together.

The one man I knew who respected me and believed in my abilities was sitting in his office (one of the good ones) with his head in his hands, his old oak desk submerged in papers, files and photos.

His body language said it all. He was under the pump. Losing Lance last night had not helped his cause. The chief had always believed in Jake and his abilities but had no option but to rake him over the coals after last night's stuff-up. Jake was hurting. My mistake had cut him deep: he had been embarrassed and I knew that if he had been with someone else, we would not have lost Lance. I had lost Lance, Jake knew I had lost Lance, yet he'd said nothing. It was just another sign of the true friend he was.

I turned my attention back to the old case reports on my desk. These were the initial reports made by friends or family members when they'd first noticed the victims were missing. I was looking for a pattern, some sort of similarity. It is commonly thought that 90 per cent of murders are carried out by someone known to the victim.

While this was the opposite in serial murders, I was certain that there was a pattern. He was targeting female police officers and I needed to look for a link in the way he took his victims.

There had to be something.

They all couldn't just be opportunistic killings.

There was no doubt in my mind we were dealing with a killer who planned everything meticulously. One who would keep killing until he was caught. It was now a necessity for him to kill. It provided him with some kind of satisfaction, a release, almost like a sexual release.

The other fact that I was becoming more aware of was that the killer would become more daring and more violent the longer he was loose.

I finished highlighting the fourth statement: 'The victim reported missing after failing to return home from a night out with friends.'

There was no pattern. All the victims had gone missing in different ways, at different times and in different places. I knew he had used the police academy several times. As for the others, I was at a loss. I decided to head home for some desperately needed sleep.

Chapter 24

Friday 7th November 2003 (6.21am)

I was interrupted by the phone ringing on my bedside table. Before I could even say hello, Jake had started talking. "Get up, we have a report of another one! I'm two minutes away."

It was more than a coincidence on the morning after we had lost Lance that there was another possible murder. A possible Slayer murder. I prayed it wouldn't be the case, however, I knew one thing was for sure, I was about to see my first dead body.

My head was so full of thoughts that it wasn't until I saw the wet road from the passenger seat of the police cruiser that I realised we were passing many of the places we had searched just hours before. We even passed the Casino.

I looked over at Jake.

He just looked back and shook his head.

We had been so close and we both knew it.

I got out in the freezing cold, realising I had left my woollen jacket on the back of my chair in the office the night before.

The apartment block had been taped off and there were two uniformed officers standing guard. "What's the situation?" Jake asked.

"Apparently a house mate found her flatmate dead. Stabbed to death. There was a note left for us. The guys first on the scene are still up there."

"Do you think it could be the Slayer?" Jake asked me.

"Let's wait and see. The crime scene will tell us," I responded, removing a jar of Vicks VapoRub from my suit jacket and placing two blobs under my nose.

"What the hell are you doing?" Jake asked me.

"Hey, I hear dead people smell. I'd rather smell this stuff than decomposing flesh!"

When we arrived at the apartment floor, uniformed police met us at the elevator door. "It's room 3316. The flatmate is in the neighbour's apartment, 3314," one of the officers told us.

We walked down the dimly lit hall.

As we approached room 3314, I paused and saw the flatmate providing her statement to another uniformed officer. She was a short, slim, blonde-haired woman with shoulder-length hair.

She was sitting in a wooden chair at the neighbour's dining table with a cup held firmly in her hands and a shock blanket, given to her by the first police officers on the scene, wrapped around her shoulders and back.

She was shaking, and her hair and makeup were a mess. Her mascara had run and the foundation had smeared.

"Let's check out the body first. Give her some time to compose herself," Jake whispered into my ear, as he led us back to apartment 3316. It was a nice place, very modern, bright and open.

At one end was a bedroom. I could smell death from the entrance. What I had been told was true. It's an awful odour. Jake put his tie to his nose. "You have any of that stuff?" he asked, his mouth muffled by his tie. I handed him the jar and Jake followed my lead, putting a dab of Vicks under each nostril.

We entered the room, which held about 15 other people, including patrol officers, ambos and forensics. "Listen up!" I yelled. "I need everyone except forensics and Jake out of the room now!"

All the various officers stood stunned for a few moments and then began to vacate the room. I stopped the last officer by placing my hand in the middle of his chest. "Who was the first police officer here?" I asked.

"Me and my partner Vince," the officer replied hesitantly.

"What's your name?" I asked calmly.

"Constable Simon Davison," the officer answered.

"What I want you to do, Simon, is ask all the neighbours if they saw or heard anything. Get as much information as you can. The smallest thing may break this case wide open. Once you've got everything, you can come back and see me."

Simon began to leave and when he was in the doorway, I called him back. "Simon, next time you arrive at a murder scene, don't let anyone in the room. Do you understand? If you want to get ahead in the force, you need to think about things."

I closed the door behind Simon and turned back to the victim. For a moment, I was stunned by the amount of blood all over the bed and the room. "I was glad you said something. I was about to blow my top!" Jake said, waking me from my trance.

"Yeah, I didn't mean to override you or anything," I said apologetically.

"Let's just get to work," Jake said, passing me some surgical gloves.

Jake went straight to the body and began to examine the stab wounds on the victim. I was just finishing putting on the gloves when I saw the uniform on the floor. I picked up the top and noticed straightaway. This was no police officer; this was an imitation uniform.

"Do we know who this girl is yet?" I asked Jake, still holding the uniform in my right hand.

"You'll have to ask the officers, they should have an ID by now," Jake replied with a puzzled look on his face.

"Simon, come in here please?" I called, as I opened the bedroom door. Did the flatmate give you the victim's name I asked.

"Lucy Akin. Her stage name is Charlie. She worked as a stripper at the Sweet Kandy Club. Her flatmate also works there and hasn't seen her since Friday morning," Simon answered, reading from his notepad.

"So she is a stripper not a police officer," I said.

Simon looked at me, puzzled, and began to flick through his notepad again.

"That's fine, Simon," I was thinking aloud. "Go and see what else you can find out about her."

Simon placed his notebook back in his top pocket and left the room, closing the door behind him.

"This isn't the work of the Slayer," I said, as I turned in Jake's direction.

"What are you talking about?" Jake asked, looking up from the body.

"This isn't the work of our killer," I said, shaking my head.

"Are you blind, Brodie? She's been stabbed in a frenzy just like the others. This is our man all right," Jake said, looking at me as if to say, 'what drugs are you on?'

"Jake, she isn't a cop, she's a stripper. Our killer has a purpose, a reason, a plan. A stripper is not part of that plan. But most importantly, our killer forgot to take his trophy. She still has her head, mate!"

"Maybe that's why he dressed her up as a cop, to get off when he killed her; maybe he was in a hurry and didn't have time to remove the head, who knows. He's a fucking psycho. That's why he's killing people and we're chasing him," Jake said in a raised voice.

"He dumped every other victim. This one he just left here. It doesn't fit. It's all wrong. You hired me to give you an insight into who's doing this, and out of all the files I've seen, nothing suggests that he would change his MO midstream. Believe me when I tell you that this is not the Slayer's work."

Jake looked up at me with an accepting look as if to concede defeat on the point.

"Are you sure it's not him?" he asked, giving his argument one last shot.

"Positive," I replied, and nodded as if confirm my answer.

"This is a copycat." I placed the police uniform into a big plastic evidence bag.

"What have you guys found so far?" Jake asked the forensics team, pathologist Dr David Lewis and Grace Edils, his assistant.

I remember Jake telling me, in the pre-Hayley days, how there was a hot girl named Grace in forensics. He was right. While I knew this was not the appropriate time to be admiring her looks, I found myself struggling to focus for the first few seconds after meeting her.

"Your friend appears to be right," David said to Jake. "Come here. I'll show you something. See how there's torn flesh around the knife entry and exit wounds? This tells me it was a serrated knife, while all the others have had a straight edge. So it's a different weapon to start with. Secondly, as your friend mentioned, her head is still intact. I don't think this guy would have left such an important part of his ritual unfinished. Finally, based on what Grace's blue light is showing up, I would say our killer had sex with her and that is a first in these killings."

Jake glanced up at me as if to say sorry for not believing me.

"There is a different lack of overkill in this case. I think it's safe to say that it's unlikely to be the work of the same person." David paused. "Well, we're done here. I'll compare the evidence to past victims when we get back to the lab. I'll call you with the results."

As the forensics team left, Simon reappeared. "The coroner is here for the body. Are you finished?" he asked quietly.

"Yeah, we're finished. Send them in," Jake said, as he removed his other glove and we began to leave the room.

We returned to the neighbour's apartment and both sat down at the dining room table. It was nothing flash, just the type of table that you buy on a budget, at a store like Ikea.

Jake started the conversation by introducing himself and then me to the young lady who was still holding the now empty cup in her hands.

"I'm Jessica," she replied in a low voice, trying to hold back tears.

"I know that you've been through an ordeal and I know you've been very helpful to the officers, I just want to make sure that we've covered everything so we can catch the person responsible for this," Jake said. "I understand that you and Charlie both worked at the same club in Melbourne? I don't want to pry but I take it that you were both strippers?"

"Yeah, we were just trying to get ahead. It paid so well, I never thought it would be dangerous," Jessica replied, crying, wrecking what was left of her makeup.

"We don't know that she met the person who did this at your club, but it is a strong possibility. Do you know if she knew anybody who might want to hurt her? Any ex- or current boyfriends, special admirers, or a client that was perhaps upset with her?"

"Not that I know of. Her ex is back in WA and I don't know about any clients. You might have to ask Midget at the club. He takes care of the girls while they're at the club and when they leave. She would have told him if she had problems with a client." Jessica was now sobbing.

"Midget?" Jake repeated, as if not sure he had heard the name correctly.

"His name is Gus and we just call him Midget, cos of his size."

"Do you know the name of the ex-boyfriend in Perth?" I asked.

She sat thinking for a few seconds. "Josh, I think, but I'm not sure. Her parents will probably know," she mumbled.

"One final question, Jessica. Did Charlie have drug issues, or anyone chasing her for money who might have done this?"

"No," Jessica replied quickly, shaking her head. Her words became inaudible from the tears. "She wasn't into that stuff," she muttered a few seconds later, when the tears subsided.

"Have you got a place you can go and stay for a while? We're going to need to seal off this apartment at least for a week or two," Jake said.

Jessica responded with a little nod.

"Simon, make sure you take Jessica wherever she needs to go and organise a counsellor and whatever else she needs," Jake continued. "Ok, thanks for your help, Jessica. Try and take care. I know it's going to be hard. Here's my card if you need anything or remember anything else. Just let me know."

"Thank you, Detective," she muttered as the tears began to flow again.

We left the apartment, leaving the officers to take Jessica to her interim home.

"Where are we off to now?" I asked as we exited the apartment block. It was still freezing cold. "It feels like it's about to snow," I said as we quickly made our way to the car.

I was hoping that Jake had pressed the remote for the central locking so I could get in without having to wait. When I pulled the door handle, it felt freezing. It was ridiculously cold for November, the coldest weather in 42 years. It was meant to be spring but it felt like winter.

I realised my wish had not been answered. Jake walked slowly to the car in his nice warm jacket and began to laugh as he watched me shivering beside the passenger door. "Hurry the fuck up and press the button. I'm freezing out here."

The indicator lights flashed.

I was very glad to get into the vehicle and out of the icy wind. "So, are you going to answer my question?" I asked as I did up my seatbelt.

Jake started the car and looked at me, before pulling away from the curb. "I think our first port of call should be the Sweet Kandy Club," he replied as he turned to check the traffic. "I think we need to speak to Midget and see if he knows anything."

Jake merged into the traffic and we headed back through the city towards the club.

Chapter 25

Friday 7th November 2003 (7.35am)

Maggie was shivering, partly because of the cold but mainly in fear.

Cuffed to some homemade torture contraption. She had been there all night.

A madman with a sword stood motionless in front of her.

She knew from the moment she had seen the heads in the jars that she needed a miracle to get out of this.

Mason was calming himself. It had to be perfect this time.

He wondered what Maggie would be thinking.

What thoughts run through your head when you know you're going to die?

Would they be of family?

Loved ones?

Would she beg? Most did.

Time to find out.

"Now Maggie, I'm sure by now you know why they call me the East Side Slayer?" Mason asked. He removed the sword from its cover, and pointed the shiny silver blade at Maggie's face. He pressed the tip of the blade onto her cheek.

The screams started as soon as the metal touched her skin.

"Please don't!" she screamed. "Please stop, please."

She begged just like the others, Mason thought.

Mason ignored her begging and went to work.

Her screams filled the room. Mason wondered if with all the screaming Maggie knew her left eye was now lying on his dirty cellar floor.

He assumed she did.

Maggie's good eye continued to weep tears, while the other flowed blood, and a considerable amount of it. Mason took the sword tip to the other eye, the screams continued, even after the other eye had joined its mate. Mason had never removed the eyes before but thought it wouldn't be too hard to stitch them back into the skull for preservation.

Her horrendous screams increased in pitch, thus increasing Mason's sexual desire and enjoyment.

Mason managed to remove her top with the sword without cutting any of her skin. He moved a little closer, and began to feel her right breast through the soft unpadded bra. He could even feel her nipple through the mesh.

Mason ripped at the bra, not showing any care, and grabbed the breast harshly in his hand. It was firm and ripe and he began playing with it like an overzealous teenage schoolboy.

Mason ripped off the rest of her bra and then removed her pants. Maggie wasn't wearing bloomers or a g-string, she had decided to go for the three-quarter boy legs, and what part of her arse Mason could see was impressive. It was as close as he would get sexually. No evidence, he reminded himself. No matter how much he wanted to, he couldn't get carried away with her.

Maggie stood in darkness, shaking with fear. As he touched her, she decided it was time to leave. While she couldn't leave physically, she could mentally. She began to think of all the good things in her life.

Happy times.

Her family.

Most of all her mum.

Even though he was still sexually aroused, Mason knew that what gave him the most pleasure was yet to happen. Mason savoured the final moment for a few seconds and then without further thought, he raised his sword.

With one quick strike, her head was rolling in the dirt at his feet.

Mason dropped the sword to the ground.

He stared at his handiwork and took in all the euphoria.

Then he went to work on his own body.

Ejaculation was his final act of pleasure.

Chapter 26

Friday 7th November 2003 (10.04am)

We pulled up outside the club. For a Friday morning, it was surprisingly busy. The patrons leaving were all in good spirits and had wide smiles, obviously impressed with the talent they had seen inside. The bouncers requested ID of any patrons who looked under age and refused entry to those who didn't abide by the dress code.

As we entered the darkened foyer, Jake asked the hostess sitting behind a large mahogany counter, "Where can we find Gus?"

"We don't have guys here. This is a girls' only bar, boys, $10 per head if you want to enter."

Jake just flashed his badge and the girl picked up the phone. "Can you come downstairs, Gus? There are two officers here to see you." She hung up the phone and smiled. "He'll be down in a second."

"$10 dollars to enter," she said to the next boys in the queue.

They gladly handed over the money. "Just upstairs, boys. Don't forget to tip well," she reminded them as they ascended the stairs.

"Have you heard from Charlie?" a voice from behind us said.

"Not yet, Gus," was the reply from the hostess as she pointed to us with her pen to indicate we were waiting for him.

"Damn that girl!" Gus said loudly, as he turned towards us. "You better make it quick, guys, because I've got a lot to do."

"We will take as long as we like, Sir," Jake replied with a smile. "Is there somewhere we can go to talk?"

"Yeah, follow me." His voice was deep and considering his size, I was not surprised. I estimated that Gus stood about six foot six and he was of very solid build. He was one person who I think Jake would have had trouble handling. Midget was obviously an ironic nickname. We went up the stairs and off to the left. To our right we could see two semi-naked women dancing and performing some sort of lesbian show. One was a brunette wearing a pink g-string with a big star on the front and the other was a blonde in a black g-string with a gold dollar sign on the front. It was only a quick glimpse but it looked like a very raunchy show.

We entered a room with a big banner hanging across that said 'Bucks Party'.

"This room isn't booked until midnight so we have plenty of time," Gus said as he took a seat in front of the round table with a long metal pole in the middle.

Jake and I positioned ourselves opposite Gus so we could both see his expressions as he answered our questions.

"Firstly, Gus, I'd like to introduce myself. I'm Detective Jake Miller. This is Detective Brodie Foxx," Jake said, pointing to me. "Charlie won't be coming into work. Gus, she was found deceased in her home earlier today. We know that you have worked with her for a while and we know that you were close. We are sorry for your loss," Jake said in a soft voice, and paused to give Gus time to take in the news of Charlie's death.

"If you don't mind, Gus, we have a few questions to ask you to try and piece together what happened," Jake continued.

"How did she die?" Gus asked, his face now ashen.

"We believe that she was murdered. We can't give too much information as this is an ongoing investigation. Can you tell us when you last saw her?" Jake had his notepad and pen ready.

"I saw her last night as she was leaving just after midnight. She was walking home with a male friend. I asked her if she knew him, and she said she did. I thought I had seen him around here getting lap dances. I can't be sure though; it's not the best lighting out the back."

"Could you describe the man with Charlie?" Jake asked, again poising his pen for the answers.

"Yeah sure." Gus described the guy. As Jake finished his notes, he turned to me.

"Do you know who this guy is?" Gus asked, puzzled.

"Not yet, but hopefully we will have him soon." Jake again paused. "Could you identify this man if you saw him again?"

"Yeah, I sure could, I'd know his slimy little face if I saw it," Gus said angrily.

"Apart from this guy, had Charlie said anything to you about anyone, an ex, an over-the-top patron perhaps, anyone who had been annoying her or stalking her?"

"No. She hadn't mentioned anyone to me. Usually the girls will tell me if they're having a problem. After all, that's why I'm here."

"Just a few more questions, Gus, then we'll be on our way," Jake said. "We have to ask, as we believe you were the last to see Charlie alive. Can you please tell us your whereabouts for the last 24 hours?"

"Yeah, after Charlie left I was here till 5am which is closing time. I escort the girls out as I do every shift. Then I went home with Vicki – she was the blonde girl on the stage when you first walked in, I'm sure you noticed her. I don't have to go into all the details of what we did when we got home, do I?" Gus asked with dirty smirk.

"No," Jake replied quickly.

"We woke up about midday and had some lunch at Donatellos on Lygon Street till we both started here at 3.00pm, and here I am."

"Thanks for your time, Gus. We just need to ask Vicki some questions now," Jake said, "can you send her in?"

"Sure," Gus replied, picking up the phone and hitting the intercom button. "Sal, could you send Vicki in to function room one?

Well, if she's on stage, then get her off now!" Gus said, raising his voice.

Within seconds, the door opened and Vicki appeared, topless and in her black g-string.

"That's all we need from you Gus, you can leave now." Jake gestured for Vicki to take a seat.

Once Gus had left and closed the door behind him, Jake began to question Vicki. Again, he first went through the standard introductions, and then asked a simple but straightforward question. "Please tell us where you were last night?"

Although a little taken aback by the question, Vicki answered it in the same forthright manner as Gus had. "I worked till 5am then I went to Gus' house where he banged my brains out for the next two hours. He was good too. I bet you'd like to have a go at me for a couple of hours, wouldn't you, Copper?" she said, looking at me as if to say, I know you want me. She purposely licked her lips.

Jake just glanced at me with a smile. "You can go now, Vicki, thanks for your help."

"No problem," she replied, smiling, "I hope to see you later, Coppers, especially you," she said, pointing to me.

As she left, Gus returned to stand in the doorway, arms crossed and leaning on the door. "Is that all you guys need?"

"We're finished," Jake replied, as he gathered his things and headed out. "Oh yes, one more thing. All we need now is the video footage of the back laneway last night, if you have it?"

"Yeah, we should do. I'll get it for you on the way out," Gus said, leading the way.

We went down the stairs and headed back to the entrance. Gus stopped at the front counter and opened a drawer below the till, sifting through three rows of tapes that looked as if they were marked in date order and with 'Rear' or 'Front' written next to the date.

"There you go," Gus said, as he plucked out one of the tapes from the drawer and handed it to Jake.

"Do you have any of inside the club?" I asked.

"We only record this foyer, we don't record where the dancers are," Gus replied quickly.

"Can we have that too?"

Gus opened a second drawer and handed over a tape.

"We'll return them both as soon as we've finished with them," Jake said.

We were on our way back to the station when Jake's phone rang.

"Miller?" he answered. "Yeah, in 15 or 20. See ya then, Captain."

"The captain wants to catch up on everything we have," Jake said to me. "It'll give us an opportunity to look at that tape too."

Chapter 27

Friday 7th November 2003 (10.41am)

We were keen to get a look at the tape from the club and see what it revealed.

The captain was waiting for us when we arrived.

"Was it him?" he asked as we walked down the hall and headed towards the media room.

"Brodie doesn't think so. He thinks it's more likely a copycat, but we have a tape from where she went missing so we'll see what that gives us."

The captain turned to me. "What do you mean it wasn't him?"

"Her head wasn't missing."

"Different MO?"

I replied, quickly and firmly, "Yes, he wouldn't change such an important part of his ritual."

We continued down the hall until we reached the media room. Jake wasted no time in switching on the TV and placing the video in the machine.

"Maybe he was rushed," the captain continued.

Before I had a chance to answer, Jake stepped in. "Forensics agree with Brodie. They think there are too many inconsistencies between this murder and the others." He Jake bent down and pressed the play button.

The digital readout at the top right-hand side of the screen showed 10.03pm. Jake hit fast forward until the counter reached 11.57pm, and then slowed the tape down to normal speed. At 12.01am, a tall male figure made his way into the bottom corner of the screen. All that could be seen of him was his right shoulder and arm. At 12.13am, from the bottom left of the screen, a girl entered the picture. "That's our girl," Jake said, tapping the screen.

"It's a pity we can't see the guy," I said.

With the counter on 12.14am, a third figure appeared. From his bulk, there was no doubt that it was Midget.

By the time Midget had headed back where he had come from, only the backs of Charlie and her possible killer were visible, and then they walked out of view.

"Shit!" Jake screamed as he hit the top of the video set.

"Settle, Jake," I said. "Go back to where that guy came into view." Jake rewound the tape. "There, in his hand," I said, "it's a bag. It has some writing on it. Do you think we could get the lab to try and enhance the bag so we can read what it says?"

"We can give it a go," Jake replied, as he ejected the tape and we headed through the double doors.

Sitting behind the biggest computer I had ever seen was Jason, the lab technician.

"Jason, could you have a look at this for me?" Jake asked as he handed him the tape.

"Sure thing," Jason replied, spinning around in his chair. Jason looked like a typical high school nerd who'd spent all of his time in computer class, not to become smarter but to be away from the bullies in the school yard. He wore inch-thick glasses of the sort that everyone at school used to refer to as coke bottles, and I thought about what Mum always used to say. "If you sit too close to the screen, you'll go blind." 'Must be true,' I thought.

"What do you need me do with this, Jake?" Jason asked as he placed the tape into his wiz-bang super computer.

"The guy is holding a bag. Can you enlarge it so we can see what's written on it?"

Jason began to move his cursor across the screen until he had highlighted the bag. He then turned several knobs and dials on the computer and before our eyes, the words 'Adult Playground' appeared.

I looked at Jake. "Let's find out what the hell Adult Playground is. Probably one of those sleazy city adult shops."

Jake replied, smiling as if he was excited at the idea of being in a room full of toys and porn. "Thanks Jason," he said, slapping him on the back.

"Let's check the entrance tape, Jake," I said, "see if we can get a match."

After viewing the video, Jake and I realised two things.

1. Lance had been at the club that night wearing a similar jacket but without a bag.
2. There were four or five other guys similarly dressed and of similar build who could easily have been the man in the alleyway.

"We need to find who was at Adult Playground last night before we go any further," Jake said, heading back to his desk. Before he had even sat down, he had Google up on his screen. Within a few seconds, he was impatiently waiting for the printer to finish.

This time I made sure I had my jacket and waited for Jake to let me know if we were going back to the city.

"You were right. It's an all-night adult shop. So let's get going." Jake scooped up his keys with his left hand.

"Don't forget your coat," Jake remarked, allowing himself a dig at me.

Chapter 28

Friday 7th November 2003 (11.13am)

The wind seemed to have picked up a couple of knots and the air felt as though it was about to snow.

"You know, Jake, the guy who did this is just as dangerous as the East Side Slayer. He thinks he's the Slayer and he can't see the difference."

"So what you're saying is, he's also going to keep killing until we catch him. Is that what you're telling me?" Jake was trying to look at me and keep his eyes on the road at the same time.

"That's what I'm telling you, buddy. He won't stop until he's caught or killed. This guy probably sees his kill as a dare to the Slayer himself."

The door chime buzzed as we entered Adult Playground. Jake immediately made his way to the counter, while I spent a bit of time wandering around the shop looking for some of the items that I'd seen at the murder scene. In particular, the police uniform. I saw it displayed on a mannequin, everything from the lycra shorts to the police cap complete with its imitation badge. "Jake," I called, "over here. This is what we're looking for." I began to take the mannequin down. Jake and the shop assistant headed to the back of the store.

The assistant was about five foot eight and had long, flowing, shoulder-length blonde hair. She was wearing a pale pink top that showed off her stomach. Her belly button had been pierced and she had a diamond belly ring dangling down towards her low-cut Levis. She was obviously told to dress provocatively to entice the customers to purchase.

"We're looking for a customer who may have purchased this recently," I said, turning to the assistant for her response, when a shiny steel object on the other side of the store caught my eye. Jake didn't have a clue as to what I was doing. I pointed to the handcuffs hanging from the shelf and asked, "Have you had anyone purchase both these items at the same time?"

"I can get my manager Dianne to check the system for you. She's the owner. I can ring her now if you like?" She punched in a handful of numbers for a mobile.

"What's your name, Miss?" I asked as she waited patiently for Dianne to answer the call.

"I'm Leah," she said, pointing at the nametag pinned to her chest.

"That's a nice name," I replied in my standard dorky fashion. (It was no wonder I had trouble meeting women.)

When she hung up, Leah said, "Dianne said she remembers a fairly tall guy coming in last night and buying a uniform and he purchased the cuffs as a secondary thought, kind of on his way out. The police uniforms only came in last week."

"Can we view last night's video footage?" I asked.

"Sure, no problem, Officer," Leah replied, as she headed towards the back room, looking over her shoulder to see if I was following.

"You can call me Brodie," I said.

She again looked over her shoulder and smiled. "Ok Brodie." She muttered something after that but I couldn't quite make it out. My hearing wasn't what it used to be.

My hearing had cost me some opportunities for sex in my younger days. I had been on a Christmas holiday just after my eighteenth birthday and being older than Jake and the only one with a licence, I was given the task of driving down to the caravan park for our holiday. We had been there about two days when he sparked up a conversation with a couple of girls who were staying about two spots over. By the third night, we were spending all of our time with them, and me being a dorky 18-year-old, I did nothing. Made no attempt to even chat to the remaining girl whose friend had quickly abandoned her for Jake. It wasn't until Jake came to me and said that she liked me and suggested that I make a move that on the fourth night, while Jake and his newly acquired friend were playing handies under a blanket, I summoned enough courage to kiss the girl I only knew as Mindy. Then I placed my hand on her breast and cheekily slid it inside her loose-fitting top. Worried about the move I had just made, I asked her if she minded. For some reason, I didn't hear her response. To this day, I still don't know what the answer was. I was so afraid she had said something like "get your hand off" that I was too afraid to ask the question again so I simply removed my hand and went no further with any advances. The next day, she left.

Jake asked me why I hadn't gone any further and I said, "I couldn't hear what she said." Jake told me what he'd heard and the words, while music to my ears, left me feeling like an idiot. "She said you could put your hand anywhere you like!"

I followed Leah into the small tearoom at the back of the store, while Jake waited patiently at the cash register to keep an eye on the shop for her. "Ah, here it is," Leah said as she ran her finger along the front of the video cassettes on the shelf in numerical order, stopping on the Friday one. "You can watch it here if you like? We have the equipment," she said, pointing to the TV and video machine used for all the store cameras.

"That would be a great help," I replied, removing the cassette from its cover. Leah removed the one from the machine and took the other one from my hand, stroking my fingers lightly as she removed the cassette from my grip. The counter started at 10am.

Leah handed me the remote, "I'll leave it with you. Call me if you need me," she said as she left the room. This time there was no second look back over her shoulder.

Jake came in a few seconds later. "I think she likes you, Brucey," he said, as he looked up at the TV screen.

"What are you talking about?" I replied, with my finger still firmly pressed on the fast-forward button. The counter had reached 7.23pm when Jake interrupted again.

"She said your name was cute. She wouldn't say that if she didn't like you," Jake continued. Jake thought it was his responsibility to find my future wife.

"Maybe you should ask her out?" Jake suggested

I hit the fast-forward button again to skim through all the costumers until the counter reached 8.47pm, when a tall slim man walked in then disappeared to the back of the store. A few seconds later, he reappeared and placed an item on the counter. It was a police uniform. He then disappeared again towards the back of the shop, reappearing again a few seconds later holding a small shiny object.

"That's him," I said to Jake.

"That's Lance!" he replied immediately. I hit the pause button and moved closer to the TV screen. He was right. It was Lance, there was no doubt about it. Jake ejected the tape and headed briskly back into the store, with me following him. "We need to take this as evidence," he explained to Leah, holding up the cassette.

"That's fine," Leah responded. "Do you have a card for my boss in case she asks any questions?" she asked shyly.

"Brodie will leave his contact details and you or your boss can call him anytime," Jake replied without hesitation. Then he walked outside to the car, smiling.

"Hey Brodie, you have to give me your contact details. Your partner dobbed you in," she said, smiling.

I handed her my card that had been recently supplied by the Victorian Police Department.

"I'll call you if I need you," Leah said, still smiling, as I walked out of the store. Jake was leaning against the car. "Let's go get this sick fuck," Jake proposed as I approached the vehicle.

"I think that we need to think about this before we rush off to arrest him," I answered, as I got in the passenger side of the vehicle.

"What are you talking about? We have him cold," Jake said with a degree of anger in his voice.

"Hear me out. I know we have him cold but we don't have the Slayer. We could use this situation to our advantage. Lance doesn't know that his killing wasn't the same as the Slayer's and the Slayer doesn't know that someone is copying him."

"So what are you proposing?" Jake asked with an inquisitive frown.

"I think we release details of Lance being wanted as the East Side Slayer. The real Slayer will see this and be furious that someone else has taken his glory. He may slip up, make a mistake, by wanting to take back the glory that's been stolen from him."

"Sure, or the Slayer could kill someone else just to prove to us that we have the wrong guy." As Jake finished his sentence, it suddenly hit me.

"If we play this right and feed the right info to the media he could possibly hand himself in and then we could arrest them both!"

"Sounds easy, no problem, are you on crack? That is the most absurd thing I have ever heard. You can't be serious? Why would he do that? He has spent 10 years trying not to get caught, suddenly he will just give up?"

I knew Jake was pissed, but I was sure I could convince him that my plan had merit.

"Jake, he's addicted to killing, he won't stop. He loves the power it gives him. However, he also believes he's better than us because he's beaten us for 10 years. Suddenly someone else will get his credit. It might just persuade him. We need to take a risk if we want to catch this guy," I finished.

Jake sat in his seat pondering for several minutes, then he replied, "We need to talk to the chief about this."

Chapter 29

Friday 7th November (12.05pm)

By the time we got back to the station, it had been just over six hours since Charlie had been reported murdered. It had been one of the saddest, yet most exciting, 24 hours of my life. I had been running on adrenaline the whole time and now I felt the urge to sleep run through my body. A 15-minute power nap would do me good, but there wasn't even time for that.

The chief had come into the station at Jake's request. He had been at home sleeping and Jake said he'd sounded a little pissed.

"This better be good, Miller," were his first words as we entered his office. "You know I didn't get to sleep until 4am and then you woke me!"

Jake ignored his boss's comments and went straight to business.

"Brodie has a plan, Chief, and I think it's a good one."

Without speaking, the chief turned his attention to me and waited.

Nervous, I hesitated a little and my voice cracked as the first words came out. "My plan is simple. The girl killed yesterday was a stripper. She'd been dressed in a police uniform. This was no doubt a Slayer copycat killing. However, the true Slayer doesn't know he is being copied. If we arrest Lance now, he will admit to all the killings even though he didn't do them and the Slayer will continue, with us being no closer to his identity. My plan is this: while we wait for Lance's DNA to come back and forensics to search his car, which we will need to prove his guilt, we front the media and release the video footage of Lance at the store and in the alley, asking for anyone that knows this man to contact Crime Stoppers as a 'person of interest' in connection with the East Side slayings."

"What does that achieve?" the chief asked in a less-than-approving tone.

"Well, the real Slayer will hopefully be pissed that someone else is about to take his glory and turn himself in, or at the least, contact us. Many serial killers in the past have contacted police to prove that they are the killer. Quite often this leads to their downfall."

"That's your plan?" the chief asked me. He then turned to Jake. "What amazes me more is that you thought this was a good idea." He pointed his finger at Jake. "What if the Slayer instead of contacting us goes out and kills another girl to prove he's the Slayer?"

"He will do that anyway, if we don't stop him. We know that for sure," I interrupted.

"What if this causes Lance to go on a killing spree?" Richard questioned.

"Anything is possible with these nutters, as you know!" Jake said.

"We will have him under strict supervision. If he leaves his house we will arrest him, Chief," I added.

"Don't call me Chief, you haven't earned that right yet! Remember, your appointment to the force can be revoked as quickly as it was given. Don't forget that! If this goes bad we will never hear the end of it. I went to the commissioner to get you approved, don't put me in a position where I have to go back to him."

The chief was now standing, leaning across his desk.

Shocked at his outburst, I put my head down and also wondered what the hell I was doing in the middle of all this. Maybe he was right; maybe I didn't belong.

"Don't start going off your tree. This case has been going on for 10 years so maybe you should take a look in the mirror," Jake fired back. "At least Brodie has a plan, which is better than you and your previous taskforce have ever done."

The chief sat back in his chair and began to rub his eyes. "All right, Jake, it's your call and your arse if you do this, and if it goes horribly wrong, you're back on traffic duty. Do you understand? As for you, Brodie, well you know the consequences."

"You don't have to threaten us, Chief, we get it."

"Jake," I interrupted, "it's ok, I understand your boss's position." I was being careful not to use the word 'chief'. "This wasn't Jake's idea. It was mine and I offer you this. If we do what I have suggested and if we don't flush out the Slayer, I'll be your fall guy if you need one. I can't guarantee that we'll catch him but I can be fairly sure that this plan will get us closer to him."

The chief, who had now calmed down, looked at me and sighed.

"You better pray it flushes him out."

I followed Jake out of the office. He turned to me in the hall. "Are you sure you want to go ahead with this plan of yours? We have a lot of information we could sort through before we resort to this strategy."

"Charlie's murder won't remain quiet for long. If we arrest Lance now, we won't get another opportunity like this again," I said. "I think it's our best chance and I'd rather try and fail than not try at all."

Jake continued walking towards his office. "Let's do this then," he said, smiling slightly.

Chapter 30

Friday 7th November 2003 (6.43pm)

"Now Maggie, it's time for you to go where you can be found," Mason muttered to himself as he again went across to his workbench. He returned a short time later, holding a large piece of extra-thick plastic normally used for ground cover to prevent weeds coming through the mulch.

Mason laid the plastic along the dirt floor of the cabin cellar next to Maggie's lifeless body. He grabbed Maggie under the shoulders, dragging her headless body onto the plastic. Laying her on the plastic, he began to wash her with a bleach solution, then wrapped her up like a cigarette. He then began to cut several pieces of orange rope from the spindle he had retrieved from his bench. He cut each piece to a length of approximately three foot. He began to tie the end where Maggie's head would have been, ensuring there was enough plastic at the end so the ends would not come free during transportation. Mason then tied a second rope around Maggie's chest. It took five pieces to secure Maggie's body fully.

Mason went outside and drove his BMW down to the cellar. He drove in through the open doors and parked on the dusty cellar floor, swiftly closing the doors behind him. Then he loaded Maggie's body into the open boot.

Mason knew that if the police ever found this place there would be enough evidence from Maggie and all the other victims to convict him a hundred times over. However, the chance of finding this place was remote.

By the time Mason drove his car out of the cellar, it was well after 7pm. With the drive ahead of him, he would be dumping the body in the dark as planned.

Chapter 31

Friday 7th November 2003 (7.30pm)

"Are you all set for this conference?" I asked Jake. "You know what to say?"

Jake nodded. Then he was on.

"We have information about the East Side Slayer and we feel it is important to let the public know some of the facts that have come to hand," Jake began. "My name is Detective Jake Miller I am lead detective of the Eagle taskforce. We are looking for this man…" they rolled the surveillance footage, "in relation to the murder of Lucy Akin and the unsolved police officer murders. We encourage anyone with any knowledge of this man to contact Crime Stoppers immediately. We believe the community will be able to help us identify this man."

We had given the public the impression that we didn't know who Lance was, which was exactly what we wanted.

Jake finished up and headed back to us. "The conference doesn't hit the air at 7am tomorrow, I'll pick you up in the morning, say at 6.15?" Jake didn't wait for an answer.

We arrived at Lance's house about 6.40am and it was good to see that our night surveillance was still there and awake. "What's the status?" Jake asked into the handset.

There was a short pause before the answer returned, "He's been inside since 10.35 last night. Before that, he was at the Crazy Horse cinemas watching porn. I'd say he's been in there spanking the monkey ever since."

"Thanks for the detail, Chad, you guys can leave now," I replied.

"So we just sit and wait?" Jake asked, as Chad's vehicle left to return to the police station. "Yep, just be patient. Soon, both Lance and the Slayer will see the press conference and then we just wait for the Slayer to contact us or turn himself in to claim his glory." At least I hoped that was what would happen. My whole plan rested on my study of serial killers and their egos preventing them from allowing someone else to take the credit. Surely he would contact us.

Chapter 32

Friday 7th November 2003 (8.00pm)

As Mason drove back to Melbourne, he knew exactly where he would dump Maggie. While he knew the location, it was impossible to plan exactly. He never knew who might be floating around. After all, the last thing he wanted when he was taking a body out of the boot was someone seeing him.

A dead body wrapped in plastic was difficult to disguise.

Mason had prided himself on dumping the bodies in different locations. He knew that it would make it harder for police to track him. His plan was simple. He wanted the police to think that he was on the move all the time and that no one in the whole state was safe. For the last decade, it had worked. They had released several suspect profiles through the media. One had suggested it would most likely be a person who travelled in his job, who had a position that provided the freedom to commit these horrendous acts. The police media spokesperson had suggested that it was likely he was a truck driver or possibly a cabbie. Both of these theories pleased Mason a great deal.

He had figured that this body needed to be dumped somewhere remote, and miles away from the last one. He had sold a couple of properties back in the old 'multi-list' days out in a suburb called the Basin, which was an area of bush.

The outskirts of the suburb abutted a national park. Mason always liked dumping in the parks. There was an abundance of walking and riding tracks, increasing the chances of the body being found within a reasonable time. Yet, at night, the parks were practically deserted, giving Mason the privacy he needed.

Mason pulled his car into the turning circle at the top of Clairveness Avenue, the Basin, at almost 8.30. It was nearing dark. He had parked where the road met the beginning of the Basin National Reserve, as some moron at the council had decided to name it. While the turning circle didn't provide any cover for getting Maggie out of his boot, it did provide perfect and quick access to the park and the dense bushland, which would protect him while he was dumping her. All Mason had to do was time his run. Reaching under the dash, he pushed the boot release button. He heard the mechanical release and the boot popped open about half an inch. Mason took a final look in the rear vision mirror and saw no headlights approaching.

He got out of his car and stood at the boot, taking a final look down the road. He could see approximately 300 metres before the road curved and vision of any oncoming vehicles became impossible. Mason swung around and looked up the road for any approaching vehicles from the rear. There was about a 200-metre view in that direction.

Mason knew that if a car came from either way once he had removed the body, he would have no time to put it back before the car was well and truly upon him. After a couple of further glances, up and down the road, he opened the boot a little more, lifted his shirt up and placed the knife, still in its leather case, down the back of his jeans. It rested against the small of his back and at the top of his buttocks.

Mason always took his knife when he was dumping someone. He never knew when he might need to cut some brush.

Mason placed his arms in the boot and took hold of Maggie's body, still with the boot only ajar, allowing him enough space to reach in. He took his final look and then prepared himself for the lift and run into the park. In a single motion, he pushed the boot up with his biceps and lifted the body out.

Maggie's feet weren't even clear of the boot as Mason began his dash for the cover of the bush, clipping Maggie's foot on the corner of the boot and tearing the plastic as he went. He carried her almost at a run and was glad when he found himself in a secluded area away from the road in the scrub. Mason left the stony path, obviously provided for mountain bikers and walkers, and trudged through the bracken, ferns and fallen bark from nearby gums, which towered above Mason and his headless victim.

Mason began to struggle to carry the body once he left the dirt track. Fallen branches and potholes made the journey more difficult.

He almost dropped Maggie twice within the first five metres after leaving the track.

The third time, Mason was forced to drop his victim when he stepped into a concealed hole, causing him to lose his balance and roll his ankle. Had he not dropped Maggie, he probably would have broken his ankle.

That would have left him in a fine mess, sitting next to the victim and unable to walk.

He had a vision of himself crawling back to the car. How stupid that would look, not to mention a great way to attract attention.

Maggie's body rolled a few metres before coming to rest against the side of a fallen gum. It was here that Mason decided to leave her, not because he thought it was the best place for her but because his ankle was killing him and he knew he wouldn't be able to carry her any further.

Mason undid the rope from the plastic and unrolled Maggie, like a rolled-up sleeping bag in front of a blazing campfire.

He tore a few branches off a nearby fern and began laying them over the package of Maggie's sprawled body. Mason had only half covered the body when he felt something wet on his back.

He turned, half startled, to see the nose of a German Shepherd sniffing his back and leg and trying to sniff Maggie. What the hell was a dog doing out here at this time of night? Mason tried to get the dog away from him.

Chapter 33

Friday 7th November (8.43pm)

Alan was heading for home at the end of his jog. He had been doing this run for a little over six months now and winter had not stopped him. Even the dark didn't bother him. Jogging had become easier over the months and the rewards were now visible. He could see that his body was more toned. His main concern was finding his dog Rex, who had gone exploring.

He had started his jog a little later than usual this evening; work had been hectic. He had almost decided not to go because it was getting too late. But he knew Rex needed the run and he always took Rex on both his morning and evening jogs, more for exercise than company.

"Rex, Rex, where are you?" he called, slowing down and scanning each side of the path for Rex. Where had he gone? He had been running nearby.

Mason heard the distant calls for the dog, which was obviously the one sniffing around behind him. The calls were coming a lot closer.

Mason knew his time was limited so he quickly tried to cover the exposed parts of Maggie's body. As he grabbed more bracken and fern branches, he knew that his time had run out when he saw Rex's owner standing on the track.

He had obviously been jogging for a while. Mason could see he had well defined and toned thigh muscles. Mason guessed he must have been close to the end of his jog because sweat was running down his face.

Alan sighted Rex and cautiously observed the stranger with the large plastic tarp. He then noticed what appeared to be a leg protruding from beneath it.

Alan quickly comprehended what he had seen and decided to flee. He began to run away as fast as he could sprint. Mason knew that there was no way he would catch him: not with his ankle in its current condition.

Reaching around his back, Mason withdrew his knife from its holster, held it by the tip and began to focus. He knew that he only had one chance and if he missed, his killing days would soon be over. He aimed at the jogger's broad back.

His target was one of the lungs. He knew the best way to stop him would be to cut the oxygen supply and a knife through a lung could certainly do that.

Taking a deep breath, he swiftly threw the knife at the escaping witness.

The knife spun end over end, compass, tip, compass, tip, compass, tip, through the air, until it hit its target. Alan felt something hit him, but couldn't understand what it was. There was no pain at first. Then his breathing became spasmodic, wheezing and slow. Had he been shot by the man in the bushes? He hadn't heard anything. His running had slowed to a stagger.

Then the taste of blood. It wet his lips, and was quickly filling his mouth. Then the pain came. With every breath, the pain increased, sharp and excruciating and becoming increasingly shallow.

His adrenaline could carry him no longer. He was dying and he knew it.

The ground was wet and muddy in places from the winter rains and the mud clung to him as his knees hit the mossy ground. Still desperate to escape, he began to crawl along the track, trying not to think of the inevitable.

His hands and knees quickly became muddy and slippery. He could no longer continue on all fours. He fell, face first into the mud. He tasted the dirt mixed with blood. He rolled onto his side, hoping he could muster the strength to call and command Rex to attack. Maybe then his attacker would not be able to pursue him any further.

Alan's breathing was a real struggle now and more painful than ever.

He took the deepest breath possible, causing himself more pain than he could have thought possible.

Rex's ears pricked up at the cries from his owner. He turned his head away from the body he was sniffing on the ground, and towards his owner. At the sound of his second weaker cry of anguish, Rex jumped into action.

Mason heard the call coming from the jogger, but he never expected the dog to attack him from behind.

Mason was halfway to the collapsed jogger who was lying on his side in the mud and gravel with the knife still embedded in his back, when he was suddenly knocked to the ground. The large dog attacked him ferociously. First, he went for Mason's throat but Mason protected himself with his right forearm. Mason felt the dog's teeth pierce the skin then tear the flesh away. He knew that his arm could not protect him for much longer and that he had to do something.

Mason used all the power he could in his good foot and what little power he could muster from his sprained one and kicked as hard as he could, dazing the shepherd temporarily.

The kick didn't seem to do it any serious harm, but it was certainly enough to stun it.

Mason rolled onto his stomach and got to all fours and then to his feet. He had only taken a few steps when the shepherd was back at him, this time attacking his foot. Mason dropped to the ground for a second time.

Mason twisted his neck around to see if he could reach his knife embedded in the jogger's back, but it was still out of reach.

He had to get this dog off him and fast. The jogger was still alive and trying to crawl away, and the longer the dog was on him, the more injuries he would sustain.

A serious injury would be hard to explain. Not to mention the unfinished business and the chances of someone coming across what had become nothing short of a disaster.

Mason reached out both arms to ward off the dog as best he could, scanning the ground for any weapon he could use. Then he felt a rock. Rolling over, he wasted no time in grasping the rock and hitting the dog continually until finally, the rock connected with the shepherd's temple and it gave a loud yelp before falling silent.

After kicking the dog off him with his good foot, Mason got to his feet. There was no doubt the dog had done some damage but not enough to prevent him from hobbling out of this mess. Mason staggered towards the almost lifeless sprawled body of the jogger. "Your fucking dog had a lot of fight in him but I sent him on a little trip and now I'm sending you there with him." Placing his knee in the small of his back, Mason withdrew his knife from under his shoulder blade and flipped him over. He wanted to see his eyes. This wasn't his usual kill but he needed to see him go. Mason wasted no more time, slitting his throat and then beginning his frenzy of stabbing. He wrenched him up by the hair and stared into his eyes as he began to splutter and wheeze. He was almost gone. Then silence, as he passed. Mason used what energy he had left to remove his head. Finally, he rolled him off the walking track, wrapped the jogger's head inside his own jacket and returned to the safety of his vehicle.

Mason had always kept a spare bag of clothes in his car in case of an emergency such as this. He removed a garbage bag, placed the jacket and the head into it, and tied it tight. He removed his bloody pants behind the cover of his car. He added them to a separate garbage bag. Dressed in his spare clothes, he placed the bags in his boot and headed home.

He had left the jogger's body barely covered, but it would have to do. He was just hoping he hadn't left too much evidence behind.

He couldn't get home soon enough. Mason entered the home still hobbling and headed straight for the powder room and the medicine cabinet.

He was so lucky his wife had gone away. How could he have explained his injuries?

He washed his foot and forearm under the tap before applying the antiseptic and adding some gauze and Betadine, hoping it would do the job. The bites didn't look deep enough to require stitches, and that wouldn't be possible anyway without raising alarm bells. Especially when the police found the dog and the headless jogger. Mason wound the bandages tight, swallowed a couple of painkillers and headed upstairs, where he watched a movie in bed and fell asleep.

Chapter 34

Saturday 8th November 2003 (7am)

Despite his injuries, Mason rose early as he had always done on a Saturday morning. Saturdays were his open home days he had to be up and out early. He stood in front of the mirror with the shaver balanced delicately in his right hand. He no longer recognised the man looking back at him. Mason leaned forward and looked deep into his own eyes. Nothing there; nothing but darkness. It even scared him. It was eerie. What had he become?

Twenty minutes later, Mason sat down at the table ready to eat breakfast.

The morning news was on in the background.

Before he had even consumed a mouthful of his cereal, he stopped, in a trance, staring at the vision on the television screen. Mason watched the police interview and listened intently as Jake introduced himself and the taskforce. His heart felt like it was about to burst out his chest. When CCTV footage appeared, his panic turned to anger. It wasn't him. The footage was of someone else. Some tall skinny bloke. Mason stood and threw his bowl from the table to the kitchen sink. It smashed on impact, sending pieces of the bowl across the room along with cereal and milk.

This was not right. All his hard work for someone else to take the glory, 'Uh ahh,' Mason thought. 'No way. It won't end like this.' He had to put a stop to it.

Mason didn't arrive at work for at least another 40 minutes. He had decided to put his open for inspection boards out early, giving him time to listen to the talkback stations, which were buzzing with excitement at the possibility of a suspect. They had even taken the unusual step of bringing in ex-profilers to prove that the police had been on the right track all along. How wrong they were.

Talkback callers suggested that the death penalty be brought back for the man found guilty of the murders. By the time he arrived at the office, the host had announced that News Limited had identified the 'man in the alley' as one Lance Silver of Kew and that his car was in the hands of forensics.

Mason was the first to arrive at the office, as was often the case. He unlocked the door, turned off the alarm and turned on the lights, immediately heading for his laptop. He had a good hour before his first appointment. His last open home finished at 2, so he would have plenty of time to act if need be.

Removing the notepad from the top pocket of his shirt, Mason entered the name into his reverse phone directory. 'Please don't be unlisted,' Mason thought. Then after what seemed like an eternity, the search brought up exactly what he needed: There were three on the list but only one 'L. Silver' in Kew. His phone number was unlisted. All Mason needed now was a plan to show everyone who the real Slayer was, once and for all.

Mason spent the next half hour doing a little research of his own. He typed into his Google search bar 'Jake Miller Eagle taskforce'. Several links came up. He clicked on the link 'Eagle taskforce restructured after 10 years'.

He read that Senior Detective Jake Miller would head up the revamped Eagle taskforce in an attempt to reinvigorate the much-maligned original taskforce. Upon his appointment, Miller had said he believed that the cases were solvable. The Victorian police would do everything in its power to ensure the killer was caught and brought to justice.

Yet, less than a week later, the taskforce had already come under fire for the appointment of criminal psychologist Brodie Foxx. Foxx's appointment was highly criticised by the state government who were now debating amending the Police Act to forbid any such future appointments.

"Can I see you in my office, Mason?" a distant but distinctive voice called out. Mason sighed. He wanted a plan and now his planning was being interrupted. Probably over something trivial.

Kurt had only been made the boss because it was his father's company, not because he was an outstanding salesperson. Kurt had tried to demand respect from the moment he'd taken the helm, without success. Mason thought the pressure of running his father's multi-million dollar business was taking its toll.

In the last two years, Kurt had gained a lot of weight and lost some hair. What little remained was now grey. He looked as if he was falling apart.

"Shut the door," Kurt said from his seat on the other side of his desk. Mason did as he was told and took a seat opposite his boss, surprised by his boss's request for a meeting. "What's going on with you lately? Is there a problem at home that I don't know about?" his boss asked, wasting no time in getting to the point.

Mason sat there, stunned. Then he replied with a stutter, "No, everything is fine." He was unsure where this conversation was heading.

"Well, it's just that your sales figures have dropped dramatically and you're never in the office any more," Kurt said, flicking through a sales result spreadsheet.

Without hesitation, Mason went on the attack. "Everything is fine. I'm just having a bad run, that's all. The reason I'm out of the office is because I'm trying to get business. Houses and land are out there, not in here. I have a lot on, that's all."

"Well, if your results don't improve by the end of the month, I'm going to have to consider letting you go."

Mason sat silently for a minute, looking at his boss's desk, still trying to come up with a plan. Then it appeared in front of him. It was sitting there staring back at him and it was brilliant. 'Opportunities always present themselves when needed,' he thought. "I understand; I'll work harder," Mason replied.

Mason stood and paused. "Is that photo new?" he asked, pointing to the photo of his boss's daughter on his desk. "Yes, she just graduated," Kurt replied abruptly, picking up his phone to dial his next call. "They grow up so fast," Mason said, as he left his boss's office and pretended to get back to work.

It would have to wait until tomorrow before it was revealed in all its glory, but it was simply perfect.

Mason spent the rest of the day doing the mundane tasks that he was required to do in order to keep his job for at least a little longer. It wasn't until around 1pm that he told his lovely receptionist that he was going to do a market appraisal after his open home, and that he might not be back that day.

Chapter 35

Saturday 8th November 2003 (10.30am)

We had spent Saturday morning sitting at the front of Lance's house. We had been there for almost four hours and thankfully, our shift was almost over. He was so stupid; he kept sticking his head out from behind the curtain to peek into the street.

We had his phone bugged and he had made two calls, both to his solicitor Dale Moreholm. His answering machine had answered both times. Obviously, it had taken the second call for Lance to realise it was a Saturday afternoon and the office was closed.

Both times Lance left the same message: 'The police have taken my car and I'm on the news. Please call me'.

We had issued strict instructions to the media that they were to stay away from here. The media had reported that police had confiscated his vehicle.

My plan wasn't going as I had hoped. I thought we would have at least heard from the Slayer by now. Maybe he was smarter than I thought. I kept hearing the chief's voice in my mind. "Don't make me have to go back to the commissioner!"

In the time we had been sitting, watching and waiting, Jake must have consumed more chocolate, chips and cola than most humans could do in a whole week. There was no argument; if Jake had a weakness, food was it.

We prepared to go back to the station to continue our investigation into other Slayer leads. Lance was a killer and as soon as we had enough evidence to gain a conviction for the murder of Charlie, he would be off the street. It was only because we were a few pieces shy of what the prosecution called 'overwhelming evidence' that he was still free.

We had spent most of our time on the other Slayer suspect leads. We needed to follow those leads just in case my plan didn't yield the desired result.

Chapter 36

Saturday 8th November 2003 (10.42am)

C had's car pulled into the empty space behind us and he turned off the engine. He and his partner, Henry, had arrived a few minutes before their 10-hour shift was due to start. Josh and Leah had the 9pm to 7am graveyard shift. Henry had been off sick the previous night. I glanced at them in the side mirror. Chad, who was observant of his surroundings, as all good cops need to be, noticed me peering at him and made a gesture with his right index finger.

Henry looked as if he had vomited very recently or was full of the flu.

Forensics had matched the fingerprints found on a bottle of beer in Charlie's apartment to Lance, through a process known as 'fuming'. The bottle was put in an oven with super glue. When the oven reached the required temperature, the glue evaporated and stuck to the oil left behind from the human print. Once removed from the oven, the bottle was lightly dusted and the prints appeared.

It was proving difficult for the forensic team to locate blood, hair or fibre samples from Lance in Charlie's apartment. Proving that Lance had been in Charlie's apartment didn't prove he'd killed her. Even the video evidence from the club and the lingerie shop, and traces of his semen, didn't prove conclusively he'd killed her. This was all circumstantial evidence, which could easily be argued against by a good defence lawyer.

Chad told us that the lab had finished testing the vehicle and that the evidence brief would be lodged with the director of public prosecutions today. We would only have until Sunday noon to flush out the Slayer.

Finding the murder weapon had been crucial. Now our submission to the DPP had substance and would outline that Lance had killed Charlie and in returning to his car, had hidden the knife inside his vehicle. They say every murderer makes 25 mistakes while committing a crime. Lance's biggest one was not disposing of the weapon.

We headed back to the station to continue our search for the Slayer. I was calmer now that we knew for sure Lance was Charlie's killer. But I was still haunted by the thought that there was someone out there planning his next kill, selecting his next victim. Such thoughts had kept me up most nights, sifting through the files looking for more answers, more clues, or both. I had found nothing yet, but I was sure that I would continue to search until the early hours of Sunday morning. I don't think I had enjoyed a decent sleep since I'd started this case.

We were only minutes away from the station when dispatch called us on the CB. "Jake, come in," the familiar voice of Kim Reynolds requested. Jake picked up the CB and replied, "Jake here. Not far away, Kim. What's up?"

"I have someone here who says she has information regarding the Slayer case." Jake almost dropped the handset to the floor. Thankfully, I was driving, preventing any chance of an accident. He recovered and replied quickly and firmly, "Kim, we're on our way. Whatever you do, don't let her go! Make her a coffee. Just make sure that you keep her there!"

We drove to the station with the siren screaming and headed straight for the waiting area. Kim had done her job. Sitting on one of the plastic chairs with a steaming drink, our informant was waiting patiently.

Kim came out from behind the counter to introduce us. "Detective Jake Miller and Brodie Foxx, Esmeralda."

"I'm a psychic," she said immediately. "I came here because I see things. I can't control what I see or why I see it but this, I can't ignore."

Jake glanced my way as if to say, here we go, another nut.

"With all due respect," I said, "we've had many psychics offer assistance but it has always led us nowhere. So please forgive my partner's scepticism. Sometimes, it gets the better of him." I hoped she would start telling us what she knew.

"Of course," Esmeralda replied, "I understand and I don't want to waste your time."

Jake gestured towards the interview room at the end of the hall. I followed closely without saying anything more. I had heard stories and seen documentaries on psychics solving crimes, but like Jake, I had my doubts. Still, anything was possible and our luck had to change eventually.

In the interview room, we sat opposite Esmeralda, who was sitting where the criminals usually sat when being interviewed. Esmeralda didn't look how I expected a psychic to look. I had pictured a witch-like character, yet Esmeralda was a middle-aged, distinguished looking lady, someone you expected might live in Toorak or Beaumaris, and who might drive an Audi rather than ride a broomstick.

"It all started last night when I had a dream; well, it was more like a vision. It felt very real." Esmeralda paused and shuffled in her seat, clearly uncomfortable with the two sceptical officers staring at her. "In the vision, I saw a man being dragged. His head had been removed. Then, I saw another body being carried under a blue tarp. Whoever was carrying it dropped it. The head was missing too. I think the body was a woman but I can't be sure. One leg was hanging out from the tarp. Then suddenly I saw a wolf."

"What makes you think that this has anything to do with the Slayer case?" Jake asked seriously but calmly.

"It may not be connected, but some deep instinct tells me it is."

Jake looked at me and gestured towards the door.

We got up and stood in the hallway under a flickering fluorescent light. "What do you think, Brodie?" Jake asked with a lost look on his face.

"Well Jake, no one knows about the Slayer removing the heads. So how the hell could she know about that?"

"Yeah, but he's never killed a man before," Jake replied. "Well, let's see what else she knows," Jake continued. We entered the room again and took up our position opposite Esmeralda.

"Is there anything else you can tell us about the dream or vision?" I asked.

"Did you see the man at all?" Jake added as he removed his notepad.

"No. Sorry, that's all I have."

Jake stood up and reached over to take Esmeralda by the hand. He could see this vision had seriously scared her. "We believe you. We will look into it, ok?"

"Can you tell us more about this girl in a tarp? Is there anything else you remember seeing?" I asked, nodding at Jake to allow me to question her further.

"No, I can't even be sure it was a girl, I just felt that it was."

"The area he dropped her in. What did that look like?" I asked.

"It was light bush parkland with shrubs and trails. It wasn't familiar to me. I didn't know the place."

Jake and I looked at each other, knowing it could be anywhere, if it existed at all.

She could tell us nothing more and so before she left, Jake said, "Please, Esmeralda, if there is anything else that comes to you, please let us know, anything at all. Any information may be vital."

"Anything at all," I reiterated.

I asked Kim to notify us of any recent missing persons in the last day or two. Minutes later, Kim reported that as of Friday 8pm, no one had been listed as missing across the state.

Chapter 37

Saturday 8th November (2.30pm)

Half an hour after his last open home, Mason stood in the driveway of his next victim. He knew that what he was about to do might increase the possibility of him getting caught. But his options were limited. It was either this or let the skinny man take the credit for his work.

Wasting no time, Mason walked up to the door of his unsuspecting victim and calmly rang the bell. Silence. Mason again pressed the bell. Silence, then footsteps. 'Jackpot, she's home,' Mason thought. The door swung open. On the other side of the security door, she beamed and asked, "Can I help you?" drying her hands on a tea towel.

Mason began his usual door-knocking speech. "Hi, my name is Mason Belic from Greenside Real Estate. We have buyers."

"Is that you, Mason?" the woman on the other side of the door asked. The security door clicked open. "It's me, Tammy Green," the girl continued as she opened the door and invited Mason in with a wave of her hand, still clutching the tea towel. "I thought you knew I lived here?"

"I had no idea," Mason lied.

"I moved in just after last year's company awards. That would have been the last time I saw you."

Mason nodded and followed Tammy down the hallway to the kitchen. "I think I must have been a little drunk back then. I'm sorry I made a pass at you, combination of my thing for an older guy and too much champagne. I hope you don't have any bad feelings towards me?"

"Not at all. It's water under the bridge," Mason replied, as he sat on a stool at the breakfast bar. She didn't know how close Mason had come to accepting her invitation at the awards night. If her father hadn't been his boss, he was sure he would have. Damn, she'd looked great that night, Mason remembered. Hair done, silky red dress that showed off all of her gorgeous features along with most of her breasts.

Tammy removed two white cups from the overhead cupboard and began filling the kettle. "So how's Dad treating you? Ok, I hope?" Tammy asked, as she removed the coffee from the cupboard and placed it on the breakfast bar.

"You know your dad. Always wanting to get more out of his workers. What boss wouldn't though?" Mason asked, not interested in an answer. "How are you going? Do you like it here?" Mason asked. This was the first real question he had asked.

All Mason had been thinking of was how he was going to kill her. But first, he might as well have a little fun.

"Well, I get lonely being here by myself, but apart from that I really like it. Do you take sugar?" Tammy asked, hand poised over the sugar bowl.

"No thanks," Mason replied. "You know, I would have said yes at the awards night. I wanted to go back to your room with you. I just thought you should know that the only reason I didn't was because you're my boss's daughter. I was worried your dad would find out and sack me."

"So that's why?" Tammy responded with her mouth open, blushing. She was stunned.

"Maybe I should go," Mason said, moving to stand up.

"Don't be silly," Tammy replied, grabbing his arm before he had a chance to leave. "Stay. Have your coffee."

Mason loved the smell of freshly percolating coffee. Tammy poured him a cup and placed it in front of him. "So what would your answer be now?" she asked.

"First, I would ask how old you are."

"Twenty-two," she replied. "You afraid you mightn't be able to keep up?" Tammy added, smiling as she sipped her coffee.

A little embarrassed, Mason could not help but laugh at Tammy's question. "I would say yes," Mason replied, as he sipped his steaming hot coffee and looked over the cup at her. Tammy moved around to the other side of the breakfast bar and pulled up a stool next to Mason. Although she wasn't dressed in that stunning red dress that she'd worn to the awards, she still looked sensational in casual jeans and a top. Her blonde hair looked amazing, even though it hadn't been done by a hairdresser as it had been on the night of the awards.

"So do I have to ask or can we just assume that I have asked?" Tammy said, as she leaned forward towards Mason.

"I don't know what you're referring to," Mason replied with a shrewd smile.

Tammy, enjoying the game playing, repeated the question of almost a year before on a crowded dance floor. His answer had crushed her heart, as rejection always did. This time there would be no such rejection. "Do you want to come to my bedroom?" she asked.

Mason simply nodded and made no resistance to Tammy, who leaned in further for a kiss. Before Mason could respond, he felt Tammy's tongue slide gently into his mouth. She took his hand and they walked back down the hallway to the front of the house. Mason hadn't seen things going this way when he'd pulled up in the driveway. He'd been expecting to get inside, stun her and get out but he thought it would be worth the small risk associated with sleeping with her.

As they walked through the bedroom doorway, Tammy lifted her arms, breaking the connection with Mason, and removed her top.

There was no bra, just firm round breasts, breasts the like of which he hadn't seen for many years.

Mason's shirt dropped to the floor as he returned the favour. His chest was still firm, but his stomach had let go a little. The remnants of his sculpted six-pack were still visible, despite a bit of flab. Tammy flicked her jeans through the air with her left foot, and they landed on the other side of the room. Her bum was round and firm and it was unlike anything he had ever experienced before, and he doubted he ever would again.

Tammy flopped onto the bed, naked, and gestured for Mason to join her.

Despite his obvious excitement, sex was the last thing on Mason's mind. He always kept his victims away from his normal life. He wanted no connection with them whatsoever. Stranger murders were always harder for police to solve. He couldn't believe he was about to break his number one rule.

Mason didn't want to admit it to Tammy but he soon realised that she was right. He did have trouble keeping up. She just kept going and going.

They were still lying on the bed when Mason decided there was no more time for fun. He had risked being here too long already.

Tammy jumped up from the bed after giving herself a few minutes to regain her breath and headed to the shower. Mason knew he had to act and act now. He began searching through the walk-in robe for a bag or suitcase. He found what appeared to be Tammy's gym bag on the top shelf. Listening out for the sound of the shower, Mason quickly began to strip the bed: sheets, pillowcases, the whole box and dice. He had risked too much already by sleeping with her and he didn't want compromise the situation any further by leaving behind his DNA.

He went out to the kitchen where he had left his jacket hanging over the bar stool and his briefcase sitting on the floor next to it. Mason removed the precious items from the inside pocket of his jacket. First, the gloves. There was no point leaving his fingerprints lying around. The second and third items were two pre-filled syringes and a 25-ml vanilla essence bottle filled with his ever-reliable Benzodiapine. This would be essential in providing him time to tidy up any trace evidence and get to his cabin. The fourth item, his favourite, he kept in its case. It was his taser, or as most people knew it, a stun gun. It was quiet and provided immediate control over the victim, giving him the necessary time required to inject his Benzodiapine..

He was glad Tammy had decided to take a shower. It would help remove any DNA evidence that he surely would have left behind. Mason knew hair and semen were the hardest to remove and while the shower would help, he would have to soak her in bleach before he dumped her body.

Mason walked back into the bedroom with his gloves on, and placed the drawstring garbage bag that he had found in the bottom kitchen drawer on the bedside table. The shower stopped and the ensuite door remained shut.

Mason opened it and placed his right hand behind his back with the stun gun firmly clenched in his hand.

Tammy had finished drying herself and was standing in front of the mirror, wearing only a pair of pink panties, her breasts free of a bra. She was just putting on foundation and lipstick. Mason moved up behind her, his right hand still hidden behind his back. "You ready for more?" she asked, pressing her lips together to ensure her lipstick was even.

Mason began to kiss her neck and caress her breasts with his left hand. She closed her eyes for a second. That was all Mason needed to strike.

Chapter 38

Saturday 8th November (5.17pm)

"Wake up, you slut!" Mason said as he slapped Tammy's face hard enough to bring her around.

"What are you doing?" she asked groggily.

Mason knelt down in front of her. "I want you to listen very carefully, do you understand?" Tammy nodded. "Now, I will explain why you're sitting naked in my bath, but firstly, you're going to wash yourself clean. I want you rid of all your filth and smuttiness. Then tomorrow you're coming with me door-knocking at some houses. The area will be surrounded by police and yet you will not try to escape. Do you understand?"

Tammy nodded.

"Just so we're clear: if you try to escape or fail to do what I've asked of you, your father will die. At precisely 11am tomorrow, if I don't make a call, he will be killed. Do you understand?"

Tammy nodded again, tears streaming down her cheeks at the thought of her father dying.

"I will let you and your father go once I have conducted my business. Do you understand?" he asked again. She nodded in agreement.

"Now, put some water in that bath. You're starting to shiver, you'll catch your death and we can't have that, can we?"

"No," she said simply. She turned on the taps to fill the bath.

"I've made up the spare room for you and here's your nightgown," Mason said, tapping the shelf in the bathroom where a red silk gown sat alongside a thick cream robe. "Tomorrow's clothes are on the bed. When you're finished, put your gown on and we'll have some food."

Mason left the bathroom. The cabin had seen so many deaths, but not tonight.

Mason knew very well that Tammy would not risk disobeying his instructions because of the fear of losing her father. Love can sometimes be one's best weapon.

He was certain his plan was perfect. After all, how would she know if her father was safe and well? Knowing him as Mason did, he guessed he would still be at the office.

For Mason, tomorrow could not come soon enough. Executing one of his plans always gave him the same feeling he'd had as a child when the next day he was going to the royal show. Pure excitement. Mason slept very little that night thinking of the day ahead.

Chapter 39

Sunday 9th November 2003 (6.30am)

It was Sunday morning. To me, that meant two things. One, I had to stake out Lance's house today with Jake and two, we were running out of time for my plan to work. There was no doubt that Lance would have to be arrested today and our chance of catching the Slayer would be gone.

I finished off my eggs and bacon accompanied by a glass of orange juice. It had been my standard Sunday morning breakfast ever since I was a child.

Over the past few weeks, I had become accustomed to picking Jake up from his unit in Hawthorn. Yet this morning, I would have to pick him up from Hayley's unit in Parkville. It appeared things had seriously progressed for him. I was glad. It had been a long time coming. I just wanted him to be happy and it appeared finally to be on the horizon.

The drive to Parkville was a lot busier than the one to Hawthorn; the closer I got to the city, the heavier the traffic became. My saving grace was that it was a Sunday and not a Monday. Despite the traffic, my mind was on autopilot. I searched for the reasons why my plan hadn't worked. Had I underestimated the Slayer? Had I overestimated my own ability? The last question was the one that rang the loudest through my head.

I pulled up at the address that Jake had given me over the phone and tooted the horn twice. In hindsight, it probably wasn't the smartest or the most considerate thing to do on a Sunday morning.

Within a few minutes, Jake was sitting in the seat beside me. "Morning, Bruce." It was a more spirited Jake than the one I had been working with over the last few weeks. I just looked at him, ready to ask the questions that all best friends do. However, his smile told me the answer and from the size of it, I knew all I wanted to know. "Let's go catch ourselves a killer," Jake said as he changed the radio from the AM band to FM. It was a constant struggle in our car; I always wanted to listen to the talkback and Jake always wanted to listen to his tunes. Flicking to the FM dial was only the start. It usually took Jake a few runs through to find a song he liked.

I waited until he stopped flicking. "Yes, we will."

Now engrossed in his song, Jake just nodded.

We were almost at Lance's when a call came in, one that sent a shivers down both of our spines.

It was Georgie. She worked the front desk in rotation with Kim and Stephanie. Georgie was by far the cutest; she had that intangible quality that attracted the other gender.

"We've just had a call from the Knox CIB. They reported a double homicide at the Basin nature reserve. They believe it may be related to the Slayer case, a missing person's report that matches a request you put in yesterday."

I looked at Jake and he looked back at me as if to say, 'oh my God'. It was chilling.

Jake radioed back to base to arrange someone to cover our shift and relieve Josh and Leah from their all-night-stint at Lance's.

Chapter 40

Sunday 9th November 2003 (7.00am)

The first sign of daybreak gave Mason a feeling that his plan would soon be realised, and that thought excited him.

Tammy had lain awake the entire night, too afraid to sleep. She had made herself a promise and a plan of her own. She knew that she could do nothing here. There was no help for her in this godforsaken place. In the morning, she would make her move; she just had to make sure her father was all right. She couldn't risk Mason not making the call and her father dying. Her plan was to go to the house that he wanted, wait for him to make his call, and then attempt to take him down. She knew enough karate and martial arts to take him down, as long as he wasn't behind her with a stun gun.

Mason instructed her to get up and put on the set of clothes he'd left for her on the bed. By the time she was dressed, Mason had made her toast and coffee.

Tammy wondered about the clothes, but dared not ask anything. Her outfit consisted of a long black dress that went all the way to her ankles, matching black shoes, a black woollen jumper, and a scarf to cover her head. He also made her wear a shiny silver cross around her neck. A large Bible finished Mason's handpicked outfit.

They headed out to the car. Both had very different plans for the day ahead.

* * *

We arrived at the crime scene about 25 minutes after Georgie had put the call to us across the radio.

A neatly dressed middle-aged man in a suit headed towards us and introduced himself as Detective Jacob Rein. He was tall and a lot fitter than most men his age. Even so, he looked as if he had been through a long night himself.

"A dog walker early this morning found his dog sniffing at a deceased body in the bush about 25 metres off the track to your right as you head up the hill. We believe the victim is Alan Simpson. His mother reported his disappearance to police late yesterday."

"So what makes you think this has anything to do with the Slayer case?" Jake asked.

"When investigating the crime scene, we found the body of a young female as well. Both victims had been decapitated."

Rein led us to the body of the male jogger.

"We organised a team to include uniformed officers, the SES and the dog squad," Rein explained, as he held up the police tape.

The body of the male jogger was lying off the side of the track, with little cover. My initial thoughts were that this had been rushed: it wasn't typical of the Slayer. Something had gone wrong.

"If this is what Esmeralda's vision was about, then where is the wolf?" Jake asked, still trying to throw doubt on the psychic's visions.

I was hunched down to study the scene. "It'll be here somewhere. I'm sure we'll find it soon."

I headed further up the track to where Rein had said they had found a deceased female. The track was wet and muddy. I stepped into a thick clump of mud that came halfway up my shoe. Then I stopped suddenly, realising there were other footprints close to me and I did not want to contaminate any vital evidence.

Bending down, I could see a few more shoe prints. They might be clear enough for forensics to take casts. I left the track and headed towards the broken bracken and the blue tarp. Under the trampled shrubs, I could see a large piece of plastic with a foot exposed.

Before I had a chance to call out to Jake, Jake yelled, "Dog! I've found the dog!" I stayed kneeling in position and called back, "Jake come here, you need to see this." It had to be the latest missing girl, Maggie, as all the other victims except the first had been found.

I called forensics and asked Rein to get an officer to go back to the car to collect my bag. It was designed to carry everything required to take evidence and protect that evidence until forensics arrived. The bag included tweezers, bottles, a variety of plastic bags of different sizes, test tubes, clean plastic sheets and body bags, camera, vacuum kit, torch, ultra violet light, tape measure, and of course, gloves.

David's forensics team arrived. He had worked on all of the Slayer victims and the copycat killing of poor Charlie.

"Good to see you again, David."

"This is becoming too common for my liking," he replied. "Another Slayer one?"

"That's for you to tell me, but we think there may be two here."

"Two? That's new for him." David looked sad at the possible escalation of violence.

"There's also a dog," I said. "I don't think the man with the dog was planned. I believe he was dumping one victim here – I think it's probably Maggie – and the male jogger and dog just got in the way. Let's hope we find something to finally lead us to this bastard," I said.

"Let's get to work then," David said, waving the rest of his team over.

Chapter 41

Sunday 9th November (10.38am)

It was mid-morning and beginning to drizzle, but that mattered little to the two Mormons who strolled the streets knocking on doors trying to help people find God.

You could spot them from a mile away, thought Ryan, who was back on duty after what seemed like a very short break. He was on his own today, as his partner was off sick. Ryan had only recently been promoted to detective, but he knew he had what it took to be one of the best.

'Haven't they got anything better to do than door knocking on a Sunday morning?' Ryan thought as he watched the Bible bashers walk from house to house, offering guidance to those willing to listen.

It wasn't long before they had almost completed the street. The next house was Lance's home, and Ryan was sure they would not get a warm reception there. The two Bible bashers approached the door and knocked. After a few moments, the door cracked open and the male Bible basher passed through what appeared to be a brochure spreading the Lord's word, no doubt.

Ryan was beginning to wonder whether he should call this in. He was under strict instructions to call in any activity.

On the other hand, he was sure if he called in two Bible bashers, he would never hear the end of it from the boys at the station. He could hear them now. "Morning, Father," they would say when he arrived at work, "do you have time for a prayer session, Father?" He could imagine them joking and was sure they would hang it on him for a long time to come.

Ryan finally decided to let it play out and see what happened first before calling it in.

He calmed himself, leaned over and grabbed his Thermos, spun off the top, and poured himself a cup of coffee.

Chapter 42

Sunday 9th November (10.42am)

Lance had received a call from his solicitor early that morning. A solicitor calling on a Sunday was unheard of. What would that cost him? he'd wondered when he'd hung up. His solicitor had advised it was best to wait for the police to arrest him. The fact that they hadn't already done so showed they were lacking evidence.

When he heard the doorbell ring, he assumed it was the police or the media. Either way, Lance was not in the mood for visitors, although he knew he had to face the consequences of his night with Charlie.

How had he stuffed it up?

He had it planned so well.

He reluctantly opened the door, making sure the chain was still on. The man on the other side of the door said nothing, simply passed him a piece of paper through the crack.

It was a brochure on 'letting the Lord into your heart' but that was not what grabbed Lance's attention. It was a handwritten passage that Lance focused on.

'You tried to copy me. Let me in and I will help you!'

Lance opened the door and let them in, quickly closing it behind them.

Ryan reached for the radio. The thoughts of taunts from his fellow colleagues filled his head again.

He decided that waiting a few more minutes would not hurt.

"You like to copy me, do you?" Mason asked quietly as he entered. Lance offered no response except a mumbled, "I just want to be famous."

"I will make you famous, don't worry about that," Mason said, opening his case and removing a bag and a CD. He handed over a CD. "Put this on and turn it up."

Lance nodded and headed for the lounge room. Soon the house was loud with the sound of scripture interspersed with prayer music.

It wasn't the music that worried Tammy, it was the fact that she was now in a house with two men and there was still no sign of her father.

"Where is my dad?" Tammy asked the new man. Lance didn't have a reply for her, but the blank look he gave her said it all.

She had been duped. She knew her dad was fine, but she herself was in serious danger and she had to get outside, somehow.

Chapter 43

Sunday 9th November 2003 (10.45am)

They were in the lounge with all the lights off and the blinds drawn. What was going on here? Tammy wondered. It just didn't feel right.

How was she to get out of this? She kept thinking she needed to separate them and race for the door. Mason handed Lance a bag. "Put these on. Hurry, we don't have much time."

Lance left the room and headed to the back of the house. They had just separated themselves. Now was her chance and she had to take it. Leaning on the dining room chair, Tammy made sure she had a good grip of it and was ready to swing. As if she'd heard something, Tammy said, "Shh, you hear that? People outside?"

Concerned it might be the police ready to raid, Mason moved closer to the wall and to Tammy. He focused all his concentration on trying to hear the noise outside.

Tammy struck, swinging the chair right across Mason's head and kicking him as she ran past. She knew that he would not stay down for long, and she rushed for the front door.

Frantically grabbing the handle, she turned and pulled it, but nothing. It was deadlocked, and she needed a key to open it.

With this realisation came the fear that she would soon be dead. She slid down the front door with tears freely rolling down her face.

Even with her eyes closed, Tammy could feel Mason's presence, feel his shadow cross her face.

Mason bent down and grabbed her by the throat.

"Who is she anyway?" Lance asked from behind him.

"She's the girl I will use to show you how to kill properly, unlike the bitch you killed in the city that's ended in this mess. Take her into the lounge." He handed Tammy to him by the throat.

Mason went back to his attaché case and removed a clear plastic coat and his favourite knife. The Wakizashi knife wasn't his usual method for removing someone's head but with the time constraints, he had no alternative. "Lay her on the floor and hold her down," he ordered. Without hesitation, Mason went to her head and without warning began his frenzied attack. The attack only finished with the removal of her head. It was short but ferocious, more horrifying than Lance could ever have imagined. Mason removed his coat and placed Tammy's head into a plastic bag and tied it to his shoulder. He then dipped his knuckles into Tammy's blood, flowing freely from her neck, being careful not to get any of the blood on his clothes. He then went across to the lounge room wall.

'Don't FUCK

with

Me!' he wrote across the wall.

Worried by now that the Mormons hadn't yet emerged from Lance's house, Ryan again reached for the radio, but as he picked it up, the music in the house stopped and the door opened. Two people emerged and as they stepped into the daylight, a van pulled in front of Ryan, blocking his line of sight. It began to reverse into the driveway of the house diagonally opposite Lance's property. By the time the truck had parked, the Mormons were out of sight.

He thought it would be best to call it in, just in case.

Chapter 44

Sunday 9th November 2003 (10.56am)

We had been studying the murder scene at the parkland for close to four hours. It was apparent that the killer had, for the first time, been forced to kill in haste for his own survival. It was this haste and his mistake that we hoped would give us a clue as to his identity.

It was a horrible way to get a lead but it could be our best chance to catch him.

David gestured me over to Maggie, where he had been examining her and taking samples. I walked over and thought what a sad sight it was. When you stepped out of the job and looked at it from a different perspective, this body only a short while ago had been full of life. Now it lay limp and discarded in a ditch of dirt, mud and ferns. It was a horrible thing to experience and I could never imagine the pain of the parents.

"It's the same guy all right. He took the head and like all the others, he took it pre-mortem. The stab pattern is also consistent with the other victims from what I can tell, although I'll need to do more tests back at the lab. Even the jogger's head was taken pre-mortem and while the knife doesn't match, the MO is the same. There are fibres and hairs but again, I need to do more analysis on them before I can give you any further information. It appears that like the last victim, Maggie had been washed prior to being dumped. That being the case, it's likely all the fibres are hers. I have found one unusual item, though." He held up a plastic bag with a two-centimetre splinter of wood.

"If you find the wood it came from, you'll know where she was murdered," David said. "It looks like the splinter entered her flesh when she was being dragged."

"What have the other guys found?" I asked David. We looked over at them.

"I was just about to find out. Come with me," David replied, heading off down the track.

David's assistant Grace had been examining the jogger and the dog.

"What information do you have for us, Grace?" David asked as he stumbled on some loose dirt at the side of the track.

"We have a Caucasian male, 28 to 32 years. The deceased died from decapitation, although the severe stab wounds to the chest, back and throat would suggest he was barely alive when the murderer took his head. The blood splatter indicates that his heart was still beating when his head was removed. I believe he was then dragged over here," Grace said, moving back up on to the walking track, "and then he was rolled into the ditch off the track. There was no real attempt to conceal him. The dog, on the other hand, was killed with a blunt instrument. We found a rock nearby, which we are having tested for blood and fingerprints. We also found blood on the dog's teeth, which suggests the dog bit someone. Our guess is that it was the assailant."

"If it's his blood, then we can get him," I said stupidly, regretting the statement as soon as it left my mouth.

"It's the strongest evidence we have, however, blood isn't much good unless we have a sample on file for comparison," David replied. "But it will go a long way towards the conviction, if you catch him. We're going to take all this back to the lab for further tests," David continued, as he and the crew began to pack up.

I stood there thinking, which was what I did best. I tried to turn myself into the killer and reconstruct the events as best I could. It was no easy task, but it was something they had trained us for at Quantico.

I walked down the track to the road, through bracken, weeds, ferns, and a whole heap of mud. I said to myself, "Here is where he would have parked the vehicle." I looked for tyre prints, but I was sure that the rain had washed them away by now. I retraced his steps as I thought it had happened.

He had carried her up the track, most likely over his shoulder, and then dumped her in the gully. But it was here where it had all gone wrong for him. I had no doubt that the jogger was killed only because he had seen something he shouldn't have. The dog had done a hell of a job protecting his owner. He'd fought and given his life to try and save him.

"Are you finished?" Jake called from the top of the hill. He seemed impatient.

"Yeah, all done," I called. I saw the coroner's team loading the bodies into those thick black plastic bags and I thought to myself, 'how lucky I am to be alive.'

Jake placed his arm around my shoulder, which broke me out of my trance.

"We have to go to Lance's house. Ryan from the surveillance team called. Apparently, Lance let some Mormons in this morning and Lance's ugly head hasn't been seen peering out the windows since."

"Fucking great, just fucking great," I replied.

Chapter 45

Sunday 9th November 2003 (11.06am)

Lance sat in the passenger's seat of Mason's car.

"So how do you want me to help you?" Lance asked Mason nervously.

"After that fuck-up you made in the hotel with the stripper, I realised that with a bit of training, you and I could be the best team of serial killers ever." Mason was playing to Lance's misguided illusions of himself.

Mason was not lying when he said he needed Lance's help. It could only be with his help that he would get the attention of the police, who were trying to offer Lance up as bait to catch him.

How stupid did they think he was?

"Where are we going?" Lance asked, as he began to remove the wig and dress Mason had given him.

"We are going to where I do all my work that you love so much. I'm going to give you a tour of my workshop and then we can select my next victim."

"You mean *our* next victim?" Lance replied, thoughts of killing again racing through his head.

"Yes, *our* next victim," Mason replied, almost letting out a laugh at the same time. He had already selected his next victim.

Mason had made good time, which surprised him considering

it was a Sunday when the Volvo drivers were usually out in force, slowing down the traffic.

As Mason pulled his car into the drive of his cabin, he still wasn't sure as to what he would do with Lance. He had a rough idea, but no clear plan.

He led the way into the cabin, with Lance following closely behind him.

"I'll take those from you," Mason said, holding out to Lance a plastic shopping bag full of fresh male clothing he had placed on the couch in the lounge. "I'll show you around after you change."

Lance nodded in agreement and excitement, like a teenager being asked by his girlfriend if he would like to see her breasts.

Lance followed Mason through the lounge and down the spiral wooden staircase that had a wrought-iron rail. The stairs led down to the cellar. Lance felt much more like himself in the clothes Mason had provided him. He felt like a serial killer again. Mason opened the solid oak door, complete with an old castle-style handle.

The door creaked and moaned as it opened and Lance felt a cold eerie presence as he took the stairs down to the damp and foul smelling room. It was dark, with little natural light filtering through some cracks. He'd thought it would be a room that he would enjoy and thrive in, yet he hated it and wanted to leave straightaway. However, he knew that if he showed any weakness, he would not see the light of day ever again.

Lance took in all the equipment in this hellhole, as he now considered it. There were chains attached to posts, all types of saws and axes locked behind a clear mesh cage, and an old coiled spring bed with the remnants of a mattress.

All the Slayer's victims' heads were lined up on the shelf like a child would display his basketball trophies. Below them was a Samurai sword, also on display. From the second Lance saw the heads, he knew the police had played him, and his next thought was, was Mason playing him too?

"I need you to help me fix some of this equipment," Mason said, holding out the chains.

"What do you need me to do?" Lance asked, a little worried.

"You're not scared, are you, Lance? Isn't this what you wanted? To copy me and be me? Well, here's your chance! But we need to get the equipment right. I need you to put these on and pull as hard as you can and I'll tighten up the bolts. The last thing we want is our prize to escape."

Lance reluctantly put his wrists inside the cuffs and watched as Mason locked the cuffs with a key he had plucked from his pants pocket. Lance's heart was in his mouth and he was scared as hell. He tried to keep his mind focused on what was going on, but the disgusting smell in the cellar was beginning to get to him.

"Now, when I say pull, I want you to pull as hard as you can." Mason was now behind the post that held Lance. "Let's test these babies." Mason was becoming excited. "Pull!" Mason yelled, and as he pulled, Lance's worst fears were realised.

The harder Lance pulled, the tighter the cuffs became. With all his attention on his wrists, he had not noticed Mason had looped a piece of rope around his legs until Mason pulled the rope tight, and the rope burnt his ankle. Lance began to pull and kick his legs, but it was too late. He knew what his fate was going to be. The same as Charlie's. "Hey, where you going, you fuck?" he yelled as Mason left the cellar.

Chapter 46

Sunday 9th November 2003 (11.33am)

We pulled in behind Ryan's car, stopped and got in, Jake in the passenger seat and me in the back.

"What's the update?" Jake asked, as he lifted the binoculars to his eyes.

"Nothing! I haven't seen him since this morning, when he let the Mormons in."

"How long did the Mormons stay?"

"Fifteen or twenty minutes, then they left."

"How long ago was that?" I asked.

"Half an hour," Ryan confirmed after looking at his watch.

Jake leaned over the passenger seat. "What do you think?" he asked me.

"Sounds strange, if you ask me. Something isn't right. There's been no sign of anyone else?" I asked Ryan.

"No," he confirmed.

'My plan has failed,' I thought.

"Let's bring him in for Charlie's murder," I said, tapping Jake on the shoulder.

Jake and I left the car while Ryan stayed in it. Jake walked up to the front door, unclipped his gun and then knocked. There was no reply. "Lance, it's the police, let us in!" Jake repeated this three more times, then he said, "Ok Lance, we're coming in!" He gently tried the door handle.

Jake had learnt long ago to always test the door handle first before resorting to kicking the door in.

As soon as we entered, the smell of blood and death hit us and we knew we were in trouble. Jake immediately checked the corners and entered the house. The sight was the worst we had ever seen. There appeared to be a sea of blood, and a headless body was slumped on a chair in the corner. There was a message written on the wall, we assumed from the Slayer.

"How did he get the woman in here and where the hell is Lance?" I asked.

"I'll call for backup," Jake said, "and then we'll search the house. Lance has to be here somewhere."

But he wasn't. By the time we'd returned to the lounge, the forensics team and the chief had arrived. The chief was the last person I wanted to see right now and I knew that things were about to get worse.

"You! Get the fuck out," he yelled at me. "You're fired!" I got up from my crouched position in front of the body and headed for the door.

"If he goes, I go, Chief." Jake stood with his arms folded.

"Well that's your call, Jake, but he's going. I don't want to lose you but I have to let him go. Look at this mess," the chief said, as he held a handkerchief to his nose.

I put up my hand to indicate to Jake that it was ok, that I wanted him to stay. He knew what I meant. It was something we had done as kids, raise a hand to offer an apology. Jake looked at me and nodded, then went back to work.

One of the patrol officers drove me home. I would clear out my office the next day, Monday. There was no hurry. I felt I had unfinished business and it was killing me not to be a part of the investigation. But I had to acknowledge that the plan I had come up with had failed miserably, resulting in the death of another innocent young woman.

Several hours after my departure, Jake rang to ask my opinion about what we had seen at Lance's. They had no new information on the deceased girl, he said. She was carrying no ID, there was no car at Lance's that the police could go off, and no one had reported her missing.

They were going to place a news report on TV, asking for anyone with a family member recently missing to contact police. Jake also told me that forensics were doing comparisons on the weapons used in the murder at Lance's house and those used in Charlie's murder. They would compare stab wounds and angles, but they would not have the results until the next morning.

Jake finished the phone call by telling me to keep my head up. He said the fact that I wasn't sitting behind the desk didn't mean I was no longer a part of the case. He promised that he would keep me up to date, and that I still had an important role to play.

I thanked him and knew that he would do all he could to keep me involved.

But I also knew reality when it kicked me in the arse and that I was no longer a member of taskforce Eagle.

Chapter 47

Sunday 9th November 2003 (4.40pm)

Lance wasn't sure how many hours he had spent chained to the post. His estimate was at least two. Daylight was still visible through the few cracks in the wood. Lance had spent most of his time trying to ignore the smell and unbind his feet and hands.

The metal cuffs had cut into his hands and wrists, which were now bleeding. The rope burn had probably caused similar damage to his legs because although he could not see them, he could feel the blood dripping onto his feet.

The strange smell was getting to him, as was the presence of death that sat looking at him through the glass jars on the shelf. He had to get out. He had his own plans and fantasies to fulfil. His killing spree wasn't over, and it certainly wasn't meant to end like this.

As the sun faded, Lance was left in darkness and all alone, except for the lost souls he could feel all around him. Now that darkness was upon him, he could feel the creatures of the night crawling beneath his feet. He assumed that rats had been attracted by the dripping blood.

Lance could move enough to get the rats off his body but he wasn't sure how long they would be so easily startled once they had the taste of blood in their system.

He had managed to drift off to sleep, when the old cellar door opened. Once his eyes adjusted to the dark, he could see Mason standing in front of him.

"Let me go. We're the same. We have the same passion to kill those skanky whores. We can still kill the sluts together and it's not too late." Lance was almost begging. His voice was quivering.

"Oh, it's far too late for that, Lance. Let me tell you something: we are not the same. I don't kill for sexual pleasure like you. I don't kill whores or strippers. I kill for revenge, for a life that was taken from me. But enough about me, Lance," Mason said, pausing briefly. "Let's talk about you. If you hadn't tried to copy me, then you wouldn't be in this, shall we say, predicament. Enjoy the night. It will be your last." Mason left Lance with the darkness and the rats, locking the door behind him.

Chapter 48

Monday 10th November 2003 (7am)

The morning sunlight broke through the cracks and streamed across Lance's face. Once it hit his eyelids, he woke, and the first thought that went through his head was that this was going to be his last day on earth.

Lance guessed that first light meant it was about 6.30 in the morning, maybe 7. Then the door opened and Lance could clearly see Mason this time, unlike the night before.

He realised Mason had come ready to do what he had promised, and it didn't look pretty.

Mason was holding a sword in his right hand. Lance watched him approach slowly and with every step he took, Lance's heart fluttered. He wasn't usually a sook but the fear had taken hold and his eyes began to swell and the tears flow. By the time Mason was in front of him, his tears were running like a river.

"It will all be over soon." Mason said, stroking his face. "It will be painful, but by the end of the day, you will be at peace." Mason raised the sword and swung it quickly and accurately. It cut a large gash in Lance's right arm.

Lance screamed. Mason then made a big x into Lance's chest.

The pain was like nothing he had ever experienced. Mason then firmly hit him in the forehead with the handle of the sword, sending

Lance into darkness.

When he awoke, the sun was bright in the sky above him. Where was he? he wondered. Certainly not in the dusty cellar. There was a lot of blood on his chest. He lifted his head. He was tied to a wooden picnic table. He could see the old cabin on the horizon above his toes. At least he had his legs, he thought. At least he could run, he thought. That thought was soon extinguished when he remembered the ropes binding him to the table.

A shadow eclipsed the sun from his eyes. "Let me go, please, just let me go," Lance begged.

"You're probably wondering what you're doing tied to a table, naked?" Mason asked rhetorically. You're here because I like to feed the kookaburras. Do you know what they like to eat?"

Lance offered no response. The only thing that Lance could think of was a passage from the Bible, which surprised him, as he was not a religious man at all. He hoped the passage was correct. *Even though I walk through the valley of the shadow of death...*

"Well, let me give you a quick nature lesson. I usually feed them fresh mincemeat but today, they're going to get a special treat. Today, they get to eat your flesh, and your intestines, not to forget your limp little cock that's dangling in this fine morning breeze."

Lance froze in horror as Mason removed a knife from his pocket. He placed Lance's hand down flat and quickly removed his index finger.

Lance's scream of agony was heard by no one but Mason.

As Mason held out Lance's clenched fist in front of him, he smiled, and said, "Goodbye." Then he opened his hand and sprinkled birdseed all over Lance's fresh wounds.

Lance had never seen so many birds fly from the trees at once. He closed his eyes and another Bible passage came to him: *Do unto others as you would have them do unto you.* 'Please forgive me for what I have done,' he thought, as he felt their pecking and their claws, before he again descended into blackness.

Mason watched as the birds enjoyed their meal en masse.

Mason scraped Lance's remains off the table with a shovel. By the time the birds had finished their breakfast, Mason the wheelbarrow was only half-full. He wheeled the barrow down towards the tree line, tipping the remains into a pre-dug hole.

Mason removed a bag of lime, emptied it into the hole and then spent the next 15 minutes filling it in.

Chapter 49

Monday 10th November 2003 (11.25am)

After burying what was left of Lance, Mason hosed his shovel and wheelbarrow, then sprayed each item with bleach and then hosed them down again. He burned the overalls he was wearing, went inside and had a nice hot shower.

He decided it was time to find out a bit more about the two officers who had been behind the Lance trap. Maybe it was time he stopped being the hunted and became the hunter.

Mason removed his laptop from its case and fired it up.

He needed to know more about Jake Miller and definitely more about this Mr Foxx. He must be good for the police to have used special authority to make him detective.

It was easy to find information on Foxx. Google was a great help. He found his profile and his qualifications as a criminal psychologist. He even found newspaper articles on him being appointed to the police force under the commissioner's powers. According to the article, Foxx had taken up studies due to a heart condition and had undergone several heart operations as a child.

Fate had spared him and led him to Mason.

The latest entry on the Google search result was a report from the morning paper. 'Eagle to undergo third revamp' was the heading. The article referred to unnamed police sources stating that "the

Victorian Government has serious concerns about the abilities of the taskforce and suggested that the taskforce undergo a review.' Another source suggested that Brodie Foxx would soon be removed from Eagle.

'Well I will have to see to that,' Mason muttered to himself.

Very little came up when he Googled Jake Miller. There were several articles about a servo shooting he was involved in and now he was head of the Eagle taskforce. Mason needed to know more information.

There was only one way he could get it, up close and personal.

St Kilda Road was the best place to start.

He decided he best get home. He needed to get there before his wife if possible.

When Mason reached the town of Yea, he thought it best to stop and get something to eat, plus he had some mail to send.

Halfway down the street and two shops before the post office, he saw two boys sitting on the curb sharing some fries.

He stopped. "Could you do me a favour?" Mason asked the taller of the two boys.

"Sure, Mister," the boy said, standing up to see him better.

"I really need to post these packages today, but the lady who works in the post office is my ex-girlfriend and I really don't want to go in. Could you post them for me?" Mason asked. "I'll give you fifty dollars each and I won't tell anyone that you were playing hooky."

The boys looked at each other with excited smiles. To have $100 to spend on their day of leisure would mean they could swap an afternoon of riding for the movies and see 'Matrix Reloaded'.

"Sure," the taller boy replied.

The boys noted both packages were addressed to Brodie Foxx, Melbourne Police, St Kilda Road Melbourne. Mason gave the boy one of the $50 dollar notes and a separate $100 note to cover the cost of postage, and promised the other $50 when they brought back the postage receipt.

"Now, boys, make sure you tell the lady that your uncle has asked you to send them and that they need to be expressed to that address today. If anyone asks you, just tell them your uncle is sick and he asked you to do it for him."

A few minutes later, the boys returned with a red slip and $55 in change.

Mason not only kept his side of the bargain, he handed over the $55 in change, leaving the boys to enjoy their day.

Chapter 50

Tuesday 11th November 2003 (11.30am)

Even though I had slept until late, I had awoken several times throughout the night, many times in a cold sweat. It had been a night I'd rather forget. The dreams had been with me since I was a child, yet last night they had taken on a form of their own and they were more horrifying than ever.

I'd dreamt of the hospital's cold, alcohol-smelling hallways, light green walls and flickering fluorescent lights. They were memories of my past that I had hidden deep in my mind. However, some nights they found the door and let themselves out.

Last night was the worst I had ever experienced, even more terrifying than those I had suffered while I was in hospital undergoing the surgery itself. It was more vivid and real to me than anything I had ever dreamt before.

I was lying on a trolley being wheeled to the operating theatre, except there were no nurses walking beside me, no machines taking my vitals, no drip leading into my vein. Only a doctor in a white coat with a green mask. A doctor who did not speak or answer my cries as to what was happening to me.

He kept his head down and continued to wheel the trolley along the cold halls until we bashed through two large swinging doors where the sign above said 'Operating Theatre'.

My neck hurt as I tried to see the doctor who had been hovering over me, but all I could see were his cold lifeless eyes.

Then I found myself on the cold metal table of the operating theatre wearing only a surgical gown with the opening at the back. The cold metal pressed against my skin. Above, a bright operating light blurred my vision. There were other patients there too but no one was attending to them.

I turned to look at the other side of the operating theatre and when I turned back, I was no longer in the theatre but in a dark dusty room that had a horrible smell, a smell that filled my heart with fear.

It was the unmistakable smell of death.

I moved my hands around to try to untie my hideous gown. As I was removing it, my hand slipped onto my chest. It was wet.

I raised my fingers to my face and saw my own blood. I felt my chest again; there was an opening.

I could feel my ribs; I could put my hand inside my chest. I softly put my hand inside my chest, careful not to poke anything. There was no pain, only blood. I felt around more.

I could feel ribs.

I put my fingers through my ribs.

It was then I felt my heart, a heart that was no longer beating.

I was dead.

I wasn't in the operating theatre.

I wasn't even in a morgue. I was in a cold, damp, dirty cellar with chains dangling from the rafters above.

There was a wall full of saws, axes and swords. It was horrifying. I stood on the dirt floor with my chest open and blood dripping down my front. Then I saw them. They had surrounded me. "Help us! Help us!" they repeated. I was frozen. I felt something cold and metallic in my clenched hand and unclenched my fist. It was a key, a handcuff key, most likely to the cuff still attached to my wrist.

Chapter 51

Tuesday 11th November 2003 (1.00pm)

When I arrived at the station to pack up my desk, the place was buzzing.

Jake was in the meeting room with some new taskforce members. One of them I recognised immediately, Peter Brown. He was a well-respected criminal psychologist. He had been one of my guest lecturers during the final year of my doctorate in criminal psychology. He was an expert in his field, and I knew he was a good choice to replace me.

I went across to my desk and began emptying the drawers into a box I had brought from home. Jake had finished his meeting. "Don't pack up just yet, Brodie. I've convinced the chief to reconsider terminating you. He's agreed to keep you on as long as I agreed to bring in Peter Brown to help. I assumed you wouldn't mind?"

I was stunned. Ten minutes before, I was off the case and now, I was back on. I had almost packed up my whole desk. I began unpacking the box.

Chapter 52

Wednesday 12th November 2003 (10am)

I arrived at work on Wednesday morning. No new leads had come to hand on Lance's whereabouts. We had identified the victim in Lance's house as Tammy Green, who had recently graduated from the Glen Waverley Police Academy.

Two packages sat on my desk.

"Who are they from?" Jake asked.

I looked at him, bewildered. "I have no idea. There's no return address." I grabbed the scissors from the top of my box and was about to open them when Jake grabbed my wrist.

"Wait, we'd better call in the bomb squad."

"Why would I get a bomb!"

It took two hours after the bomb squad arrived to open the boxes without incident. When they were done, the hysteria in the department was worse than if it had been a bomb.

Still in full armour, Sam, the head of the bomb unit, came out to see us. "You guys had better come and look at this, right now. It's no bomb, but it's something you need to see."

We followed Sam back into the station from our kerbside evacuation point. The opened parcels were sitting on my desk. Jake and I looked at each other, unsure what we would find. Nothing could prepare me for the horrible sickness I felt when I saw the contents.

It was a severed finger in a plastic bag surrounded by Styrofoam.

The second box contained one photo and a yellow envelope. The photo showed Lance's lifeless face. I placed on my gloves.

Then we went to open the envelope.

The note was neither typed nor handwritten; it had been created from newspaper headlines. All different letters from different papers, I assumed.

It would have taken the person a long time to put it together.

It read:

Brodie Foxx

Well, Brodie, congratulations on being the first cop to ever get close to me, except you're not a cop, are you? Maybe that's why you've done so well. If only you had been watching the house instead of that meathead, this could have all been over by now.

I know you would have been there if you could, I know that you were attending a crime scene, probably one of mine. The jogger one, I guess. Could you pass on an apology to his family for me? He wasn't in my plans. Just came along at a bad time.

Strange how fate works.

I read you may be getting replaced and I must say I don't approve. I would like you to pass on this message to your employer. Either you stay involved or one of the premier's family will be my next victim.

I expect to be able to reach you!

I hope I have made my point.

I'd better go. I have things to do, murders to plan. I look forward to meeting with you soon. To save you some time, the parts I sent you belong to the copycat idiot who didn't even have the brains to get it right.

He won't be attacking any more women I can tell you

that. Sorry I couldn't send his head but as you know I collect them.

It looks good on display. Oh, before I go, tell Jake that I am glad he has finally found love. I approve of his choice.

I must say I bet you're still wondering why I am doing what I am doing? Or as you profilers would say what was the triggering event that caused me to begin my killings? I would tell you but it might give me away

The letter finished abruptly.

I didn't know why he wanted me on the case.

He was warning us by making Jake aware that he had been watching him as well, and his girl.

We believed that he had sent the message to tell us he had disposed of Lance and to taunt us, saying he knew more about us than we knew about him.

The overriding message, however, was that he hated the police with a passion. Something had caused this; something had triggered this hatred.

We sent all three items off to forensics and then asked one of the other task members to find out where the item had been posted.

Finally, Jake ordered a uniformed patrol be sent to guard Hayley and informed the premier about the latest threat.

Jake then rang Hayley on his mobile to let her know what had occurred. I could hear her panicked voice at the other end of the line. "Is he after me?" to which Jake replied, "We're sure he's just trying to scare us all," although I wasn't sure Jake was convinced of his answer, let alone Hayley.

Chapter 53

Wednesday 12th November 2003 (12 noon)

Mason had spent several hours following Jake over the previous two days, getting to know his routine. For a detective, he was not good at picking up the signs that he was being followed.

Maybe Mason had become good at following people and looking like he was an ordinary person, going about his ordinary day.

His surveillance had uncovered a lot of information.

Useful information.

Where they both lived and what cars they each drove.

He now knew he had a girlfriend, she was a nurse, she worked at the Alfred Hospital.

He thought it best to know a little about her too. You never knew when it might come in handy. He followed her to work, to ward 8 west, the post-operative ward. "Excuse me? I'm lost," Mason appealed to her, checking her nametag. "My mother came in for an operation and she's meant to be here to be picked up. Am I in the right place?"

Hayley smiled. "Was it day surgery?" she asked in her always-pleasant voice.

"Yes, she came in this morning, my sister dropped her off."

"Ok, then you need to go to the day surgery ward, second floor.

Exit the lift and it's just on your left."

Mason now had all the information on Jake's girlfriend that he would need. It would be Jake's weak point.

Mason felt good again. His plan had gone off without a hitch and he was ready to show them who the real Slayer was once again.

He was smart. His confidence had risen. He was ready.

Chapter 54

Wednesday 12th November 2003 (2.17pm)

In light of the letter, we went to the home of the last Slayer's victim to see if we could find any leads that might shine some light on Tammy's killer.

While Lance's house had yielded little evidence, we were hopeful that more would be found in her house. We believed she had been abducted from her home. It was her last known sighting.

When we arrived, the property had been sealed off with crime scene tape. We met her father, Kurt Green, out the front of the property. It was important that we have some inside knowledge on how Tammy's house should look.

The three of us entered the property. Her father was a tall man but not as fit as he must once have been. A liking of beer and chips must have got the better of his stomach. Once inside, we began the questions and the inspection of the residence.

"Thank you for meeting us here, Mr Green, I am so sorry for your loss," said Jake. "Anything you can tell us could help us catch this guy. Does anything seem unusual or out of place here? Do you know if Tammy had a boyfriend or if she was seeing someone?"

"No, not that I know about. She was very focused on her police training." He was struggling to keep it together as he stood in the hallway of his dead daughter's house.

"Do you know anyone who disliked her or who might have wanted to harm your daughter?"

"No, she was a lovely caring girl," he said, clasping his hands together.

"Let's have a wander through then, shall we?" Jake suggested.

I stopped and faced Mr Green. "If this gets too hard for you at any time, please tell us. It's understandable. Just let us know if you can't continue."

Mr Green nodded and we continued. The first room was the master bedroom. "This is where we believe the attack occurred," Jake said. "We found a little patch of blood in the ensuite. We believe she may have hit her head on the vanity when he grabbed her."

"She would not leave the bed unmade. She always made it. We taught her that when she was little. 'Keep your room tidy,' her mum would always say."

She was fastidious, Jake noted down, but he already knew that the sheets had probably been taken by the killer, possibly because she was bleeding and so he'd used them to wrap her in. We weren't sure yet. Mr Green pointed out that the gym bag he had bought her was also gone. "She usually keeps it in her wardrobe."

Jake noted down the missing items. "What colour was the bag?" Jake asked.

"Blue," Mr Green replied, "it was a Nike bag with the logo across the sides." As Mr Green walked into the ensuite, he noticed a vibrator on the bedside table. Clearly embarrassed, he asked, "Do you think that this scumbag raped my daughter?"

"We are not sure at this point and we won't be until the lab results are back," I responded.

We continued into the kitchen where we found one cup but two saucers, which meant that a cup had been taken. The only reason he would take a cup was if he had had a drink. It was the only logical conclusion. It also made me wonder if he had been known to his victim, and invited in.

This was very rare for a serial killer. I'd also considered the possibility that he might have had sex with her. That would explain why he'd removed the sheets and why there were adult toys in the bedroom. If she'd been expecting guests, she would have put them away.

Unless he was the guest, I thought.

When Mr Green saw his daughter's police academy photo on the fridge, he broke down and had to leave.

Once Jake knew Mr Green was out of the house, he asked me, "What do you think?"

"What I think scares me. It scares me a lot. Firstly, I think that our killer knew Tammy. How or why I don't know but he knew her. I think he had sex with her, most likely consensual sex. If you raped someone, you wouldn't have time to put porn on and use the toys. Then I think he took the sheets to cover his tracks and he probably put the stuff in the bag to dispose of it all."

"What makes you say he knew her? He didn't know any of the other victims," Jake said.

I picked up the saucer and held it up to him. "See this? It's a saucer without a cup."

Jake added quickly, "Yes, and you only get saucers out for guests you're trying to impress. You think it was him?" Jake asked. Then he continued, thinking he had found a loophole in my theory, "What if the guest was someone else and our serial killer came in just after the other person left?"

"Then why would he take a cup, Jake? If it wasn't his I can't see a reason for it."

Jake agreed that I was most probably right and the theory made sense. We both liked it when our theories made sense.

Chapter 55

Wednesday 12th November 2003 (4.00pm)

Stephen Sutton had spent all day on the couch with a phone and beeper beside him. He knew he was dying and there was nothing he could do about it. He would either die by the end of the month or have the transplant that would save his life.

Cardiomyopathy was what they called it, and for a 33-year-old guy who hadn't been sick a day in his life apart from the odd common cold, he was devastated when the doctors had told him his heart was diseased and failing.

The only treatment option left to him was a heart transplant.

His doctor was nice enough. They said he was the best in Australia, well, the best since Doctor Victor Chang had been brutally shot dead.

Stephen thought that Hanam was of Middle Eastern origin. He came across as very quiet and very smart. The only thing that he didn't like about Professor Hanam was his mumbling. Stephen had a great deal of trouble understanding what the hell the man was saying to him.

Two weeks before, Hanam had said to him, "This is not good. We won't be able to continue like this for much longer," as he removed the stethoscope.

"How long is not long?" Stephen asked, scared out of his wits.

"About a month, I am afraid," Hanam said, as he adjusted his comb-over with the palm of his hand. "But there is a lot that can change in a month. Just keep as fit as you can; it's important to be in good shape for the operation. I also suggest that you do the things you want to do now. Go out for dinner, go to the movies, do the things you enjoy, because if you haven't had the transplant within the next few weeks, you will be confined to your home or hospital with oxygen tanks and you won't be able to do much," Hanam said as he sat back at his desk.

"Let's hope I get a new heart before that happens," Stephen replied.

"Let's hope. Now I want to see you again in two weeks and remember, keep an eye on your weight. If you put on a couple of kilos within a day, call me straightaway."

"What does it mean if I put on weight quickly?" Stephen asked, trying to work it out.

"It means your heart is about to fail and the weight is all the fluid building up," Hanam responded.

Hanam had been right. Soon he would be confined to bed. All his energy was gone and had it not been for the oxygen tank, he assumed he would have been out of breath as well.

Stephen didn't know how much longer he could live like this. He guessed two more weeks, maybe three, but if he didn't get another heart then, he would be dead.

He often thought he should try praying, but he had never believed in God and didn't see why God would help him now after years of being ignored. God would consider him someone jumping on the bandwagon.

He had almost given up hope.

Cassie came in with his plate of hot chicken wings and barbe-que sauce that she had kindly made for him. She was an amazing girl, full of positive spirit and cheerfully helpful. Stephen paused the movie he was watching. He had been trying to stay happy, so he was watching some of his favourite comedies. This one was 'Planes, Trains and Automobiles'. He loved anything with John Candy.

Cassie put down the plate of wings. "Do you know what you can have for dessert?" she asked him. Stephen shook his head.

Cassie lifted her top to reveal her breasts. "You can suck on these and I'll suck on something of yours," she replied, smiling. A rare smile crossed Stephen's face. That was another good thing about Cassie; she always knew ways to lift his spirits.

Sex was out of the question. Long past him. Even a BJ could be dangerous.

Best to pass, he thought.

Chapter 56

Thursday 13th November 2003 (11am)

My dream had been bothering me for two days now and I decided to call Esmeralda and run it past her. While I was telling her, she replied by saying she too had had a horrible dream. This concerned me a great deal, even more than my own dream. Two horrible dreams on the one night. We decided to meet at the Crown for lunch and discuss them further.

We met out the front of the Crown and decided on JJs Bar and Grill, a casual eatery with good food. We placed our orders and before our entrée arrived, we were already discussing the dreams.

I described mine to her first.

"They say premonitions come to us to tell us something, warn us in some way. From the dream you described, I think the key may actually be the key," Esmeralda said.

"So what are you saying? I'm confused," I said.

"Make sure you keep a handcuff key on you all the time for now. Will you do that for me, dear?" she asked, touching my hand from across the table.

Her request chilled me but I nodded.

Esmeralda began to describe her dream, then she stopped. "What's wrong?" I asked.

"I have to tell you something about Jake," she said, almost as if she was about to burst into tears. This time I offered my hand by way of comfort. Now I knew why she'd wanted to meet without Jake.

"I misled you, Brodie. I didn't have a dream. I thought it was best that I tell you this in person. I had another vision."

"Was the vision about Jake?" I asked calmly.

Our food arrived but neither of us even looked at it. She nodded and then spoke softly. "I am worried I have seen his death."

"What did you see?"

"I saw him being buried alive in the woods somewhere. There was a dam or a lake nearby. Jake was in a clear coffin but he couldn't get out. He was trapped. He had vomit all over his mouth and neck. He was struggling to breathe. I felt the tightness across his chest."

I sat there stunned and I must admit, very worried. After all, the vision of the jogger had been real. I took a deep breath. "We can't let that happen. Was there anything else in the vision that could help us prevent this? Do you know who did it?" I said, asking the second question before she had even had a chance to answer the first.

"I'll answer the second one first. I think it was the Slayer, but I can't be sure. The other thing I saw in the vision was an old cabin and a huge tree. It was an oak."

"Esmeralda, I know that you have experienced many visions, but have you ever had a vision from evidence? What I mean is, if I showed you items belonging to the victims, do you think this would help you have more visions that might lead us to this bastard?"

"I have never tried it, Brodie. I don't think any cop has taken me seriously enough to try it."

"Ok then," I replied, "let's keep the Jake thing between us and see if any of the evidence will give you some visions. I'm hoping that the reason for your visions is to help us in the future, not necessarily be of the future," I said, hoping for the best.

"It doesn't normally turn out that way," Esmeralda said with a little sigh.

Chapter 57

Thursday 13th November 2003 (6.30pm)

Mason had spent the remainder of the week working hard to make up for the days he had been away at his so-called conference. He arrived home to spend some time with Jamie, one eye scanning the Sky News channel for any updates. He enjoyed being at home with Jamie, who was his one and only true love in his pathetic existence.

They had spent the time just before dinner playing with his wooden Thomas the Tank Engine train set. Jamie loved the trains and he loved it even more when his dad did the voices of the trains and the Fat Controller. Between the trips around the track, Mason kept his eyes and ears firmly focused on the news.

It wasn't until the main news bulletin at 6pm that Jake's press conference aired around the country. Mason was pleased with the outcome. He was glad Brodie was still on board. The end was near and the final challenge excited him. The caption along the bottom of the screen read – 'Taskforce Eagle add Forensic Psychologist Peter Brown.'

Jake went on to provide an update on the case. "We are still seeking the public's assistance in locating Mr Silver. We believe he has vital information regarding the East Side Slayer case. Should anyone know of Mr Silver's whereabouts, they are urged to call Crime

Stoppers." Jake then introduced Dr Peter Brown.

"It is with great honour that I take on this position. I am hopeful that together with the other members of the taskforce we will soon have this case solved.

"Do you really think it will be solved? It's been over a decade and there doesn't seem to be an end in sight," a young reporter from the middle row asked.

"I believe we are on the right path, I believe all the work the police have done up until this point has been exceptional. While we may not publicly identify all persons of interest, that doesn't mean they don't exist. I can tell you we have hundreds of leads and several dozen persons of interest at this stage."

"Do you think the taskforce made a mistake putting Brodie Foxx on the case? Would you have been a better choice from the start?" an older journalist asked from the front.

"Let me say this, the taskforce is a team and we help each other. We are not here, I am certainly not here, to take over. It is common sense to have people in the same field helping each other. That's what I am doing with Mr Foxx. If it takes a hundred forensic psychologists to solve these murders, then that is what we will do."

With that answer, the interview ended.

Mason was very pleased to see both Jake and Brodie at the news conference.

It was time for him to kill again. His body was telling him it was time. The rage had built up again. The anger was crying to get out. Even though it was so soon after Tammy and Lance, the feeling was there stronger than ever. He was at boiling point again.

This time, it would be perfect.

Jamie sat with his mother on the couch after dinner while Mason headed to his study to begin planning. This time he had to plan for Brodie and Jake. He knew that they were close and with the letter he had sent, he knew they would be closing in soon.

Mason needed some insurance.

Chapter 58

Friday 14th November 2003 (9.30am)

With no new leads arising, the latest murders were starting to go cold. We had discussed at lunch that we needed to try something different.

I had decided to take Esmeralda with me to the latest crime scene to see if she could provide any new information, or at least confirm some of my original suspicions. Esmeralda walked into the master bedroom of Tammy's house. She stood in the doorway for a few seconds and then made her way around the hall. She touched the cup that was still sitting on the bench. No vision came to her this time; her mind remained blank.

Esmeralda returned to the master bedroom and then she went into the ensuite. It was only when she touched the basin that a vision came, except it was more than a vision. She could sense what the poor victim had felt. She felt a sharp shock to her right kidney.

"Ouch!" she cried, as I stood at the ensuite door.

"Are you ok?" I asked her.

She was clutching the basin with her left hand and her kidney with her right. "It was here," she said. "Here is where he took her and it was someone she knew. They had just had sex. She was happy, excited by the romance, until the shock at least."

"The shock?" I asked.

"I didn't have a vision this time, but I could feel a presence in the room. Her soul maybe, it was chilling whatever it was. She was having a fling with someone, and that someone is our killer, that someone came up from behind while she was doing her makeup or whatever and shocked her. I also felt a sharp pain in my neck."

"I think that the shock you felt to your kidney was most likely a stun gun he uses to subdue his victims. We believe he uses the stun gun in combination with an injection. We think that the shock gives him enough time for the injection to take effect."

Esmeralda watched me in the mirror as I explained.

"And I'm sure the pain in the neck you felt was the needle when he injected his sedative."

Esmeralda nodded as I finished.

"May I ask how you know that she had sex?"

"I can feel it when women have sex. There's a feeling that lasts after an orgasm. Just trust me; she had made love to her killer. I think you will find that's why the bed clothes have been removed. To remove the evidence, I would guess."

"Could you see who the man was?" I asked eagerly.

"I'm afraid not. I can only feel what she felt, not see him. But if you find him, you find the Slayer."

I had called Jake to let him know that Esmeralda had confirmed our suspicions and that we were on our way to Tammy's father's office to see if he could give us any of his daughter's possible acquaintances.

We only had to wait a few minutes before being met in the foyer by Mr Green. He led us into his office. "How can I help you today?" he asked, still visibly shaken by the loss of his daughter.

"We believe that your daughter may have known her attacker; we believe this may have been on an intimate level."

Taken aback by the news, Mr Green leaned forward and poured himself a glass of water.

"Are you saying my daughter was sleeping with this serial killer?"

"Yes, but to her, he may have just been a boyfriend or someone she met in a club. She would never have known what she was getting into, unfortunately."

Leaning over the desk, Mr Green looked at me in such a way that I knew immediately I had offended him. He let me know it too. "You may be a police officer but that doesn't give you the right to insult my daughter. I'll have you know that my daughter is not the type of girl to pick up a guy in a bar and then bring him back to her house. She was also a police officer."

"I did not mean to offend you, Mr Green."

"Can you think of anyone that she may have been with, an old boyfriend? Someone from here maybe? Anyone you know who she may have been willing to be intimate with?"

"She never talked to me about boyfriends. Since she'd been in the academy, she hadn't worried about boys. She was too focused on passing and becoming an officer. As far as I know, there was no one she was seeing. I'm sorry, but I can't help you with that. She may have confided in her best friend about that stuff. I can give you her number." Mr Green went through the contacts on his phone.

"Is this her graduation photo?" I asked picking up the photo from his desk.

"Yes, she gave it to me as a gift."

He took the photo from my hand, replacing it with a number written on a post-it note.

"That's great, thank you, and if anything comes of it, I'll let you know of course."

Chapter 59

Friday 14th November (10.44am)

Mason had just finished several back-to-back appointments. It had been a good start to the day. He had a buyer for the Lucas road property. No sooner had the buyers left than his mind turned back to his other life.

He wanted to visit his mum for morning tea, but he decided that he first better put in an appearance at the office. Firstly, he wanted to see his pig of a boss wallowing in misery, misery that Mason was sure he deserved. Secondly, he wanted to see if there was any office gossip about Tammy.

"Who are the people in the boss's office?" Mason asked the secretary, making out he had no idea. She was standing at the photocopier, running copies of the rental list.

"The police, asking him questions, I guess."

"It's so sad what happened to Tammy. I hope he's coping all right?" Mason said, trying to make out that he gave a shit.

"He seems to be struggling, to be honest. Who wouldn't though." She picked up the copies and raced off to answer the phone.

Inside, Mason was shaking.

Were they here for him?

Had they found something that had led them here? Had he made a mistake?

If they weren't here for him, he was certain they were getting closer.

Only one way to find out, he thought. Mason walked straight down the hall and opened his boss's office door, "Sorry, I didn't realise you were with people. I just needed to ask you a few questions about the Lucas Road file."

"I'll be with you in a few minutes, Mason," Mr Green responded.

Mason closed the door and headed back to his desk. He now knew they were not here for him. They were just doing their investigation, and it was good to see his letter had been taken seriously. Brodie was on the case all right, he was pleased to see. Mason was sure he would see Brodie on a more personal level before all this ended.

A few minutes later, Mason had a second meeting with the cops, except this time it was unexpected. They crossed paths in the car park as he was getting into his BMW. "How you going?" Mason spoke as they passed his open driver's door.

"Fine thanks," the older lady replied.

He wondered where Jake was and then thought, 'of course, looking after his girlfriend.' In the week since his threat, Mason had often visited Jake's home where he knew Hayley was receiving around-the-clock supervision. It usually came in the form of a patrol car sitting just outside either her or Jake's home. This week had been mostly Jake's. Shifts were usually four or six hours.

By his calculations, the next shift was due to end at 2pm and for his plan to work he had to be there by 1.30.

Chapter 60

Friday 14th November 2003 (11.15am)

"Something was strange about that agent. I got a very cold feeling when he came into the office," Esmeralda said as soon as we were in the privacy of the car.

"He's a real estate agent; what do you expect?" I joked. "Maybe that's just the way he is. Did you have a vision about him?" I asked.

"No, nothing like that, I just felt a cold presence around him. Can you run a check on him or something? I just have a feeling that I can't explain! It may lead you up the garden path, it may be totally unrelated to the case, but on the other hand, there may be something and if there is, it's worth following up."

Esmeralda's concerns with the agent bugged me all afternoon. I arrived back at the station and ran his name through the database. No criminal history existed; he was clean. I let it go but something kept nagging at me. I decided to ring Mr Green to see if there was anything to go on. "Excuse me, Mr Green, it's Brodie Foxx from the Victorian Police. Really sorry to bother you again but I'm just eliminating some suspects at the moment.

"Was Mason Belic working last weekend?" The phone was silent for a few seconds and then he replied, "Um, he was away Thursday and Friday at a conference in Brisbane and Saturday he was here but left early. He seemed lacking in interest that day. Sunday was his day off and Monday he was sick. But I would need to double check with HR."

"No need," I said. "Thank you. Can you send me his employment file please? Just so I can confirm a few things before I rule him out?"

"Sure, but I won't be back in until just after 2 and the files are locked in my office. Can it wait until then?"

"That's fine," I replied and hung up.

Something still nagged at me. I called Qantas to check for flights under Mason Belic to Gold Coast or Brisbane. "Sorry Sir, I have no bookings under that name. Maybe try Virgin."

I dialled Virgin and after a few seconds of typing, the voice came back to me. "I have a Mason Belic booked on flight VA663 Melbourne to Gold Coast. The 7.15 flight on Thursday 6th November."

That cleared him, was my first thought.

"Except he never boarded the flight," the voice at the other end said.

"When was he due to return?" I asked, thinking he might have caught another flight up for some reason.

"The return flight was VA459 Gold Coast to Melbourne 8pm Friday night. He also failed to board. We don't have him listed on either flight."

This had my mind ticking. Maybe I was getting somewhere. Things were starting to add up. This might just be our man.

I rang Corrections Victoria to see if they had any record of Mason Belic being incarcerated in 2000. Sometimes when updating the crime database, records occasionally fell through the cracks.

I rang Jake and explained that Mason had not boarded either of the two flights. I asked if he could organise a crosscheck on Mason. The purpose of the crosscheck was to verify where the suspect was at the time of each offence. Obviously, with so many abduction and murders, it would take some time. We needed to have more background on his movements before we could bring him in for questioning.

Jake told me he would be back just after 2pm as he was guarding Hayley until then, but he wasted no time in organising the taskforce to get the crosscheck underway.

Chapter 61

Friday 14th November (11.30am)

Soon after his second brush with the police, Mason arrived at his mother's house. She had purchased a simple, low maintenance unit recently. She had opted for a unit instead of a townhouse because her knees were shot and she didn't want a lot of garden to maintain or stairs to climb. She wasn't getting any younger, she said.

His mother, a grey-haired lady in her early 70s walking with a cane, answered the door. She was always delighted to see a child of hers but she was especially surprised and excited to see Mason. Friday had always been her day for shopping, the day after the pension arrived in her bank account. She had just returned home and was ready for some morning tea.

Mason spent the next half hour having tea and biscuits with his mother.

He had never told his mum the truth about his father. He knew it would destroy her, so he'd simply kept it to himself.

"Mum, I need to borrow Dad's uniform, if I can? I have a dress-up party on the weekend and I would feel privileged if you would let me wear it."

"You know how I feel about that uniform."

"Mum, it would be a great privilege. I will have it back early next week."

"I am sure your father would want you to wear it, but please look after it. Make sure you have it dry-cleaned before you return it." She dunked her biscuit into the remainder of her tea.

Mason left with the uniform folded over his arm, with an hour and a half to get home, change and be at Jake's in time for the shift changeover.

Chapter 62

Friday 14th November (1pm)

While I waited for the crosscheck to be done, I continued with the other leads.

I headed to see if David, who always seemed to be working, had come up with any results. David confirmed my suspicion that Tammy had slept with her attacker. "What did you find out?" I asked.

"Well, the case is building. I can tell you that we found a trace of semen in Tammy's vaginal cavity, despite the body having been recently thoroughly washed. I am hoping the sample will be enough to get a DNA profile. I've sent it to the lab and I've also sent the blood sample we found on the German Shepherd's teeth. If they match, we'll know that we at least have the same guy at two different murder scenes and you'll be able to test the sample against any future suspects."

He paused, sipped his coffee and continued.

"While I don't have the DNA yet, I can tell you his blood type is B-positive. I also got the toxicology results back on both Maggie and Tammy. They both had traces of Benzodiapine in their systems."

"Same as all the others," I said.

"There's enough evidence to suggest that Maggie was a victim of the Slayer. The stab pattern matches."

David dunked the doughnut into his coffee, bit off the soggy piece and continued.

"We've also done the cast of the tyre track recovered at Maggie's dump site as well as a partial sneaker cast. I've sent off a copy of the print to get an exact make of tyre. We know it's a medium size car by the diameter and width of the tyre." David finished off the doughnut and placed the empty cup on the desk next to him.

"When do you think that we will have the DNA results from Tammy Green? I was hoping for tonight," I said nervously.

David laughed as if to say, 'you're dreaming'.

"Those lab rats are slow, it may be a day or two. I'll see if I can give them the hurry-up."

I headed back to my desk to see if Jake had arrived. My conversation with Esmeralda had really worried me. The thought of Jake being buried alive terrified me.

I feared that this case could kill us both if we didn't act with extreme caution.

Chapter 63

Friday 14th November 2003 (1.50pm)

Mason, who was now dressed in his father's police uniform, knew that this was going to be the hardest part of his plan. Yet once done, it would give him the upper hand.

Sitting in his car, Mason kept his head low, waiting for the patrol car to arrive. He knew that he would have to be quick and precise. One mistake and it would end here with his death. The thought of his own demise was quickly erased as a patrol car pulled into the curb on the other side of the street.

Mason got out of his car and casually walked over to the patrol car. He could see the officer leaning over, fumbling around in the back seat for his cap. Mason calmly tapped on the window. The officer was a little startled at first, yet when he saw the uniform, his fears subsided. The officer switched the engine back on and pressed the button for the electric window. By the time the window was half-way down, Mason's plan was almost complete. He fired three rapid shots from his silenced Beretta. It was the perfect weapon when a quick kill was required. All three bullets pierced the officer's chest, killing him almost instantly.

Mason quickly reached through the window and pushed him sideways to prevent his lifeless body from collapsing onto the horn and bringing unwanted attention. Then he leaned in and removed the nametag. 'Sergeant Slater', it read. 'Pleased to meet you,' he thought, as he pinned it on his shirt. Mason pressed the window button to wind it back up and removed the keys. Then he turned and headed for Jake's home, on the other side of the street.

Chapter 64

Friday 14th November 2003 (1.55pm)

Jake was sitting at the table drinking coffee with Hayley safely beside him drinking her cup of Milo. Ever since her early 20s, she had had migraines, and her doctor had suggested she cut down on her coffee intake. Since she couldn't stand 'that decaf crap' as she called it, Milo was her best alternative.

Although he was anxious to make sure Hayley was protected, Jake was also anxious to get back to the station and follow up on the only lead they had. While it was a long shot, or what an experienced detective would call playing a hunch, a hunch was a great lead when you had absolutely nothing else.

Jake kept running scenarios through his head, trying to imagine why the Slayer had suddenly struck so close to his domain. Why had he made his boss's daughter one of his victims?

"So do you think he will come for me?" Hayley asked softly, looking into the bottom of her empty mug.

Jake wasn't entirely sure yet but he thought Hayley might be 'the one'. "I don't think so. I think he just wanted to get Brodie back on the case. It was a stunt. He's playing games, but don't panic, I'm here. Once I leave, there'll be another officer here to protect you. You will be safe, I promise."

But Jake knew that this was not enough to ease Hayley's fears.

Who was he to make such a promise? He tried to sound confident. "Babe, don't panic. We may have found him. We might have him soon."

Hayley smiled and reached for his hand.

Focused on his job, he knew that Brodie was onto something and that he needed to be there too. Impatient, he rang the chief. "Chief, where the hell is this guy who's supposed to be coming to guard Hayley?" he asked.

The chief was in his office with the phone resting on his shoulder, trying desperately to find the relieving officer's details. "He should be there soon. Traffic have sent, umm…" he fumbled through the notes on his desk, "…Sergeant Slater."

Jake was about to suggest that he ask Suzie to get traffic on the two-way to find out where the hell he was, when a knock came at the door. "It's all right. He's here," Jake said, ending the call.

Jake glanced through the opaque side window and saw the man in uniform standing there waiting patiently to be let in.

Jake opened the door and invited the officer in. "Hi. I'm Sergeant Slater. Traffic advised me to be on guard duty here. Is there anything I need to know?" Mason asked calmly.

"No, just watch her and ring me directly if anyone shows up. We think that this nutter was fucking with us. I don't think she's under any threat but as you know, we have to take every threat seriously."

Jake kissed Hayley goodbye and explained to her that the officer would watch her until he returned.

"I missed your first name?" Jake asked.

"Sorry, my mistake, Peter Slater," Mason replied, beginning to panic. He had no idea of the dead copper's first name, or if Jake was onto him. Peter was the first name that had popped into his head.

Jake picked up his jacket, holstered his gun and headed for the door. The guilt of leaving the safety of the only girl he had ever loved to a stranger, hit hard, but he swept the guilt aside and focused on the job ahead.

Chapter 65

Friday 14th November 2003 (2.07pm)

Mason watched Jake get into his car and speed off. He had been in such a rush that he hadn't even glanced at the squad car.

Mason turned his attention to Hayley. He was hopeful he could complete the rest of his plan without any hiccups. He wanted to take Hayley alive and without force if possible. If not, then force would be used.

As soon as Jake had left the property, Mason put his plan into action. He stepped into the kitchen and selected a ring tone on his phone, and then pretended to begin a conversation. "Yes, Jake, I can do that, and what time would you be there? Ok, uhh, huhh, really? The premier's daughter?" He walked back into the lounge to gauge Hayley's reaction. "This guy is sick. Do you want to speak to her? Ok, I'll let Hayley know."

With that, Mason pretended to hang up the call. Turning to Hayley, he said, "You might have guessed that was Jake. Someone apparently tried to abduct the premier's daughter from school. Jake wants me to take you to the police safe house where he'll collect you later tonight. Quick, come with me." Mason took Hayley by the hand and headed for the front door. He ushered her right past the squad car and escorted her into the front seat of his BMW.

"Why aren't we taking the squad car?" Hayley asked, as she tried to compose herself.

"We're undercover," Mason replied, as cool and as calm as usual.

"This doesn't seem right. I'm going to ring Jake." Hayley shuffled through her bag looking for her phone but before she could reach it, a sharp pain hit her in the kidney and she hit her head against the side window. Mason injected her without her even knowing.

Mason's plan was almost complete. Only one more stop to make before he headed back to the cabin.

Chapter 66

Friday 14th November 2003 (2.20pm)

As I waited for Jake to return, I couldn't believe how our investigation had taken on a new direction so quickly. I had received a call from David, who had confirmed that the tyre cast had also come back as fitting a 1992 BMW.

I had received Mason's work records from Mr Green and at first glance, nothing had stood out. Then I turned to his absence roster. He had been away a lot, sometimes for days at a time. The other thing that stood out was that beside many of these multiple days, 'conference' was written beside them.

His police check with photo attached had come back all clear. He had no previous record.

I then flicked through his resume and stopped suddenly.

His vehicle was listed as a BMW.

I printed the email and added it to the file.

So far, it was all circumstantial evidence, but it was enough for us to detain Mason for questioning. Most likely, it would be enough to receive a court order for a compulsory DNA test.

Where the hell was Jake? I wanted to go and pick up this guy. I tried Jake's number again. No response: 'the number you have called is currently out of radio range, please try again later,' the automated voice said.

"Can you try Jake on the two-way?" I asked Suzie. "He's not responding to his mobile."

Jake picked up the two-way almost immediately. "I'm pulling into the car park right now," his voice crackled back.

I practically ambushed Jake as he entered the station. "Found a lot of circumstantial evidence on that guy that works for Mr Green." I handed him the file. "He has a BMW. David just verified it was a BMW that left the tyre cast taken from Maggie's dump site."

Jake nodded, trying to get his head around everything that I was telling him. Then as he was flicking through the pages, he suddenly stopped.

I was speaking at a million miles an hour about the conferences and his work history.

Jake's face turned ashen and his eyes began to well with tears.

"What's wrong?" I asked, as his look went from surprise to horror and then anger.

"I met him," Jake stuttered, lost for words, probably for the first time ever.

"You met him?" I asked.

"He came to my house, to guard Hayley. I left Hayley there with him."

"What the fuck are you on about?" I asked, totally confused.

Jake repeated what he'd said. While I was still trying to understand what he'd said, he ran out of the station back to his car, and I had to run to keep up. I only made it about halfway before Jake drove up and slowed down just long enough for me to get in.

"What the hell are you on about, Jake?"

We were travelling at high speed, weaving through the traffic, with what appeared to be a total disregard for our lives.

"He has her!" Jake replied sharply without taking his eyes off the road for a second.

"Mate, we're not going to be of any help to her if you kill us trying to get there."

Jake sailed through the third consecutive set of red lights. "If you want to jump out at the next lights, I'll stop." He said this without allowing the conversation to distract him from driving.

"I'm not fucking going anywhere, I'm here for the long haul, whatever that may be," I said, my grip tightening around the Jesus handle. I was holding on so tightly my knuckles were white.

Jake pulled the car over to the gutter outside his apartment building. He left the car half on the footpath and with the driver's door wide open, and sprinted up the stairs of his apartment two at a time.

Inside his apartment, there was no sign of a struggle or disturbance, no sign of anything unusual at all. "Where the fuck are they?" Jake screamed.

"For what it's worth, I think she's still alive. He'll have taken her as insurance. She's not a cop, she doesn't fit his profile."

"If he's not going to kill her, then why take her?" Jake groaned. He was on his knees with his head in his hands.

"We know who he is, now we just have to locate him," I said.

We were on our way back to the station when I told Jake to pull over. He pulled into the emergency lane on the freeway, looking at me with an expression of pure hopelessness.

"Keep your head up, mate. Hayley needs you focused. Now let's go through what we know. He works as a real estate agent in the burbs, he drives a white BMW. I assume you've already put out an APB for the vehicle?"

Jake nodded.

"He's married with one child, according to Mr Green. So why did he start killing policewomen? What triggered him?" I asked.

"Because he's a fucking nut bag and he finds this stuff sexually exciting."

Without replying to Jake, I flicked through the file looking for Mason Belic's address.

"Ok Jake, let's go there now." I punched the address into the sat nav system.

"Why are we going to his house? I don't think he's stupid enough to go home," Jake said.

"I agree. But we can find out something about his childhood, which may give us a clue as to where he might be headed."

Chapter 67

Friday 14th November 2003 (3.10pm)

Mason pulled into the drive of the woman he thought of as his final victim. The only photo he had of her was over 20 years old.

He left his car. Hayley was slumped in the passenger seat with her head against the window.

Mason rapped his knuckles on the security door. He knew that she would be home. He had rung her yesterday, pretending to be from the gas company and saying that they needed to check the meters in the area. Some of them had been reported as faulty, he'd explained.

Samantha came to the door soon after she heard the knocking.

"Excuse me, just wondering if I can ask you a few questions about the neighbours and the robbery last night?" Mason knew the fact that he was dressed in a police uniform would erase any fears Samantha might have.

Samantha unlocked her security door so she could answer his questions. In doing so, she sealed her fate. She was the final piece of his hatred. Finally, he would fill the void that he had been seeking to fill.

A void that all the others had failed to fill. Surely this time it would be perfect.

It had to be.

Samantha unlocked the latch. Mason pounced.

Stunning her in the kidney had the instant effect of dropping Samantha at the front door step.

Mason quickly injected his serum and dragged her inside, closing and locking the front door behind him. From the inside, Mason pressed the garage remote clipped to the holder on the inside wall and opened the garage. Then he went back to his BMW and parked alongside Samantha's blue 2002 Holden Commodore. Popping the trunk of Samantha's car, Mason began removing the contents from his BMW into her Holden. Then he dragged Hayley into the boot of the Commodore.

Mason spent only 10 minutes at Samantha's home. He dragged her bound body and laid her on the back seat. Then he drove out of Samantha's drive and headed for the cabin.

Finally, it would be perfect; he could feel it in his bones.

Chapter 68

Friday 14th November 2003 (3.17pm)

Jake commented that Belic's house didn't look like the type of home that a serial killer might reside in. However, it was everything I'd imagined. The lawn was well trimmed. The plants were perfectly nurtured and the drive was free of oil stains. The home was situated opposite a delightful lake, in the leafy suburb of Berwick. It reflected the personality of a neat, meticulous person. I had no doubt his car would be the same. It was no coincidence that the murders had all been well planned and meticulously carried out. One was a reflection of the other.

When we rang the doorbell, through the half-glass half-timber front door we saw a toddler approach.

A woman appeared and opened the door as far as the security chain allowed. She asked, "Can I help you?"

"Mrs Belic. It's the police. We would like to come in and ask you some questions about your husband." Jake showed the petite woman his police badge.

"Oh, ok, come in then," she replied, closing the door first to unlock the chain. "Is he all right?" she asked, as she sent her son off to play in his room.

I had told Jake on the drive to Mason's home to let me handle the questions.

We were sitting on the couch in the formal lounge.

"Mrs Belic, we believe that your husband may have some information on the East Side slayings. Do you know where he might be?"

"He would be at work, or you could get him on his cell phone. Sometimes he switches it off if he's in a meeting." Her reply was matter of fact.

"He hasn't been at work all day. Does he have a friend whose house he might go to, or a parent? Somewhere else he might go?" I asked.

She frowned, becoming more uncomfortable with each question.

"No one that I can think of," she replied, "why do you need to speak to him?"

"He may have information that's of use to our investigation, that's all," I replied, smiling and trying to ease her concern. "Does he have family close by?"

"We see his mother quite a bit but she lives in a townhouse in Melbourne."

"His father?"

"His dad died when he was about nine. He died in the line of duty and…"

"How did his dad die?" I asked.

"He was in the police force, he was shot by his partner. She was only young, a rookie, and, well, she thought he was a robber. That's the way Mason tells it anyhow. Mason didn't cope with the death of his father. He still gets upset about it sometimes, which I don't understand."

"Well, I'm sure the death of a parent must have been very hard to cope with, as a nine-year-old," I said sympathetically.

"I am not heartless, Officer, if that's what you're insinuating. I just don't understand how Mason cared so much for someone who sexually abused him and spent his spare time beating him. If it had been me, I'd have been glad not to have him come back home."

We tried to remain impassive as we heard Mason's likely motive being spelled out for us.

"Mrs Belic, is that your husband's study?" I asked, pointing to the room with the double doors.

She nodded.

"Do you mind if we have a look around?" I asked, hoping she would be cooperative. If she asked for a warrant, it was a waste of precious time, time we just didn't have.

"Of course you can. Why do you need to speak to Mason?" she asked again.

"We just need to ask him some questions." I didn't want to let on he was a wanted man.

"This picture, is that your holiday house?" I asked, picking up the photo from the desk.

"Far from it. I haven't been there for years. Mason goes up often. He's renovating it so we can sell it. It belonged to Mason's father." She seemed more and more concerned by our questioning.

I picked up the other photo of Mason and his wife at what looked like the Grand Canyon. "When was this?" I asked.

"It was back in 2000. We decided to go on holiday and tour the USA before we had children. My parents lived over there at the time so it was a family visit as well."

"Must have been fun. Have you seen them since?" I asked, placing the photo back in its original place.

"Oh, they live here now. So I see them all the time."

I had seen and heard all we needed. "Thanks for your help. If you see Mason, could you please ask him to call us?" Still smiling, I handed her one of Jake's cards.

It was lie, but a necessary one. The last thing I wanted was her thinking we were about to arrest him. I'd rather her thinking we were just making routine enquires. That way, if they did speak, she wouldn't be in a panic.

Chapter 69

Friday 14th November 2003 (3.30pm)

Back in the vehicle, I radioed Suzie.

"I want you to search for a policeman who was killed between 1975 and 1985. He had a female partner who survived, I believe his name was Belic."

She cut me off mid-sentence.

"I know that case. I studied it at the academy. He was killed during a robbery, accidentally shot by his junior partner. What do you need to know?"

"What was the young police officer's name and where does she live?"

"I'll do a search and get back to you."

"Suzie, I also need a title search done on Mr Belic. I need to know any properties he had or still has. You will need to ring the titles office. Tell them we need them urgently."

I placed the receiver down and leaned back in my seat.

"We're supposed to be finding Hayley!" Jake shouted at me.

"We will find her, I promise, but I think that the girl who killed Mason's dad is his real target. I think he's been killing these girls at the cabin in the photo. David found a piece of wood stuck under Maggie's finger. David believed it was from trying to grab a door or a veranda rail. What type of wood do you think that cabin is made out of?" I asked Jake.

He pondered. "Looked like cedar, or western red cedar."

"I agree. We sent the piece of wood off to a botanist and he said it was an old piece of cedar. Cedar isn't used to build houses today, but 50 years ago, cabins like that were made from the trees that grew in the area. "

Jake sat quietly. "He would have all the time in the world to spend with the girls up there."

"Exactly. We find that cabin, we find Hayley," I answered.

"Let's just get the address from Mrs Belic." Jake opened the car door.

I grabbed him by the jacket. "Wait, we don't want to alarm her. We don't want her to know that we know about the cabin. If she talks to him meantime, she'll tell him we've been asking questions and that'll tip him off."

Jake closed the door.

We waited in silence for Suzie to give us the address of the cabin. She also provided the name and address of the police colleague who had mistakenly killed Mason's father all those years ago.

Mason was most likely hunting her as we waited.

"The officer, her name is Samantha Bond. We sent a squad car around to her home. Front door was open, no one at home. She's gone. The officers found Belic's BMW parked in her garage. So we know Belic was there. Her car is a 2002 blue Holden Commodore. It's gone. Do you want me to put out an APB on it?"

I looked at Jake before responding, "Not yet, we don't want to scare him. He has Hayley and now Samantha. He will kill them if he sees a cop. Now that we know where he's headed, we'll call for backup when we get there. Thanks Suzie!" I said, placing the two-way back in its cradle.

Jake had already punched the cabin address into the sat nav.

"Where is that property?" I asked.

"Central Victoria," Jake replied.

"Before we go, we need to organise backup, we need SWAT to go in," I said.

Jake sat there in silence, then he said,. "I'm one for doing everything by the book but if we send SWAT and he catches even a glimpse of them, then the girls are dead. You said so yourself: if he sees a cop, he'll kill them."

I thought it over. "One thing is clear. He wants to finish this his way. He wants to take his time killing Samantha. That I am sure of. The death of his father was the trigger. The fact that he never had the opportunity to exact revenge on his father has led to his misguided belief that killing policewomen will give him the satisfaction he desires. He won't rush this one."

"I'm concerned that if we try to apprehend him now, or on the way to the cabin, he'll kill everyone he can, including Hayley. He'd have no reason not to," Jake said.

"I agree." I paused, contemplating whether to tell him about Esmeralda's vision. I decided it was best not to bring it up now, but I warned him about the dangers. "You know, if we go in alone, then we could all end up dead."

Jake nodded solemnly. "But he won't know we're coming. We'll have the element of surprise on our side. We can't allow it to become a hostage situation. Why don't we head up there, see if he's there first, then call for backup. No point sending SWAT if he isn't even there."

"I agree. Let's assess our next move when we get there."

Chapter 70

Friday 14th November 2003

Overnight, Stephen's condition had deteriorated rapidly and he was fighting for his life. His heart was rapidly giving in to the disease and his worst fears were being realised: he might soon be dead.

His heart had gone into systolic failure. It wasn't pumping hard enough and the beat had become slow and irregular.

By the time Stephen was wheeled through to the emergency ward at Alfred Hospital, his doctor was there waiting for him.

He was immediately sent to radiology for an MRI of his heart, then to cardiology for an echo. Cassie had ridden in the back of the ambulance with him and she now sat patiently awaiting Stephen's return to the cardiology ward. She tried to keep her mind occupied by reading the latest copies of 'Women's Day' and 'New Idea'.

"Cassie," a soft voice called from the door. "May I have a seat?" Doctor Hanam sat down beside her. "I am afraid that Stephen's condition has worsened quicker than I expected. Unfortunately, from the results of the MRI and the echo, I think we only have up to five days at the absolute outside before Stephen will require a heart transplant. We will need to keep him here until we find a heart."

Cassie burst into tears at the news of Stephen's predicament. Hanam held her hand.

"I have already told Stephen the news. He is coping quite well. He will be back in his room shortly. I have arranged with the nurses for you to stay. They will set up a bed in the room for you." Hanam clasped Cassie's hand tighter. "All you can do is hope. You have to have hope, Cassie." Hanam stood up, adjusted his comb-over and left the room.

Chapter 71

Friday 14th November 2002 (5.20pm)

By the time Mason reached his cabin, his excitement was at fever pitch. He had spoken to his wife, who had rung him in a panic.

"They were asking all sorts of strange questions. What's going on, Mase? They were even asking about the cabin, asked if I'd been there recently. What do you know? Why are they bothering us?" she asked him.

Mason as usual played it cool.

"I'm sure they're just investigating everyone who may have known Tammy," Mason replied. "It's just routine. I don't know anything, babe, I'll give them a call and clear it up."

He managed to put Sophie's mind at ease.

She read out the number that the police had left.

He guessed he was a good hour ahead of them.

He assumed Jake would be coming for Hayley, and he was ready.

Mason had already locked Hayley in a cage in the cellar, before he'd even attempted to move Samantha from the car, but now, he dragged Sam by the hair all the way from the car to the cellar. She only came to as she felt the cold cuffs around her wrists. She began to kick and scream and Mason cuffed her to two of the support beams.

Once in place, Samantha was hanging a foot off the ground with her hands and legs spread wide, held only by the chains, as if she was attached to an invisible cross.

"I'm glad to see you're now wide awake. I would hate for you to miss any of the fun," Mason said, in an almost jocular fashion. "Do you know why you're here, Samantha? Do you know why I chose you?" Mason asked, as he removed the Samurai sword from its place on the wall.

"I haven't done anything to you. I don't even know who you are!" Samantha screamed, spit flying from her mouth. "Let me go, please, just let me go before you do something you will regret." Samantha was trying to talk her way out of a bad situation.

"Look up at the shelf, Samantha. I have already done a lot of things. People like me don't feel regret."

Samantha looked up at the shelf and saw all the horrified lifeless faces looking back at her from their respective jars. She lost control of her emotions and continued screaming.

Mason raised the sword and cut away Samantha's clothes, cutting her skin several times. "Normally, I would apologise for cutting you. Under the circumstances, I am sure you would consider the apology insincere. I wouldn't want to be seen as fake." Mason picked up a clear bottle from the table next to him.

"Now, I will ask you again; tell me why you are here?"

"I don't know!" Samantha screamed.

"Maybe you should think a little harder before you answer next time, Samantha." He began pouring the clear liquid onto the cuts on Samantha's skin. "This is just good old-fashioned vinegar. It might sting a little, so hold on."

Again, Samantha screamed, louder than before. The pain was agonising. "Stop, please. I will think. Stop, please stop," Samantha begged, her tears flowing freely.

Mason stopped pouring and asked the question again.

Trying to compose herself and think of an answer, Samantha paused, thinking. 'What have I done? 'Why would he want me here?' Maybe it was just a trick question. She was now down to her bra and briefs. She mustered up all her courage to and said, "I am here because I was lucky and you chose me. Thank you."

"Wrong again," Mason answered, "and I don't care for you being a rude insincere little bitch either." Mason picked up the sword, this time cutting the bra straps from her shoulder and then down the middle, causing the bra to fall to the ground in tatters, leaving Samantha bare chested.

Mason spent a little time assessing the breasts. They were still nice and firm and held their shape well for a woman heading into her mid-40s. It was a shame he was going to have to disfigure them. Without another word, Mason raised the sword and made two quick strikes, cutting off the nipple from each breast. Samantha went into a screaming frenzy, the like of which he had never heard before, and Mason had heard more than his share.

"Leave her alone, you prick, leave her the fuck alone!" Hayley screamed from her cage.

"Don't worry, I will save some pain for you, my dear," Mason replied, showing her his overexcited smile. He placed his sword down on the bench and removed his gun. Then he turned and fired a bullet, which just grazed Hayley's right thigh. "Speak again and the next bullet will be between your eyes, you understand?" Mason still had the gun pointed at her.

Hayley nodded and moved to the back of the cage.

Mason returned his attention to Samantha. "Now, for the last fucking time, why the fuck did I pick you?" he screamed, at boiling point.

Without any delay this time, Samantha replied, "Because you're sick and twisted."

"Well, let me fill you in!" Mason shouted in his rage. "You killed my dad. Is it coming back to you now, you little bitch? You let him die! You didn't even fight to save him. What sort of cop were you?"

Samantha now realised who Mason was and why he was in a

rage. "I'm so sorry," she sobbed, "I am so very sorry, I didn't mean for you to lose your dad."

"I didn't care that you let him die. He was a monster!"

"Why are you doing this to me then, if you wanted him dead anyway?" Samantha cried through her pain.

"It was my duty, my right, my revenge that you took away from me that night. Do you have any idea what he did to me? What punishment he deserved? Your stupid actions freed him from that punishment and now you will suffer his fate for him."

In silence, he raised his sword and in one quick motion, removed Samantha's head. It flew from her shoulders and landed on the dusty floor of his cellar, eyes peering directly at Hayley. Hayley screamed and would have moved away further if she'd had anywhere to go. Mason stood motionless with his sword still tightly grasped in both hands, with the tip touching the ground.

Hayley realised that Mason was in a place void of all that is decent in a human being, a place that didn't exist in ordinary people, a place that terrified her.

Motionless, Mason watched as the blood sprayed out of the neck. Only when it became a dribble did he awake from his trance. He picked up her head and placed it on the bench next to him. As Hayley watched him, she knew there would be no negotiating with this man.

Chapter 72

Friday 14th November 2003 (7.30pm)

Jake pulled the car into a track well off the road. It was hidden from the road in the undergrowth and in a heavily forested area.
The GPS showed the cabin to be off to our right about 500 metres. We guessed it was around a five-minute walk through the bush.

Jake grabbed my arm before I had a chance to exit the car. "This is a walkie-talkie radio. You place this part in your ear no one else will be able to hear us and you clip the microphone on your shirt so when you talk I will hear you and you will hear me, get it?" Jake demonstrated. "This doesn't connect to the station so if you need help and I'm dead, then it'll be useless. If you get into trouble or manage to bring the girls back here, call SWAT from the car. Leave that fucker for me, you understand?"

I nodded and went to get out of the car, but Jake held me back again. "On second thoughts, if you do see the fucker, shoot him; don't hesitate." Before I had a chance to tell Jake I didn't have a gun, he handed me a black pistol, butt first. "It's a Glock. Holds 10 shots, just pull the trigger. It does the rest. It's exactly the same as the gun you used at the range. Now, I'll take the front. What I want you to do is just go to the back of the cabin. Stay well hidden. Tell me what you see. I want you to be my eyes from the back as I come in the front. That way I have less chance of getting ambushed," Jake said.

"Can you give me a cuff key please? In case I need to unlock the girls."

Jake handed over a key, which I placed in my right pants pocket. "Be careful, mate," I said.

We left the car simultaneously. Jake headed east while I headed south. Night hadn't fallen as yet; it was overcast and the sun was low in the sky. Even though it wasn't pitch black it was already getting dark and seeing ahead was becoming difficult. There were no street lights out here. Our torches were off to keep our presence hidden. The only lights we could see were from the cabin.

I turned once, to get a visual on Jake's location, but he was already gone. I headed further south past the cabin. I could see it on the horizon but I wanted to head towards it, through the bush, rather than straight at it from the road. "Make sure you keep an eye out for snakes here, Jake," I said into the walkie-talkie, but I felt as if I was talking to myself. The thought had only just entered my head when Jake responded, "Do you really think there would be snakes out here, mate? I fucking hate snakes."

"Just watch where you walk. You'll be fine. They go down their holes at night." I was trying to calm Jake's nerves. In hindsight, it would have been better if I hadn't opened my fat mouth at all.

My eyes took a little while to adjust to the dark. "Ok Jake, I'm 20 or 30 metres from the back door. The cabin looks like a double storey, with a big garage or cellar underneath. It has large double doors that lead out the back. There's a broad clearing beyond the house before you hit the state forest." In the clearing, I noticed a big oak tree. It didn't belong here, a sole oak where all the other trees were pines. That was when I remembered Esmeralda's dream. "Hey Jake, out the back there are a few old cars. I can't see any lights on downstairs, but it looks like someone is upstairs."

"Ok, thanks mate, I'm only metres from going in. There's a blue Commodore in the drive. I would guess it's Samantha's. Brodie, try and get a bit closer so that when I go in, you can look for the girls," Jake's voice crackled back.

"Sure thing," I replied, although I was not keen on going in without Jake.

I headed a little closer, hiding behind a clump of bushes and some heavy bracken. My heart rate, if not high already, increased significantly when I saw the cellar light come on. "He's in the cellar," I radioed through to Jake, who replied with, "I'm going in the front. You wait there for my call."

I moved a few steps closer, still under the cover of large trees, when I noticed a red glow flash in the cellar. 'What's he doing?' I wondered, and saw another red flash.

Chapter 73

Friday 14th November 2003 (7.52pm)

The red light in the cellar was triggered by a sensor at the front of the cabin. Mason now knew he had company. No doubt, the guests he had been expecting. He was prepared. He retrieved his two pistols, both with laser sightings. He then removed a pair of goggles from the workbench. "Now the real games begin. Say goodbye to your boyfriend," he said as he passed the cage in which Hayley lay bleeding.

With his goggles on, Mason flicked off the power to the cabin. Then he headed for one of several trapdoors he had specially created. This one led from the cellar to the first floor.

Mason could hear whoever was in the cabin stumbling around. Obviously, the person's eyes had not yet adjusted to the darkness. The person's steps were slow. Mason assumed whoever it was would have a torch and that was the reason for the delay in the movement. He also assumed that the person in his cabin was Jake. He doubted that Brodie would be in the house. It was more likely that he was on lookout duty.

Mason waited patiently for the footsteps to move past his head. Slowly he lifted the door, aimed at the leg and fired. Seconds later, he heard Jake – he assumed it was Jake – fall to the floor. It was a lot quicker than Mason had anticipated and he was scared he had overloaded the tranquiliser. He had wanted to bring him down quickly but he didn't want him dead, not yet anyway.

Mason opened the trapdoor again to see Jake sprawled out on the floor with his gun and torch a short distance from each hand. Mason could see him breathing so he was confident his plan was still on track.

Mason dropped back down to the cellar and fired his other pistol, twice. The shots rang through the cabin and out into the darkness.

Chapter 74

Friday 14th November 2003 (7.55pm)

The shots made me jump and for the first time, I was truly scared. "Jake, are you there?" I asked into the walkie-talkie, but there was only silence. "Jake," I tried again, "are you there?"

He had told me to go for help, to call for backup if everything went bad, but I couldn't leave him in there possibly dying. I had to go in. I got up slowly and then sprinted for the cellar doors.

I had my torch and my gun hand over fist, just as Jake had taught me. I gently pushed the door open with my left foot and slowly moved the torch around the cellar floor.

Immediately, the strong smell of death hit me. We were at the right house. As I moved the torch from each corner of the cellar to the other, I was more horrified with each sight. My heart was beating very fast now. I saw the jars sitting on the shelf proudly displayed, just as a child would display a basketball trophy in his room. Each jar contained the head of a missing policewoman, all in order, all labelled with names and dates. All were tagged, except the first.

I moved the torch to the second corner where I saw a rack with another headless, naked body. The head was sitting on the bench beside it, a hobby in progress.

My guess was that Jake had interrupted him. Where the hell was

Jake? As I moved the torch around, I saw a cage. Hayley. I had found her. She was covered in blood and dirt, but she was alive. The cage had a padlock on it. I put my finger to my lips, and Hayley acknowledged my gesture by nodding.

I looked on the bench and only centimetres from the severed head were two silver keys on a small plain ring. I put the gun on the ground beside me, the torch in my mouth, and began to fumble around with the lock on the cage.

The killer was somewhere in the house, or, from the gunshots I'd heard, dead. I had heard no movement at all so I felt relatively safe. I was confident I would hear if anyone started moving around.

Then I heard a sound. It was like a door closing. I reached for my gun but before I could locate its metal handle, I felt the pain in my neck. My vision was going, my mouth was dry. I was slipping away. It took every bit of energy I had to keep my eyes open. I continued to feel around in the dirt for the gun. As I touched the metal butt, everything went black.

Chapter 75

Saturday 15th November 2003 (8.56am)

I awoke to a feeling of sickness, as if I was about to vomit. I went to sit up but my arms were chained.

Where was I?

My vision was still blurry but I could make out a figure in a doctor's outfit wearing a green surgical mask.

Then everything came flooding back. "How are you feeling, Brodie?" the deep voice behind the mask asked.

"Sick," I replied as the bile flowed up into my throat and then out of my mouth.

"I think I'll give you a few more hours to regain your senses. I want to make sure you feel every bit of what I have in store for you."

I vomited again. This time, I could feel it run down my neck.

This was like the nightmare I'd had, except now, it made sense to me. I wasn't in a surgery with a doctor, I was in a cellar with a madman. A man who was about to cut me up and pull out my heart.

"I will leave you to recuperate a little; give the effects of the tranquiliser a chance to wear off. Then I'll be back. I read that you have a heart condition and that you have undergone several operations. I will be back to have a firsthand look at what those doctors did to your heart. I even have a special jar for it."

Mason walked away from me and out of sight. I felt like I was going to vomit again at any moment.

I wanted to live. I had to get out of this somehow.

Chapter 76

Saturday 15th November (9.45am)

"**M**orning Jake, nice to see you're awake. You were out for quite a while. I can't stay long. I have to take care of your friend and then I have to spend some quality time with your woman. I'm sure you wouldn't want me to rush what I'm going to do to her. My only disappointment is that you won't be there to witness all the fun."

Jake was starting to feel like his normal self again, except that he was in deep trouble.

He was lying in what appeared to be a glass or Perspex box. He presumed the box was in the ground as all he could see out the sides of the box was dirt, the blue sky above, and a nice oak tree providing his feet with a little shade.

His hands were cuffed, not to each other but to either side of the Perspex box. Jake guessed he had only a few centimetres of slack on either side from his wrist to the side of the box. He could almost touch his hands together; his fingers met but he could not clasp them together. His feet were loose, no binding there. He could breathe quite easily, as there were hundreds of small holes in the Perspex top of the box.

Jake had begun to wonder, why had he put him in here. What was planned for him? Was it going to be a slow painful death by way of starvation? That was the only thing Jake could think of. Whatever he had in store had been well planned out, that was certain.

"You can't get out of there," Mason said as he lowered his face down to the top of the box. "You can squirm all you like, but that shit is solid. It won't break. I reinforced all the corners with steel and those handcuffs are police issue. Somehow, a lot of the women I picked up had them around the house."

"You fucker, I'll get you!" Jake screamed as he tried desperately to break the box with his feet, but he knew Mason was right. He couldn't break it.

Mason laughed as he watched Jake try to fight his way out.

"I asked myself, what would be the worst death imaginable. The answer I came up with was starvation. Having your stomach eat itself, chewing off your tongue for food. Lying there for days knowing no one was coming for you, knowing you are going to die and being unable to do anything about it. That would be horrible, wouldn't it, Jake?" Mason's face was almost touching the top of the box. "You've been a good cop so I thought you deserved better – a quick death, shall I say. So I have a choice for you to make. In this bag…" Mason placed a large hessian bag on the top of Jake's box, "is a big eastern brown snake listed as one of the world's deadliest. Now, what makes these snakes dangerous is they are very aggressive. If they were trapped in, say, a Perspex box where it's hot, they become more aggressive and might strike out. Actually, I am sure it will strike out. So the choice you have is to provoke it so it will strike you, causing you to die within an hour, or ignore it and prolong your death, in the unlikely hope that someone will stumble upon you before you starve to death."

Mason placed the bag into a small secondary box that adjoined the Perspex box containing Jake. Mason removed the bag and watched the snake slide into the box and down the clear tunnel that joined the two boxes. Once the snake was in the tunnel, Mason pushed down the piece of tin that blocked off the smaller box. The only place the snake could go now was into Jake's box.

"My money is on the snake," Mason said, laughing.

Mason walked back towards the cabin as if he didn't have a care in the world, as if he was a farmer going in for his supper.

Chapter 77

Saturday 15th November 2003 (10am)

"We have Stephen in ICU now," Hanam told Cassie. "His heart has given out, so we have him attached to what we call a mechanical heart. It's used mostly for heart attack victims to provide time for the victim's heart to recover. However, as you know, Stephen's heart will not recover because it's diseased. We're using it until we can find a donor heart. Unfortunately, we don't have long. Maybe two days at the most. The longer he's on the machine, the higher the risk of rejection if we do locate a donor heart." Hanam brushed his comb-over back into place. "All we can do now is pray we find a donor heart before the rest of his body gives up."

Cassie began to cry.

"The nurses will come to collect you when he is settled," Hanam said just before he left.

Cassie put her head in her hands. What was to become of her soul mate? They were young and in love, their lives were supposed to be full of fun, romance and excitement. Now, it was full of sadness and possible death. Even though she had known for months that this day would come, she had never really let herself believe it. Now it hit her hard.

It was a good couple of hours before the nurse came to collect

Cassie. By that time, Stephen's mother had arrived. Shelley was in her mid-40s but looked far younger, and some people had mistaken them as sisters when they had been out together. They sat in the waiting room across from each other, waiting to be shown into the ICU. They both knew what the other was going through but had no idea what to say. They sat in silence, each hoping the other would start the conversation.

When Cassie set foot in the ICU, she almost fainted at the sight of Stephen. It looked as though he was hooked up to every machine ever invented.

"Now don't panic about the machines," the nurse said reassuringly, "let me explain. It might help ease your fears. Stephen is hooked up to a normal blood pressure machine. This is the sats machine, which tells us how much oxygen is in his blood. That is the mechanical heart. It's the noisy one." She pointed to the machine in the corner.

"Finally, the tubes are the oxygen: just to help take the pressure off his lungs. We'll be with him here in ICU all the time. We never leave the room. We check on him at 15-minute intervals. Have a seat next to him. Try and relax. He'll probably come around soon. He will be groggy but I am sure he would love to hear your voices."

Cassie sat down, looking from Stephen to Shelley. "He's going to need both of us to get through this."

Shelley looked up with tears in her eyes and nodded.

Chapter 78

Saturday 15th November 2003 (10.05am)

I was lying on the trolley in the cold damp cellar, which smelt of blood and death. My vision had cleared and my vomiting had ceased. I was cuffed to what felt like an old hospital trolley. One hand was cuffed to each side rail and my legs were strapped to the sides, as if I was in a mental hospital. I kept thinking about the nightmare I'd had that night, the one that had made me call Esmeralda to discuss it. I remembered the mask and those piercing eyes. I also remembered the one thing in the dream that I hadn't been able to work out: the silver handcuff key in my pocket. Esmeralda had told me that day to keep a spare and thankfully, I'd remembered to ask Jake for it. Now, I hoped I could reach it.

I moved my body slowly over towards my right hand. I could only reach the tip of my fingers inside the pocket. Searching, I could feel the key but I couldn't get hold of it to grab it. I pulled as hard as I could on the cuff to try and gain those few extra centimetres. The cuff dug into my skin. It felt as if there was blood running down my wrist, but there wasn't enough time to check. He would be back soon.

I pushed hard again, one last go at the key, then I had it, balanced delicately between my pointer finger and index finger. I placed it on the trolley where I could pick it up in a more useful grip by holding the key between my forefinger and thumb. I managed to slide it into the lock of the cuff that was attached to the rail. I could see the blood running from my wrist. Now how to turn it? I knew I had to be careful. If I fumbled and it fell to the floor, my fate was sealed. The fate of the three of us was sealed. If the key didn't turn, it was the same deal.

I moved my thumb and forefinger, stretched out as far as I could, and tried to turn the key, but there was not enough give. I only had one option. I put my hand outside the rail. If I dropped the key now it would hit the floor and be out of reach for good. Unable to see the lock, I moved my hand around, feeling for the keyhole in the cuff. There, it was in. Now to pray for it to turn.

Click! The sweetest sound I had ever heard. My right hand was free, now for the left. I pulled my hand back inside the trolley. The tip of the open cuff clipped the rail of the trolley. Then it happened. It dropped. I had dropped the key with only one hand free.

There I was on the trolley, with my left hand cuffed, my right hand free, with half an open cuff dangling from my wrist and the key to freedom on the floor. There was no way I could reach the key with my left hand still cuffed to the bed.

On my left, my gun sat on the bench close to Samantha's severed head, but several metres away from me. I stood up with my left hand still cuffed to the bed and pulled on the trolley. The brakes were on. I could not reach the brake release pedal at the end of the bed. I had no other choice but to try to move the trolley with the brakes on.

I pulled, using all my weight. The trolley began to move. The wheels didn't turn, they just dragged in the dirt of the cellar floor. I had managed to move the bed a few metres before I began to feel fatigued. I was worried I wouldn't be able to move it much further and there was no way I would be able to move it back. Just a few more metres in order to reach the gun. I took a deep breath, gathered myself and pulled. I could touch the bench but not far enough to reach the gun.

If Mason were to walk in now it would all be over. Suddenly, I heard laughing outside, not far away but not too close either. I had to hurry.

I held onto the bench and pulled with all my strength.

Finally, the cold metal of the revolver touched my fingertips and soon, the gun was safely resting in my palm.

Over the bench, I could finally see inside the cage that held Hayley. I had not called out to her for fear of Mason hearing voices and returning. I could see she was still breathing but her eyes were closed and the pool of blood had increased. My guess was the loss of blood had decreased her blood pressure and she was possibly unconscious. I didn't know how much time she had left.

Still with the fear of getting caught, I gathered all my remaining strength and pushed for as hard and as long as I could. I managed to get the trolley back to its original position. My chest was sore, I could hardly breathe, and I needed to slow my heavy breathing down quickly.

I lay back on the trolley, breathing deeply, trying to return my heart rate to normal.

I hadn't worked out yet how to kill him. Should I shoot him as soon as he walked into the cellar? If I fired at the door from here, it would mean I would need to hit him from 10 metres away. I had only been to the range with Jake twice. That wasn't enough training for me to be sure I would hit him from that distance.

If I missed, I had to hope he wasn't carrying any weapons. I knew I was not likely to win a gun battle, half cuffed to the bed, from where I had no cover. I needed a better plan.

Then I heard footsteps on the loose gravel.

I needed that plan now.

Chapter 79

All that occupied Jake's mind now was how he could kill a two-metre brown snake without getting bitten. The snake had hardly moved. It lay coiled up in the outlet tube just centimetres away from his feet. 'If I'm calm and quiet, it will just sit there, surely,' Jake thought. 'Why would it come up here if I don't move?'

Then he realised it would only be a matter of time before the snake became too hot in the Perspex box. Then what would it do? It would look for shade or water. Jake answered himself, but what shade was there? His pants leg? he answered himself again. Fuck, what then? How long would it be until the snake sought refuge up his trouser leg?

As it turned out, it was only ten more seconds before the snake began searching the air with its tongue and then it began to move. Jake was sure it was looking for escape inside his trouser leg.

Except it didn't.

It crawled along the floor and side of the Perspex box as close to the cool soil as possible. It headed straight for Jake's head. 'What if it senses my breathing, smells my breath? What if it wants to drink the saliva from my mouth?' With these thoughts, Jake closed his mouth and pushed his lips together.

He didn't know a lot about snakes but he knew a few things: if it felt fear or felt it was in danger, it would strike. If you stepped on it, it would bite.

Again, with its tongue leading the way, it made its way further up Jake's body, looking for food, shade or water. Jake wasn't sure which.

In the short time Jake had, he had devised a plan. It wasn't a great plan. Hell, it wasn't even a good plan, but it was the only chance he had. It was simple. Once the snake reached his hand, he would try to grab it around the neck and snap it before the snake had a chance to move into an attack position.

The snake climbed up Jake's left arm and across his face. Jake closed his eyes and held his breath. He could feel the head of the snake on his right shoulder. It began to move down his right arm.

Jake opened his eyes to see the head of the snake cross his elbow. He had trouble seeing its head fully as the body was still moving across the bridge of his nose.

Jake slowly opened his right palm. He was poised ready to strike and he guessed the snake would be too.

He had never touched a snake before this. The skin was different to what he'd expected; it wasn't as slimy as he had imagined, or as scaly.

Jake could feel the sweat drip down his brow. Surely the snake could feel Jake's nerves vibrating through his body.

Jake glanced at the snake again. His moment of truth had arrived. Only one question remained. Was he quicker than a brown snake?

Chapter 80

Saturday 15th November (10.10am)

The gun was hidden and at the ready, with the safety off.

"Good to see you awake. I wanted to tell you how much I respected you, before you meet your demise," Mason said, as he approached the trolley I was chained to.

"You know, I'm surprised that such a smart man got caught by such a novice," I said, trying to provoke Mason, "'cos I mean, this is my first case. Sure, you have the upper hand now but really it must worry you that I managed to catch you." I hoped to provoke him into losing his focus.

"You really shouldn't take credit for other people's work. If I'm not mistaken, it was me who actually sent you the evidence, so you could find me. So I wouldn't flatter yourself if I were you, Brodie."

Mason ripped open my shirt, causing the buttons to fly everywhere.

My plan wasn't working yet so I had to do something soon. Something that would rattle him. Something that would send him over the edge. "Do you know what surprises me, Mason?" Without waiting for the answer, I continued, "With all six girls…" I said, purposely reducing the number of his victims.

He snapped. "It was nine I killed, nine of those bitches, and once I'm done here with you, I'll start on her," he looked over at Hayley, "and then I'm going looking for my next one. No one can stop me."

He sounded triumphant but his rage was increasing. My plan was beginning to work.

"Ok, nine, I stand corrected. It makes my point worse really. Out of those nine, how come you never got it right? How come it was never the way you wanted it? I didn't think you could fuck it up nine times!"

"Fuck it up? I'll fuck you up in a minute. I think you're forgetting where you are and the predicament you're in, Brodie. I never fucked it up. They were all perfect." Mason was beginning to move around, forgetting his task, which I was glad of because his task was me.

"You say they were all perfect, except we both know that's not true. That's why you had to keep going. They were never perfect. They will never be perfect because the person you really want to kill is already dead."

"You don't know me; don't pretend you do." He was starting to show his anger.

"The one person on this planet who should have protected you, didn't, and yet she's still fine. Why isn't her head in a jar?"

He knew I was talking about his mum.

I was getting to him. His face was becoming redder. The veins in his neck were bulging. Now that I had found the button, it was time to push it.

Chapter 81

Saturday 15th November 2003 (10.20am)

Jake took a deep breath and grabbed as fast as he could. The snake reared and struck. Jake only felt a small scratch but he knew immediately that it had got him. He had to keep going. The last thing he needed was to get bitten again and to have an angry live snake in his box with him. Jake managed to pinch the snake's neck between his thumb and forefinger. Then he wrapped the chain attached to his wrist and the side of the Perspex box around the snake's head and jaw. He had the snake trapped. He increased the pressure with his thumb and forefinger and then pulled on the chain. He pulled harder. Snap! Something had broken. Blood began flowing from the snake's neck. Jake was hoping the extended pressure of the chain had done enough.

He'd lost count how many times he'd pulled the chain but when the snake's head finally fell off and landed on his leg, he guessed it was safe to let go of the headless serpent.

He lifted his head and saw what only looked like a scratch on his hand. But he knew it was serious, even though he could not feel anything yet. The effects would take hold of his body soon.

Now that the snake was out of the way, Jake turned his attention to getting out of the box. He tried to keep thoughts of being buried alive away. He knew that as long as Brodie was alive, there was hope that he would get out.

"Think positive thoughts, stay still, think positive thoughts, you're going to be all right, you're going to be all right," Jake kept repeating to himself.

The box had hinges secured by screws, and the handcuff chains were screwed to a metal plate on the box, so Jake was not going to bust them off anytime soon.

Jake looked around the box to try and find a solution to his problem, when he noticed next to his decapitated serpent friend a crack in the Perspex. It had been caused by pulling on the chain to strangle the snake. It was only a small crack, but it gave him the idea that he could perhaps crack the Perspex around the hinge.

However, Jake knew that if he started bashing the hell out of the Perspex, the venom from the brown snake would travel though his bloodstream faster. He didn't know a lot about it, but he knew that a lot of movement and exertion would increase his heart rate and that would only expedite the effect of the venom.

Chapter 82

Saturday 15th November 2003 (10.28am)

"Don't tell me your mum didn't know what your dad was doing to you!" I shouted, pushing the boundaries hard. "She knew he'd abused your brothers before you and yet she did nothing about it. She did nothing to protect you either. Don't you think she noticed the man lying beside her kept leaving in the middle of the night? Of course she did! But she left you to deal with the problem. She ignored you, left you all alone in the dark with that monster."

"Don't you ever say my mum was to blame!" Mason said furiously. "She tried her best to protect us. Dad was scum."

His rage was growing but not enough. I needed him to fly off the handle. I wanted him going nuts. I knew I wouldn't be able to distract him when he was focused on cutting me to pieces, so I turned up the anger dial. "Your dad didn't make you into this monster. You're not killing these girls because your dad molested you. You're killing these girls because you're exactly like your dad. Your dad liked seeing you beg, just like you enjoy watching the girls beg. You're just like him except worse."

Then he started to lose it, giving me the distraction I needed.

"I'm nothing like him! Nothing..." he began to mutter, clearly losing his focus. Then he picked up the scalpel, still muttering, and jammed it down into my shoulder. The piercing pain was excruciating but I did my best not to show him any weakness. My mind and my mouth were not in sync and I let out a thunderous scream to make him think I was at his mercy.

"I am nothing like my father, you understand?" Mason said, as he twisted the blade embedded in my shoulder.

He stared at me squarely in the eyes. He was truly rattled, and I knew that now was my only chance. I purposely looked behind Mason and then shouted, "Run Hayley! Run!"

She was still in her cage but I knew that Mason would turn and check. He did, and I had only a split second but it was all I needed. By the time Mason swung back to face me, I had already fired the first shot and before I even realised, I had pulled the trigger again. The first hit Mason on the side of his head just above his left cheekbone, while the second hit him just above the right eye, as his head recoiled from the first hit.

By the time he hit the floor, he was dead.

It was time to go and find Jake. By God, I hoped he was alive tied up somewhere waiting for Mason to return. I put the barrel of the Glock to the keyhole of the left handcuff that I couldn't unlock and fired my third shot. Metal flew everywhere and the cuff spun open.

I stepped over Mason's corpse. Blood had pooled around his head and turned the dusty floor into a mess of bloody mud. I went over to Hayley's cage and fired another shot into her lock, then opened her door. Tears were rolling down her face as she crawled out of the cage. I held her up but she couldn't walk. She sat outside the cage, her head facing Samantha's headless body.

"Don't look," I said, helping her up the stairs out of the dark cellar and into the bright sunlight. It took a minute or two before our eyes adjusted. I sat Hayley down on a nearby log, "Are you all right?" I asked, kneeling next to her on a soft patch of grass. "I'm going to look for Jake."

"I'll be fine," Hayley answered.

I looked at her wound and while there was a lot of blood, it wasn't as bad as I'd first thought. I took her socks off her feet and tied them both around the wound. "Keep pressure on it. I'll be back."

She continued to wipe the tears away. "Go and find Jake," she said.

I headed up the front stairs to the door of the cabin, praying I wouldn't find Jake dead on the floor.

Chapter 83

Saturday 15th November (10.32am)

Jake had been pulling on the cuff and then slamming his fist against the cracked Perspex, for what seemed like an eternity. It had hardly made a difference.

He felt sick and had a thumping headache. He didn't think he had much longer. If he was to live, he had to get out of there, and fast!

Vomit was making its way up his throat, and then he could no longer keep it down. By now, he guessed he had performed about 30 hard pulls on the handcuff. Then it suddenly cracked. Jake pulled again and the hinge and surrounding Perspex fell inwards.

Jake vomited again and his vision blurred. He was sure his time was running out.

He began kicking the end of the box but he had no more strength and had to stop. He vomited for a third time but this time his vomit was white and foamy. His eyes began to close. He was losing the fight. He couldn't go on, the venom had taken hold quicker than he'd thought. He had to rest for a moment.

His eyes closed again.

Chapter 84

Saturday 15th November 2003 (10.35am)

I had been through the laundry and the kitchen and had seen no sign of Jake. I entered the lounge and saw a few drops of blood. It looked fresh. I was hoping it didn't belong to Jake.

As I was kneeling there, a tree moving in the wind caught my attention out of the corner of my eye. Then it was as if Esmeralda was speaking to me directly. "An old oak in a forest full of pines." I remembered now that I'd seen it when Jake was about to go into the house. I ran to the kitchen window to get a better look and saw the big old oak tree in the middle of a paddock.

Esmeralda had been right: about the jogger, Mason and the key. She had to be right about this.

The oak was only 300 or 400 metres away but by the time I got there, I was stuffed. My heart felt as if it was going to seize up or explode. I could hardly breathe. I couldn't see anything at the base of the oak. Where the hell was he? Maybe Esmeralda was wrong. What if he was buried? What if he had been buried since yesterday? If so, surely his oxygen supply would have run out by now.

I double-checked around the trunk of the oak. Had I missed it?

Nothing!

Exhausted, I slumped down against the trunk and looked towards the thick forest at the bottom of the gully.

I decided to head for the car and call for backup.

I got to my knees. Then a reflection caught my eye. A refection of glass or steel. Whatever it was, it didn't belong out here. I ran, despite the fact that I thought running was no longer an option.

It was a simple Perspex coffin. Jake lay lifeless inside with vomit all over his shirt and chin. He looked like a ghost. I had never seen him so helpless and vulnerable. I called Jake's name several times and then saw the snake.

Without hesitating, I removed the gun from the holster, fired at the latches on the coffin and lifted the lid. I was ready to unload a few rounds into the snake before I realised it was headless. It was then I realised the vomit was the after-effects of a snake bite. Jake was too heavy for me to move. I had to get the doctors to him, fast, and the only communication for help was located 800 metres away in the police car. I leaned down and felt his pulse. It was very weak.

I knew we were running out of time, but I had no choice. Still puffing from my previous exertions, I began the run across the field towards the car. I wasn't even halfway and I thought I was going to collapse. My heart was pounding, it hurt badly, and my lungs and legs were burning. I had to keep going. It might already be too late but I had to do my best. I continued without even slowing and soon I was amongst the thick bush leading to the rear of the cabin. The bracken brushed my legs and whipped against my ankles. I felt a sharp pain in my left ankle. I had stepped on a stick and half of it had flicked up and stabbed me. It was not enough to slow me down. By the time I got to the car, my heart had gone into palpitations and I was struggling to remain conscious. I knew that the palpitations could cause my blood pressure to drop and make me collapse. I lay across the driver's seat, clasped the handset and radioed in for help.

I was guessing my heart was going about 200 beats per minute. There was no way that I could walk back to Jake in this condition. I had to drive. I didn't care if I wrecked the car, I had to get back and help him.

I decided to drive around the front of the house and head down the side of the cabin to where the big old oak stood.

"We are sending in the helicopter," I heard the voice on dispatch say. "Can you tell us what type of snake it was, Brodie?"

I picked up the radio receiver. "It looked like a brown," I replied.

"They have the anti-venom on board. They'll be there soon, Brodie."

I pulled the car to a halt just in front of the oak.

The car tyres slid in the mud as they struggled to grip the soil. My heart was still palpitating. I held my breath, trying to slow my breathing down.

It was to no avail.

I fell out of the vehicle and moved fast towards Jake. I placed my two fingers on the side of Jake's neck near his jugular. His pulse was present, weaker than before, but still there nonetheless. "Jake!" I called again, but there was still no response.

My palpitations began to thud and thump, thud, thump, thud, thump, hard against my chest. Every beat felt as if it was going to be my heart's last. I was starting to struggle. I headed back to the car to grab some water. I took the water and tipped some over my face. The rest was for Jake.

Hayley was limping her way over, and by the time I had finished wetting Jake's lips and washing his face, she was standing over him. She too checked his pulse. I could tell by her body language that he was still alive.

"The air ambulance is on its way, Hayley, all we can do now is wait," I told her. She took Jake's hand and sat on the dirt with his hand clasped in hers. "Give him some more water," I said, tapping the bottle on her shoulder. She poured some over his lips and a little over his forehead, trying to cool him down. She took a sip herself and handed the bottle back to me.

"Are you all right? You're very pale."

I explained that I had palpitations but reassured her I was fine. Hayley knew palpitations were not to be taken lightly.

Chapter 85

Saturday 15th November 2003 (10.51am)

It was only 12 minutes before the helicopter appeared overhead and within another minute, it had landed safely.

Both Hayley and I waved the ambulance officers over to Jake. They were no sooner at his side than they had him hooked up to an intravenous drip. As I lay on the grass close to unconsciousness, I could hear the ambo medic tell Hayley the drip was full of saline and anti-venom.

"Hopefully he'll be all right. The next few hours will be crucial. He's lucky to be such a big guy. It really gave him more time."

Unmarked police cars pulled up around Jake's car. One of the ambulance officers approached me about the same time as some of the local cops. Even though I was sprawled out on the ground, I pulled out my badge and instructed the local cops not to go anywhere near the house or the cellar.

The ambulance officer wanted to take me to Melbourne to treat the palpitations. He was a nice enough sort of guy, mid 50s, fit and caring.

"I'm not going anywhere."

"We have to get you to hospital, mate, you can't do anything in this state."

"Give me some verapamil and then I can get in there and sort out the crime scene. I have to make sure everything is done right. So stop stuffing around and give me some verapamil to get rid of these palpitations."

He looked at me. "Ok, lie in the back of the ambulance and I'll give you some verapamil but if they don't stop with that, I can't leave you here like this, ok?"

I nodded. I knew I wouldn't be able to do my job in this condition anyway.

He helped me onto the stretcher and drew the verapamil into a 10-ml syringe. He removed my shirt to connect the ECG. He noticed the stab wound from Mason's scalpel. "We'll get these palpitations under control and then sort that cut out." He started attaching the leads for the heart monitor. My heart rate jumped around, 188, 194, 191. It was all over the shop. Brian injected the first mil through the cannula in my wrist. It was one mil per minute and after 10 mils, they would stop and then take me to hospital for more drastic treatment, including an anaesthetic and then shocking my heart back into a normal rhythm. I was lucky. Up until now, it had never come to that. The verapamil had always worked.

We were up to the fifth mil when I told Brian the palpitations had gone. He looked up at the screen and watched as my heart rate dropped from 192 to 123 to 88 and now 74, which was an unusual rate, but normal for me.

Every time my heart dropped that suddenly, the initial feeling was it had stopped altogether. While the verapamil had done its job, it would take me a while to feel completely right again. But for now, I was right to do my job and finish this mess.

The ambo removed the cannula and again asked if I wanted him to look at my shoulder, but I politely waved him away.

David was being flown in to search and examine the grim finds.

The scene soon became very cluttered. There were patrols arriving from Yea and Seymour, even from as far as Shepparton. From what I knew, the Melbourne taskforce was on the helicopter with

David. The chief had rung me and told me very clearly that I was the only one permitted to enter the crime scene until he and David arrived.

I closed off the whole cellar until David and the chief arrived. It wasn't the crime scene that interested me. I needed to know what had made this guy tick. Mason had told me it was revenge against Samantha for killing his father, when he'd wanted to take his own revenge for what his father had done to him when he was younger, but to me that was just his excuse. He killed because it excited him. He liked the control he had over the women and well as the sexual gratification after their deaths.

The cabin was two hours from city headquarters by car but only 20 minutes by helicopter. The chief and his entourage didn't take long to arrive.

My thoughts went back to Jake who was now on his way to Alfred Hospital. More than anything, I wanted to be with him but I also knew that he would want me here to finish this. Anyway, Hayley had gone with him. I would be there soon to see him. He would be all right. Somehow, I just knew it.

"You all right?" the chief asked as he offered his hand to help me up. I nodded in acceptance. I couldn't be bothered with a lot of talking, I was so tired.

"You did a fantastic job, but you should have told us what you were doing."

Again, I nodded. He was right. We should have called for backup. Nothing like hindsight. "Lead the way, Detective," he said, motioning towards the cellar doors. I couldn't believe it. He had called me 'Detective'. Maybe the fact that we had solved the case had made me one of them. Maybe now I would be accepted.

Chapter 86

Saturday 15th November 2003 (11am)

I opened the doors to the cellar, flashed my torch around a few times. It caught Mason slumped in a pool of his own blood at the bottom of the trolley, where he had put me, ready to cut me to pieces.

Slowly, we all entered. The medical officers began taking photos. Flashes kept going off. I saw one of David's team picking up my bullet casings with tweezers. It was like being in a CSI show. It felt surreal.

David left his team to join me. We stood motionless, saying nothing for a while. I think we both had the same thought going through our heads. What type of person would do this? The victims' heads were displayed on a shelf in large round jars. They were all there, all labelled. It was the second time I had seen them.

I knew for sure that the first girl who'd gone missing was one of his victims. With no body, there had been doubts. Obviously, there had been a reason he hadn't dumped her body; not that we'd ever find out.

"Just think the world is a better place because of you. He can no longer kill. You stopped him." David put his arm around me. "Just think how many girls you saved. He would have never stopped."

The crime scene guys had finished taking their photos of Mason and Samantha, and their bodies were bagged. My gun was taken into evidence. I was told I would have to make a full statement to internal affairs, but not to worry. The coroner came in and removed both bodies, placing them into separate vans and taking them to Melbourne for further examination.

The magnitude of what Mason had done finally hit me. It was a torture chamber. I was sure he'd visited the cabin frequently between killings. It was the place he came to remember. Relive his past glories. Relive the murder and the torture and most likely masturbated to the memories of his victims. He would have found it sexually gratifying. I was sure he did a lot of reliving until the memories faded, thus igniting the need to kill again. The wall contained what seemed like all the newspaper articles ever published about him. He obviously enjoyed being the hunted as well as the hunter. The shelf that held the heads of his victims also held plastic lunch boxes that contained the personal effects of each girl. Some had just a few items of jewellery; others had wallets and keys as well. One had a whole bag of items. I continued to look at the wall while the crime scene guys photographed everything. There were dates listed on the wall and next to each date were names.

What took a lot of my attention was an article about Lance. His photo had been marked with a red circle. As we'd expected, Mason hadn't liked someone else taking his limelight.

I had seen this all before at Quantico. It was nothing new to me. A killer's shrine was common amongst serial killers. I had all the answers I needed.

The sunlight that shone on my face as I walked out of that cellar was the best feeling I had ever had. The sadness was still heavy in my heart for the victims, but the fact that I knew no one else would suffer at his hands made me happy. Now, it was time for me to check on Jake.

I was helped into the back of the ambulance and we asked the driver to radio the hospital to find out how Jake was doing. He agreed and we headed off to the same hospital.

As we started moving away, with the movement of the ambulance swaying me from side to side, I suddenly felt tears roll down my face. Yet I had no idea why they'd come.

Chapter 87

Saturday 15th November (11.30am)

Cassie ran to Stephen's side. "They've found you a new heart! You're going to get your operation, baby. You're going to get your new heart!"

Hanam strolled through the door with a slight smile, adjusting his comb-over before he spoke. "Well, Stephen, your new heart is on the way. Do you want me to go over the operation again before theatre, or are you comfortable with what I've already told you?"

"I'm fine. I just didn't expect it to happen so soon."

"We never know how long it will take. Some take months; some never happen. The lucky ones have it happen when they need it."

Cassie began to cry.

"You're lucky because you're still healthy enough to cope with the operation. Had it been much longer, you might have been too weak to survive the operation. I'm sure everything will go very well. Don't worry, ok?"

Stephen looked at Cassie and she smiled. "You're going to be fine, baby. I'll be here waiting for you. It'll all be over soon and then we can get on with our lives together." She kissed him on the lips. It was a sweet and lingering kiss, one that made Stephen happy, even if it would be his last.

Cassie tried not to cry any more, but it got the better of her and it was Stephen's turn to comfort her.

"Hey baby, I'll be ok. Don't cry, I'll see you soon. This is a good thing for me. It's a great thing for us. I love you. See you when I wake up."

Stephen looked across from Cassie to his mother. "We'll be here, darling," his mum said, grabbing his hand.

"We have to take him in now," the orderly said. "We'll take good care of him."

Cassie and Shelley both gave Stephen a kiss on the cheek and Cassie finished with one on the lips, surpassing the previous one.

He waved to them as he was pushed through the double doors to the operating theatre.

Cassie and Shelley were now well out of sight and Stephen was on his own. As they wheeled him along the corridor under the flickering fluoro lights, the possibility that there would be no tomorrow filled him with fear.

The surgeon had explained that this heart operation was risky. Stephen knew that but he simply had no other choice. Die now or next week.

Stephen turned his head from the fluoro lights above him to the pale green walls of the corridor.

The orderly's eyes were focused straight ahead. Having done this hundreds of times before, he was calm and collected. He reminded Stephen of a prison warden, walking the prisoners to their death. It made Stephen wonder if what he was feeling was similar to how prisoners felt on their final walk down the green mile. Full of panic and nerves, and helplessness.

"We're here. We're just going to move you onto the table now, Stephen," a voice behind the green mask said. "One, two, three," the voice counted, as they slid Stephen from the bed onto the table, using the sheet to help.

"Stephen, we're just going to put this anaesthetic into your IV now." This was a new voice and a different set of eyes. They were very kind. "I have the anaesthetic here. I'll let you know when we're ready to use it and I'll get you to count back from 10, ok?" he said, as he tapped Stephen on the shoulder.

Stephen nodded, looking into his kind eyes.

"Ok, we're going to put you to sleep now; everything will be fine. We'll see you soon. Stephen, start counting back from 10 now, slow, deep breaths." Stephen began to realise what the prisoners on death row must feel like. Seven…six…but before he could say another number, a mask was placed over his face and he slipped into darkness.

Chapter 88

Saturday 15th November 2003 (1.45pm)

When I arrived at the hospital a few hours later, my body had recuperated a little and I was feeling a lot better. My emotions, on the other hand, were still all over the place.

They took me in to see Jake. He was sleeping when I went in. His parents were already there at his bedside. He had a drip in his left hand. He looked a lot better than when I'd seen him last.

Jake's mum came over and gave me a hug and an update. He was recovering well, the anti-venom had started to take effect and no major tissue damage had been done. He was a lucky boy. Had he not been so solid, the doctors suggested he wouldn't have survived the bite.

His parents were about to leave. I told them that I would stay with Jake until he woke up.

His mum left after giving her son a kiss on the cheek.

My heart palpitations always brought on an appetite. Maybe it was because my body thought it had run a marathon or driven a Formula 1 GP. Whatever the reason, I was bloody hungry and needed a nice cup of tea as well, so I headed for the cafe while Jake slept. I was hoping he wouldn't wake up while I was downstairs.

I picked up some food for the two of us. I put Jake's food next to him on the dining tray at the end of his bed. Jake was still sound asleep and hadn't even moved. I sat back, grabbed my chicken roll and began to read the paper.

I tried to relax and not think about what had happened to both of us today and how close I had come to being dismembered by Mason. Keeping the thoughts away was almost impossible in the end. I closed the paper, leaned over to Jake and said, "We've got him, mate, you, me and Hayley are all ok. He's dead. I killed him!"

"Good job, Bruce," Jake responded in his half-asleep half-drugged state. He rolled over and went back to sleep. With that said, I knew he was going to be all right.

I pulled the second visitor's chair over for my feet, laid my jacket over my chest and tried to sleep too.

Chapter 89

Wednesday 21st January 2004 (9.00am)

Stephen had recovered well from his transplant. The anti-rejection drugs seemed to be working. He was now only required to visit outpatients for a biopsy every six weeks, providing everything remained stable.

Stephen was enjoying being able to shower independently again and the scar down the front of his chest, the zipper as he called it, was almost fully healed. The scar was still a little raw and he had to be very careful in the sun, but it was free of scabs and he no longer needed to use Betadine.

He couldn't believe that he felt so well. He had never felt this alive. Yet at the back of his mind, he felt different and he had no idea why. Everything about him seemed different since the operation.

He didn't like some of the foods he'd previously liked, he no longer felt the same attraction towards Cassie that he'd had before. He found her a little too chubby for his liking now. He couldn't work out why this was so.

He had even started to have horrible dreams, or were they memories? He couldn't tell, but he had them often.

He kept seeing women he didn't know, dying. He kept seeing places he had never been to.

A cabin was the most frequent image that flashed up in his head.

Stephen shook the dreams from his mind and tried to focus on the positives, how strong and well he felt. His breathing was easy, and his skin had become a normal colour without the blue tinge of before the operation.

Stephen dried himself off and stood in front of the steamed-up mirror. He wiped away enough of the steam so that he could see his face and chest. He leaned forward and stared intently at his reflection.

"Who are you?" he asked. Without thinking or forethought, he wrote one word in the steam, a word he didn't understand, a person he didn't know.

Mason

About the Author

Jasper Wolf lives in Melbourne with his wife and two children.

He has a background in Criminology and Law. 'Hunted' is his first novel.

Having spent much of his childhood in hospital, he has drawn on many of his own experiences within this book.

Become a fan of Australia's newest crime thriller writer. See Jasper Wolf on Facebook for further new release titles and dates.